A WALLFLOWER NEVER SURRENDERS

THE WEATHERBY WALLFLOWERS
BOOK ONE

COURTNEY MCCASKILL

HAZEL GROVE BOOKS

MORE BOOKS BY COURTNEY MCCASKILL

The Weatherby Wallflowers

Book 1: A Wallflower Never Surrenders
Book 2: Snowbound with the Scoundrel
Book 3: One Bed for the Bluestocking (Coming Soon)
Book 4: How He Won His Wallflower (Coming Soon)

The Astley Chronicles

Book 1: How to Train Your Viscount
Book 2: What's an Earl Gotta Do?
Book 3: The Sea Siren of Broadwater Bottom
Book 4: The Duke's Dark Secret
Book 5: Let Me Be Your Hero
Book 6: Romancing the Rifleman
Book 7: A Laird for Lady Lucy (Coming Soon)
My Favorite Mistake: An Astley Chronicles Novella

The Wicked Widows' League

Book 1: Scoundrel for Sale
Book 2: A Very Roguish Boxing Day

Other Books:

One Fine May (The Rake Review)

For more information, visit www.courtneymccaskill.com.

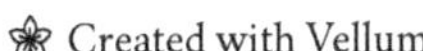 Created with Vellum

PROLOGUE

September 1823
Village of Boroughbridge
Yorkshire, England

It started as an ordinary breakfast.

As the eldest of the four Weatherby sisters, Eleanor had the honor of sitting near the head of the table, just to the left of the seat reserved for her father.

It was a dubious honor, at best.

Their father, Kenneth Weatherby, proved her point by striding into the dining room and snapping his fingers. "Eleanor, my toast."

She bit back a sharp response. As if she needed a reminder. As if he didn't demand that she toast his bread for him each and every morning.

Across the worn oak table, the second oldest Weatherby sister, Clarissa, glanced up from her precious newspaper just long enough to give Eleanor a commiserating look. She immediately buried her nose again. The paper might be yesterday's edition, saved for them by their more prosperous neighbors, the Ramsays, but Clarissa would read every line of it, including the weather report from the Outer Hebrides and the minutes of the Post Office's quarterly meeting, with avid interest.

Eleanor set her own book, a well-worn copy of *Twelfth Night*, aside and went to work on her father's toast. Three minutes later, she handed him a plate of crisp, golden slices with a forced smile.

Kenneth Weatherby began buttering his toast. "An opportunity has arisen."

Eleanor saw the alarm she felt mirrored in Clarissa's eyes. Their father was a naturalist, which was a respectable enough occupation, at least, the way his peers practiced it.

But Kenneth Weatherby had no interest in meticulously cataloging every conceivable variety of birds, bees, fish, or flowers. Oh, no—he was determined to make a *breakthrough*.

And that determination to chase after rainbows usually led to disaster not just for him, but for his four daughters.

"What sort of opportunity?" Eleanor asked, unable to mask the tension in her voice.

Their father did not look up from his toast. "It is an around-the-world voyage. Smithers is organizing it. I will be leaving next Friday."

"An around-the-world voyage!" the third oldest Weatherby sister, Kate, exclaimed. "How exciting."

Kate was the only one who would think so. A talented artist, Kate served as their father's assistant, creating exquisitely lifelike watercolor illustrations of his specimens. Kate's paintings had been featured in the handful of scientific exhibitions in London in which their father had been invited to participate.

Privately, Eleanor thought that Kate's illustrations were

the most remarkable thing about her father's work and the only reason he had been invited to participate in those events.

But while Kate seemed thrilled by the prospect, Eleanor felt nothing but alarm. "An around-the-world voyage? How much does that cost?"

Kenneth Weatherby took up his chipped teacup, then scowled. "Philippa! My tea!"

Philippa, or Pippa, as she was usually called, was the youngest of the four Weatherby sisters. Seated next to Eleanor, she was busy cooing to her three cats, Pepper, Ollie, and Crumpet, and feeding them morsels from her own plate.

At her father's recrimination, Pippa snapped to attention. "Sorry, Father," she said, taking up the teapot and preparing their father's cup just the way he liked it, with two lumps of sugar and a splash of cream.

After taking a sip of tea, Kenneth Weatherby went right back to buttering his toast, seeming to have forgotten all about the rather startling announcement he had made just moments ago.

"What is the cost of the voyage?" Eleanor asked sharply.

"Only a thousand pounds," her father said, reaching for the jam.

Clarissa froze with a spoonful of soft-boiled egg halfway to her mouth, her eyes wide with horror. Eleanor suspected she was making much the same expression. A thousand pounds? This year, they'd only managed to afford fabric enough for two new dresses amongst the four sisters. Those had gone to Pippa and Kate, whose wardrobes were the most threadbare. And they could only afford sugar for their father's tea. His four daughters had to go without.

Not that Eleanor really minded. As Clarissa would explain, whether someone asked for her opinion or not, everyone should still be boycotting sugar, because even after the abolition of the slave trade, money spent on sugar still flowed to the plantation owners who continued the cruel practice in the West Indies. Eleanor had to admit that her sister was right, even if she yearned for sweetened tea.

But the point was, they didn't have anywhere near a thousand pounds! Eleanor should know. She'd been managing the household budget for years.

"Where on earth did you get a thousand pounds?" Eleanor asked, hoping against hope that her father had somehow managed to find a benefactor.

"I sold the house," he replied calmly while spreading gooseberry jam on his toast.

Clarissa's spoon clattered against the flagstone floor. Pepper, Ollie, and Crumpet abandoned Pippa to race beneath the table so they could nibble up the fallen eggs.

Eleanor could scarcely think. The room around her seemed to sway. Sold the house? He couldn't have *sold the house*. Even her life could not possibly be this horrible!

Eleanor drew in a steadying breath. "I think I must have misheard, Father." Her voice sounded far away, as if someone else were saying the words. "For a moment, I thought you said that you had sold the house."

"That's correct," he replied, reaching for the ham.

"This was *Mother's* house," Clarissa said, her voice shaking with rage. "It was part of *her* dowry."

"And surely Mama would have wanted it to go to us someday?" Pippa asked, glancing at Eleanor uncertainly.

Eleanor gave her a firm nod. Elizabeth Weatherby had died bringing Pippa into the world, so her youngest sister had never had the chance to know their mother.

But Pippa was absolutely right.

"The marriage settlement included no language to that effect," their father noted. "The house is legally mine, to dispose of as I see fit."

"Nevertheless, she would have been furious," Eleanor said in a clipped voice.

Their father looked baffled by this reception. "This is the chance of a lifetime. I couldn't possibly turn down such an opportunity."

He said it so guilelessly, that the notion popped into Eleanor's head that things could not possibly be as bad as she was assuming. That, for once in his life, her father must have given a thought to his daughters and made accommodations for them, rather than leaving everything for her to figure out.

She therefore asked, "Who will be taking the four of us in?"

"How should I know?" her father asked before taking a bite of toast.

"But where will we live?" Clarissa burst out.

Kenneth Weatherby continued chewing his toast, leaving his four daughters to stare at one another in horrified silence. When he finally swallowed, he said, "Eleanor will figure something out. She always does. And you have two weeks until the buyer comes to take possession."

Eleanor wanted to scream. Two weeks? How on earth was she supposed to find a new living situation for the four of them in *two weeks*?

And yes, it was true that she had become good at figuring these things out, good at finding ways to stretch their meager budget until it all but burst at the seams. She'd had a great deal of practice, as she'd been doing it ever since their mother died twenty years ago.

But just because she always managed to make a silk purse out of a sow's ear didn't mean she should have to.

Eleanor fought to keep the panic rising in her breast from creeping into her voice. She had to be strong for her sisters. "But we have no close family to turn to."

Her father paused as if considering this for the first time, but just as quickly, he shrugged. "I suppose you'll have to marry, then."

"That isn't such a simple matter!" Clarissa snapped.

This was a rather spectacular understatement. The four Weatherby sisters were not only penniless, but they were also not particularly well-connected. To be sure, their mother's second cousin had married an earl, but any benefit that could be wrung from that tenuous connection had been negated by their father's eccentricities.

To make matters worse, they were bluestockings, all save perhaps for Pippa, whose great passion—cats—was fairly conventional. Pippa had the added advantage of being pretty with her wavy blonde hair, green eyes, and delicate features.

Truth be told, Clarissa and Kate were pretty, too, although they cared little for their appearance and put no effort into it.

Unfortunately, the same could not be said about Eleanor. There was nothing feminine about her. She was tall—taller than half the men of her acquaintance—but she wasn't tall in a willowy, elegant way. The word that came to mind was *sturdy*. She had once been told that she would've made a good farm wife, and she couldn't honestly disagree. She had the sort of build that made people think, *I'll bet she could churn a lot of butter*. As for her face, at best, it was plain, with a nose that might euphemistically be described as "Roman."

And so, Eleanor had accepted years ago that no man would ever want to marry her, a truth that had been confirmed by the fact that she was now firmly on the shelf at the age of seven and twenty.

But hope remained for all three of her sisters, and in fact, their mother's countess cousin had once even managed to arrange a match for Clarissa with Rupert Dupree, the second son of the Earl of Rottenbury. This had seemed like a blessing at the time, but really, it had been the prologue of their latest disaster. Because Rupert had jilted Clarissa, and the papers had picked it up, turning the four Weatherby sisters into laughing stocks.

Or, more specifically, turning them into the Weatherby Wallflowers, which was the nickname the gossip rags had gleefully adopted.

It was a good thing Rotten Rupert, as they had taken to calling him, had decamped for the Continent immediately after jilting Clarissa. Were Eleanor ever to pass him in the street, she was confident that she would wind up committing one or more acts of violence upon his person for which she would face, at a minimum, transportation.

And that was nothing compared to what Clarissa would do. Clarissa would not settle for mere murder; Clarissa would desecrate Rupert Dupree's corpse, and she would cackle while she did it.

So, when her father suggested marriage, as if this were a simple solution, as if Eleanor had not been trying to find respectable husbands for her sisters for *years*, something inside her snapped.

"And have you found husbands for us, Father?" she asked, for once not troubling to conceal the sharpness of her tone.

Her father looked startled. "No. I assumed you would prefer husbands of your own choosing."

"*Husbands of our own choosing.*" Eleanor laughed, but not in an amused way. "A curious turn of phrase, considering we have no choices."

Their father frowned. "What do you mean, you have no choices? You could choose any man in the world. I wouldn't stand in your way."

"You would not stand in our way, but nor would you do anything to aid us, such as making sure we have dowries, giving us a Season, or even making sure we had decent wardrobes. It is no simple matter to find a husband with the 'advantages' you have provided us, Father."

Kenneth Weatherby looked bewildered. "We didn't have money for any of those things."

"No," Eleanor snapped. "No, we didn't. Not after you undertook that voyage to Cyrene, in order to search for basilisks. Then, there was the trip to Eritrea to hunt for a Pegasus. And the summer you spent looking for sea serpents off the coast of Aberdeen. And the time you went to Tatarstan in search of wyverns. And—"

Her father's ears had turned red. Although Clarissa could be snide, he was not used to having Eleanor defy him. "Scientific discovery is not always a linear process, Eleanor. The careers of the greatest naturalists are littered with false starts."

She surged to her feet. "A Pegasus, Father! You spent hundreds of pounds—money that could have gone toward giving Clarissa a Season, Kate a dowry, or Pippa a proper wardrobe, to chase after a *Pegasus*!"

Her father scowled. "It's easy to point the finger after the fact. But had I found any of those creatures, it would have been the making of my career."

"There is a reason no one has found those creatures," Eleanor snapped. "Because they do not exist! I have known that since I was a six-year-old child!"

"Even *I* know that," Pippa added, slicing a morsel off one of her kippers and feeding it to Crumpet.

"As much as I hate to contradict you, Father," Kate said, "I agree with Eleanor. Although this is truly the voyage of a lifetime, it isn't right for the two of us to take it if it means that my sisters will be without a roof over their heads."

Across the table, Clarissa caught Eleanor's eye, and they exchanged a look of alarm. In Eleanor's opinion, Kate had never seen their father with clear eyes. Whereas Eleanor,

Clarissa, and Pippa understood that he would abandon them in a heartbeat if it meant he could go chasing after fairies in Albania, Kate thought the world of their father. In fact, the reason she had honed her artistic talent so meticulously was so she could be of use to him.

And so, Kate's assumption that their father would be taking her with him on his around-the-world voyage was not entirely implausible.

But when had Kenneth Weatherby ever thought of anyone but himself?

Eleanor held her breath. God, how she hoped she was wrong. Kate would be crushed if their father abandoned her. At least Eleanor, Clarissa, and Pippa had grown used to it.

Their father did not look at Kate as he said, "You seem to have made an erroneous assumption, Katherine. The sale of the house did not generate enough money to cover the cost of two passages. Well, strictly speaking, I suppose it did, but I would not have been able to afford a private cabin. I will therefore be going alone, and you will be staying here with your sisters."

Eleanor watched the blood drain from Kate's face. "But… but you need me. You need me to illustrate your findings! We're a team, a duo, and—"

"I will not deny that your drawings do add a negligible amount of value to my work. But you would do well to remember, Katherine, that *I* am the scientific expert. You are, at best, my assistant."

Kate looked as if he had slapped her, but she recovered quickly. "And that is all I want—to assist you! Let me come with you, Father. I can be of help to you. I know I can!"

He shook his head. "The voyage is expected to last a minimum of two years. I refuse to make it in discomfort. No, you will stay here with your sisters."

Tears streamed down Kate's face. One dropped onto her

wrist, and she started, touching her cheeks as if she did not realize she had been crying. Kate was by far the most stoic of the four sisters. She could sit in a copse of trees for hours, still as a fawn hiding in the grass, waiting for an animal she wished to sketch to emerge. She would not complain of cold, nor heat, nor rain, nor boredom. In fact, Eleanor could not recall the last time she had seen her second-youngest sister cry.

But Kate had genuinely thought that their father loved her. And this was the moment she finally realized she had been wrong.

Clarissa stood, wrapping an arm around Kate's shoulders and urging her to her feet. "Come, Kate," she said, glaring venomously at their father. "We'll finish our breakfast in the front room. Pippa, would you bring the teapot?"

Pippa stood and began placing the tea things on a tray. Eleanor gathered her sisters' half-finished plates and started to follow them.

Just before she strode through the door, she paused to deliver a final parting shot. "You are the worst father imaginable. If Mother could see you now, she would be disgusted."

Her father said nothing in response as Eleanor sailed out the door.

In the front room, Eleanor found Clarissa and Pippa sitting on either side of Kate on the tattered brown sofa, arms around their sister's shoulders while she sobbed.

Eleanor set their plates on a side table, then knelt on the floor so she could take her sister's hands. "I'm so sorry, Kate."

"I thought…" Kate sobbed. "After everything I've done…"

Eleanor rubbed the back of her sister's hand with her thumb. "I know, dear. I know."

"Eleanor," Pippa said, her voice quavering, "what are we going to do?"

Her three sisters looked at her expectantly.

Eleanor was no stranger to this moment. She had been just seven years old when her mother died, and she'd been looking after her three sisters ever since. She had never failed them before.

Nor would she fail them this time.

"We're going to stick together," Eleanor answered, trying to infuse her voice with a confidence she did not feel. "Our father has abandoned us, but this isn't new. In truth, he abandoned us years ago."

All three of her sisters, even Kate, nodded sadly in agreement.

"But," Eleanor continued, rising to pace the room, "we are *not* giving up. I am going to write to every distant relation, ostensible friend, and casual acquaintance I can possibly think of. Who knows—maybe one of them will offer to shelter us. But we must not rely upon the generosity of others." She made a point of holding each of her three sisters' eyes for a beat. "We must look to ourselves and think about how we might earn our own livings going forward."

"I could offer drawing lessons," Kate said, her voice scarcely above a whisper. "I'll have time now that I won't be helping Father."

"Yes!" Eleanor exclaimed. "That's an excellent suggestion. We would need to move to a larger town that would have a better pool of potential students. But it looks like we'll be leaving Boroughbridge one way or another."

"I could offer lessons in French or Spanish," Clarissa noted. "Or find work as a governess."

"I think becoming a governess or a companion might be a

good option for me as well," Eleanor noted. She swallowed. "Or perhaps even a housekeeper."

It would be a step down, to be sure. A governess existed in the shadowy realm between servant and family. A gently bred woman could contemplate taking a position as a governess.

A housekeeper was something else entirely. Still, Eleanor would be good at it. She knew she would.

And if becoming a housekeeper was her only option to keep her sisters from being turned out into the streets, she would do it.

"I don't think I could do any of those things," Pippa noted miserably. "I'm not clever like the rest of you."

"Yes, you are!" Eleanor insisted in the same breath Kate murmured, "That's not true."

"You're perfectly clever," Clarissa said with a note of finality. "You're just not a dyed-in-the-wool bluestocking like the rest of us."

"Perhaps I could find work as a nursemaid, though." Pippa gave a smile that did not reach her eyes. "All I've ever wanted to do was to marry and have children of my own."

"Marriage isn't a bad goal. Quite the opposite," Eleanor noted. "If any of us can manage to catch a husband, that could pull us all back from the brink." Her eyes fell on Clarissa, and she noted her sister's drawn expression. "What is it, Claire?"

"It's not that I disagree with anything you've said. These are all good ideas, and of course, we have to try everything." Clarissa slouched back on the couch, rubbing her brow. "But we only have *two weeks*! What are the odds that you and I can find families in need of a governess, Kate can line up a dozen art students, and Pippa can catch a husband in *two weeks*?"

"We just need one bit of luck," Eleanor countered. "Just one distant relation to offer us shelter for a month, or for one of us to find a position. I won't lie—it's not going to be easy. We may have to sleep four to a bed in a dismal little room. Our stomachs will probably be rumbling for the first few months. But things are going to turn around for us. I know they are."

Clarissa looked unconvinced. "When have things ever gone right for the Weatherby Wallflowers?"

"There are worse things to be than wallflowers," Eleanor countered.

Clarissa's face was a portrait of skepticism. "Are there?"

"There are," Eleanor said firmly. "Wallflowers are tenacious. No one bothers to tend them. They are relegated to the cracks between the paving stones, yet still they find a way to bloom."

"Unlike hothouse flowers," Pippa said, "wallflowers don't merely bloom in perfect conditions. They can survive the frost, the drought, whatever the world throws at them."

"Wallflowers are more interesting than hothouse flowers," Kate added. "Every variety of rose is basically the same. But wallflowers are fascinating in their variety."

Eyes shiny, Clarissa stood, snagging her teacup from the tray. "And wallflowers have thorns and sometimes even poison. Pity the man who thinks they will be easy to pluck." She raised her cup in a toast. "Because a wallflower never surrenders."

"Hear, hear!" Eleanor called, grabbing her own cup from the tray. "A wallflower never surrenders!"

"To the Weatherby Wallflowers!" Pippa cried, lifting her chipped cup.

"To sisterhood," Kate added, raising her cup.

And that was how the four Weatherby sisters came to be hugging one another, raising toasts and sloshing tea upon the carpet in the front room of the house that would be their home for only two more weeks.

As she hugged her sisters, Eleanor's gaze fell upon the miniature of their mother where it stood on the mantelpiece. She closed her eyes. *Help me, Mother. I cannot let my sisters down.*

That very moment, a beautiful pale-yellow butterfly fluttered past the window.

It was probably her imagination, but Eleanor fancied that it lingered there.

CHAPTER 1

Northamptonshire, England
Three Weeks Later

"Come, Pippa," Eleanor said for the sixth time, "we must return to the house so you can dress for dinner."

As she had done the previous five times, Pippa did not rise from her place kneeling in the straw. "Just a few more minutes," she said, burying her face in the downy-soft fur of a black and white kitten.

Eleanor sighed. She hated to rush her sister. When they'd left Yorkshire one week ago, they'd had no choice but to leave Pippa's three cats, Pepper, Ollie, and Crumpet, behind. The family that had bought the house had kindly agreed to look after them. They had two girls and a boy, and the children seemed delighted by their new pets. The oldest daughter had even pledged to write to Pippa each month to let her know how Pepper, Ollie, and Crumpet were faring.

But, even knowing that her cats were in good hands, Pippa had been distraught. Eleanor had not been the least bit surprised that, upon overhearing a maid mention "the kittens in the barn," Pippa had come straight out, not even bothering to change out of the plain taupe muslin gown that had been dingy even before it became dust-stained from four days of travel on the mail coach.

As much as they needed to get Pippa cleaned up so she could make the right impression at dinner, Eleanor didn't have the heart to begrudge her this moment of respite. This was the first time Eleanor had seen her youngest sister look happy since they had left her cats behind in Yorkshire.

They had just arrived at the country estate of their mother's second cousin, the Countess of Milthorpe, and her husband the earl. Lady Milthorpe had come through for the Weatherby sisters yet again, with an invitation to attend this house party. Although her husband had forbidden her from offering her Weatherby cousins a permanent home, this invitation provided them with two weeks of shelter, and Lady Milthorpe had provided some additional intelligence.

The seventy-two-year-old Baron Oglesby, who was also to be a guest, was in search of a fourth wife. Lord Oglesby had produced an heir and a spare four times over, so finding a bride with a noble lineage was less pressing than it once had been. The baron's estate was also productive, so he could afford to choose a bride without a dowry. He wanted someone pretty and sweet-tempered to look after him in his dotage, and the Weatherby sisters stood as good a chance of catching him as anyone.

Buoyed by this news, Eleanor had suggested they go straight upstairs and dress with care for dinner. Unfortunately, on their way up, they had passed a pair of maids who were chattering about the four orphaned kittens out in the barn.

A brace of oxen could not have dragged Pippa up to her room after hearing that.

And so, this was how Eleanor and her sisters had come to be standing in the old thatched-roofed barn Lord Milthorpe's staff used to store fodder for the horses, when what they needed to do was leave said barn with all possible speed, so Pippa could clean herself up and attempt to ensnare a man old enough to be their grandfather.

"Pippa, dear," Eleanor said yet again. "We really must go."

Ignoring her sister, Pippa held the kitten aloft, touching its nose to her own. "If you were mine, I would name you Wellington. Because you don't just have socks, you have boots!"

"The kittens will be here for our entire stay," Eleanor noted.

Settling Wellington in her lap, Pippa reached for one of his sisters. "I would call you Lavender because your fur is so grey it almost has a lavender hue."

"Help me," Eleanor entreated Clarissa and Kate, who were watching in silence. Clarissa's only response was a shrug. Meanwhile, Kate continued staring at the far wall of the barn, not seeming to have heard at all.

"You would be Midnight," Pippa continued, oblivious, scratching the solid black ball of fluff behind the ears. "And you would be Bathsheba," she cooed at the grey tabby with a white belly that had crawled into her lap, "because I've always wanted a cat named Sheba."

"Pippa!" Eleanor exclaimed. At last, her sister deigned to glance up. "I know how much you want to play with those cats. Truly, I do. But it is imperative that we get you freshened up so you make your very best impression upon Lord Oglesby at dinner."

Frowning, Pippa returned her attention to the kittens. "You seem to have misspoken, Eleanor. *I* do not need to get freshened up to make *my* best impression upon Lord Oglesby. *We* need to get freshened up so we can *all* make our best impressions upon the baron. After all, we do not know which of the four of us might catch his eye."

Eleanor sighed. Her sister did have a point. She was eaten with guilt to be offering her youngest sister up like a sacrificial lamb to a man four times her age. But really, what were the odds that Lord Oglesby would choose one of the three older sisters?

Clarissa was actually quite beautiful, with blonde hair, brown eyes that sparkled with intelligence, and a classical symmetry to her features. But ever since her jilting at the hands of Rupert Dupree, she had developed a deep cynicism when it came to the male sex, and she was more likely to use her daunting intellect to cut a man to ribbons than to entice him with her quick wit. Compounding the problem, she insisted on dressing in what Pippa referred to as dirt-colored dresses, preferring to bury her charms beneath a swath of ill-fitting brown muslin. Clarissa put on a good front, but Eleanor knew she had been wounded by Rupert's rejection, and she wore her brown dresses like armor. By making sure that men did not notice her, Clarissa ensured they could not scorn her, and that was all she cared about.

Kate was equally pretty, tall and slim with brown hair, blue eyes, and delicate features. Kate had always been taciturn by nature. She was never going to be the belle of the ball, but a bookish sort of man who wanted a peaceful home would find Kate's quiet nature tremendously appealing.

But Kate was suffering through even more than their father's abandonment. Before he departed to catch his ship, he had attempted to extract a promise that Kate would never mention the fact that she was the creator of her own watercolor illustrations. Kate had always signed her works *K. Weatherby.* It turned out that their father had given people to understand that the "K" stood for "Kenneth." He had been claiming credit for Kate's work all along.

Kate had always assumed that she was building a reputation as a scientific illustrator, much like her idol, Sarah Stone, who had been the in-house artist responsible for documenting the Leverian collection back before the museum had closed.

Instead, it turned out that she had no reputation, as no one in the scientific community knew she existed.

Kate hadn't agreed. She had been on the cusp of speaking when Eleanor had snapped, "She isn't promising you anything, and you should be ashamed of yourself for taking credit for her work!" The four sisters had once again stormed out of the breakfast room.

Since learning of this new betrayal, Kate had been not merely taciturn, but morose. At the moment, she was about as lively as a funeral—not the sort of demeanor likely to catch a man's eye.

And as for her? She was the ugly duckling of the family, except she had passed the point at which she might grow into a swan. No man wanted a bride of seven and twenty who was built like a farmwife and had a beak for a nose.

As if her looks weren't disqualification enough, Eleanor very much doubted Lord Oglesby wanted a wife of her temperament. Eleanor had been forced to take over the running of her father's household at the age of seven, and to say that his household ran on a shoestring budget was a grave insult to shoestrings. Most seven-year-old girls of good family spent their days reading, sewing, and playing with dolls. Eleanor, on the other hand, had spent hers browbeating the butcher into giving them a joint of pork for a quarter of the usual price, hectoring the neighbors until they agreed to loan their books to Clarissa and their art supplies to Kate just to get rid of her, and transforming an old brocade tablecloth from the previous century into a Sunday dress for Pippa.

These were household skills, of a sort, but not the right sort. Most gentlemen wanted a wife who was accomplished on the pianoforte, not one who could negotiate like a fishwife. Just as bad, after twenty years of having to demand that the world make a place for her and her sisters, Eleanor was intimidated by next to nothing. Instead of being demure and ladylike, she was outspoken and brazen.

For Pippa's sake, she would try to feign a little feminine modesty. But she doubted she could keep up appearances all week. The truth had a way of coming out.

Clarissa finally spoke up. "You're the pretty one, Pip."

Pippa gasped, looking a thousand times more wounded than she would've done had the insult been directed at her. "I think you are all very pretty," she said with quiet dignity.

Eleanor sighed. Lord Oglesby would be a lucky man, getting a wife as kindhearted as she was beautiful. "It's a fair point. We will *all* go and freshen up and see what the party might bring. Now—"

She was cut off by the creak of the barn door. The four sisters froze, spines straightening.

Eleanor turned to see who had interrupted their solitude but couldn't make out much of the figure who stood framed in the late afternoon light, beyond the fact that he was a man.

"Oh, dear," a sonorous voice said. "I hope I'm not interrupting."

CHAPTER 2

The man who stepped into the barn was young, probably around Clarissa's age. He had a mop of wavy caramel-colored hair and was smartly dressed in a charcoal grey coat and aubergine waistcoat. He was of average height with a trim figure, and Eleanor found him handsome in a boyish sort of way.

He chuckled at the sisters' silent reception. "I'm sorry, I didn't mean to startle you. I heard there were kittens, so I thought I would, er…"

"There are indeed kittens," Pippa exclaimed from her seat down in the hay. She held the grey tabby aloft. "Aren't they adorable?"

Clarissa watched the young man's face transform as he beheld Pippa for the first time. He froze, his features going slack. The word *thunderstricken* came to mind.

Pippa did not seem to have noticed. "There are three more—plenty to go around. I would never deny a fellow cat-lover the chance to enjoy them."

Shaking himself, the young man crossed the barn. Heedless of his expensive clothes, he sat right down in the straw next to Pippa. He scooped up the black kitten with the white face and feet. "Look at this handsome fellow! Yes, you're a handsome fellow. Yes, you are."

"I've been calling that one Wellington," Pippa noted.

A broad smile broke across the young man's face. "Because he has boots!"

Pippa beamed at him. "Precisely!"

"That's very clever." He set Wellington down in his lap and scooped up his solid-black brother. "Now, this one should be Cinder."

"Oh, dear." Pippa laid an apologetic hand upon his wrist. "I'm afraid I've already dubbed that one Midnight."

"Midnight is good," he said agreeably. "I like Midnight even better. And what about these two?"

"This is Lavender, and this is Sheba. Bathsheba for formal occasions."

The corners of his mouth twitched up. "For when she's presented to the queen."

"For when the queen is presented to her," Pippa countered.

He laughed, a full-throated, resonant sound that Eleanor found tremendously likable. He held out his hand to Pippa. "I'm Felix. Felix St. James."

Pippa seized his hand eagerly. Neither of them were wearing gloves. It was the *height* of impropriety. "I'm Philippa Weatherby, but everyone calls me Pippa."

He bowed his head. "A pleasure, Miss Weatherby."

Pippa gave him a dazzling smile. "Likewise, Mr. St. James."

Eleanor had to bite back a groan, because this man was no mere mister. She was surprised Pippa didn't recognize the name Felix St. James. He was the younger brother of the Duke of Norwood, whose estate was only around twenty miles from their home village of Boroughbridge.

"I believe it's 'Lord Felix,' dear," Eleanor said gently.

"Oh!" Pippa exclaimed, eyes going round as those of the kittens. "I'm so sorry. *Lord* Felix."

He waved this off. "Eh. My brother, Jasper—he's the duke. He likes to stand on ceremony, but I don't care about such things. I'd be pleased if you'd call me Felix."

Eleanor would have absolutely refused. To call the son of a duke by his first name after an acquaintance of three minutes was unheard of.

But Pippa merely smiled. "Only if you will call me Pippa."

He leaned his forehead toward hers. "We have an accord."

"Oh, and these are my sisters." Pippa pointed to each of them in turn. "Eleanor, Clarissa, and Kate—Katherine, I should say."

Felix somehow managed to make an elegant bow from his cross-legged position in the straw. "How do you do, Miss Weatherby, Miss Clarissa, Miss Katherine?"

Eleanor smiled and curtseyed, but the honest answer was that she was not doing nearly as well as she had been doing five minutes ago. Because Felix St. James was precisely the type of man they were looking for—young, rich, and eligible. He even seemed taken with Pippa.

But his first impression had been of her sitting on the floor of a barn, wearing a tattered, dusty dress! Would that he could have met her that evening, in one of the gowns Lady Milthorpe was loaning them for the duration of the house party. Those were a season or two out of date, but at least they weren't fraying at the hem!

To make matters worse, Pippa proceeded to tell Felix everything, and Eleanor did mean *everything*. She started by waxing on about how desperately she missed her own three cats. Felix responded to her sadness with a tender concern that spoke well of him.

But then, Pippa had proceeded to explain in excruciating

detail *why* she had been forced to leave Pepper, Ollie, and Crumpet behind. Their father selling the house. The fact that they were penniless and desperate. The necessity of finding a husband to support them in the space of two weeks. The probability that one of them would have to marry Lord Oglesby.

Dear God, if their threadbare clothing hadn't put Felix St. James off, the admission that they were destitute and that their entire purpose in being at this house party was to ensnare a husband to support them would surely send him running for the hills!

But Felix was too polite to let his disdain show. He even offered Pippa his arm as they made their way back up to the house. He glanced back at the barn. "I know we have to dress for dinner. But they're so wonderful, it's hard to leave them behind."

"I know exactly what you mean." Pippa glanced up at him, slightly awestruck. "I've never met someone who loves cats as much as me."

"Well, I don't love cats, precisely." A horrified expression swept over Pippa's face, and he laughed. "I do love cats! I promise. What I meant was, I have a deep love for *all* animals. In fact, I'm even involved with an organization dedicated to protecting them."

"Oh!" Pippa looked up, surprised. "I didn't know that such an organization existed."

Felix rubbed the back of his head. "It doesn't yet. We're working on getting it off the ground. It's going to be called the Society for the Prevention of Cruelty to Animals. I know it probably sounds like a pipe dream, but some very prominent men are involved—Richard Martin, William Wilberforce—"

"You know William Wilberforce?" Clarissa burst out.

Eleanor's mouth twitched. In most things, Clarissa was

deeply cynical, but she was a great admirer of the famous abolitionist.

Felix nodded. "I do. He's a great man. A very great man. It is the involvement of men such as him that makes me confident that we will succeed in founding the organization."

"What will your organization do?" Pippa asked breathlessly.

"For starters, we're going to focus on carriage horses. You see..."

Felix proceeded to enumerate the cruel conditions under which carriage horses labored in the capital. "They have to work without food or even water. Whether it's boiling hot or freezing cold. If they collapse in the street, their drivers will start beating them to get up—"

"That's terrible!" Pippa cried, eyes full of distress.

"It is," Felix agreed. "But we're going to do something about it. We just need the money to get the organization off the ground. It's actually why I'm here. I need to speak to my brother. You see, I'm due to come into my inheritance when I turn twenty-five. I just turned twenty-four last month. So, I need him to release some of my funds. Then we'll be able to make our start."

"I honestly didn't know people did that to carriage horses," Pippa said ruefully. "I'm from such a tiny village, you see. No one would ever treat their horse that way in Boroughbridge."

"You're from Boroughbridge? In Yorkshire?" Felix asked. At Pippa's nod, he laughed. "That's only a stone's throw from where I grew up! Imagine us meeting all the way down here."

"It almost feels like fate!" Pippa said brightly.

Eleanor caught Clarissa's eye and saw her own horror mirrored on her sister's face.

But Felix seemed unperturbed by this spectacularly gauche statement. "It does, doesn't it? But... What was I saying? Oh, yes, carriage horses—I was ignorant as to how poorly they were treated for many years. My brother is a duke, you see, so all our horses are expensive animals and well cared for." He shook his head. "Until I went to London, I didn't realize how cruelly the world can treat innocent animals. But don't you worry." He laid his hand upon Pippa's where it rested on his arm. "We're going to do something to help them."

Pippa was now looking at Felix with something close to awe. "How I wish there was something I could do to help. But, as I mentioned, we don't have two pennies to rub together." She looked away, crestfallen.

Eleanor watched as Felix squeezed her sister's arm. "I'm certain there's something you could do, whether or not you have two pennies."

"Do you really think so?" Pippa breathed.

"Absolutely." They had reached the house. Felix nodded to the footman holding the door. "Once we get started, we'll be holding all kinds of fundraisers. We'll need people to help organize them. There will be plenty to do if you're interested."

"Oh, I am! I am very interested." She gave him a rueful look. "If I ever make it as far as London, that is."

Felix gave her a wry look. "Oh, I have a feeling you'll make it to London one day. I have a feeling you'll be visiting all kinds of marvelous places."

They had reached the base of the stairs. Felix bowed over Pippa's hand, brushing his lips across her knuckles, both dirt and decorum be damned. His eyes were bright as he said, "I'll see you at dinner." He released Pippa's hand, then gave an elegant bow to the remaining sisters. "Miss Weatherby, Miss Clarissa, Miss Katherine."

He jogged up the stairs and headed off toward the east wing.

Eleanor noted that Pippa watched him the entire time.

"Come, dear," Eleanor said, taking her youngest sister's shoulder. "We must make sure you look ravishing at dinner."

Pippa did need to look ravishing.

But now, Eleanor wondered if her sister might be able to set her cap for a husband with whom she would be better suited than Lord Oglesby.

CHAPTER 3

asper St. James, the Duke of Norwood, was almost done receiving a shave from his valet when his brother Felix strode into his room, face glowing with happiness.

It had been a few weeks since they'd seen each other. At the end of the Parliamentary season, Jasper had retreated to the family seat at Harrogate, while Felix had opted to stay in London.

"Brother," Jasper said, careful not to swallow as Stephens was currently running the razor over his Adam's apple. "You look… happy."

"I just met the girl I'm going to marry," Felix burst out.

How fortunate that Stephens happened to have lowered the razor for a rinse because Jasper whirled around. "You've *what?*"

He would have to wait for his answer, because at that moment, the mastiffs went bounding up to Felix.

Felix immediately bent down to greet the dogs—not that one had to bend particularly far when it came to the mastiffs.

Benedick came up to the top of Jasper's thigh, and Jasper was not a short man.

"Bea!" Felix exclaimed, scratching her behind the ears. "Benny! It's good to see you! Yes, I missed you. Yes, I missed you, too."

Jasper frowned. "Their names are Beatrice and Benedick. They don't like being called that."

"Of course they don't," Felix said as Benedick rolled over on his back, looking up at Felix hopefully. Felix complied by scratching the dog's tawny belly.

"Beatrice! Benedick!" Jasper pointed a commanding finger toward the pair of large corduroy cushions positioned beneath a window. "Bed! Now!"

The dogs both gave him a woeful look… although, honestly, their wrinkly, squished faces always looked woeful, even when he gave them each a joint of beef.

Whatever their feelings might have been, the mastiffs both obediently trotted back to their beds.

Felix was definitely giving him a woeful look, but Jasper ignored it. Accepting a hot towel from Stephens, Jasper sought to bring the conversation back on course. "What was that you said about meeting a woman?"

Just like that, Felix was glowing again. "Yes, and not just any woman—the future Lady Felix! I can't wait for you to meet her."

Jasper groaned. This wasn't the first time Felix had informed him that he had found his future bride.

Far from it, in fact.

"Who is she this time?" Jasper asked, wiping his face with the towel.

Felix recoiled, looking wounded. "It's been seven years. Are you ever going to let that drop?"

"Apparently not. Nor do I think that I should, considering

that you were convinced you were going to marry three different women in the space of a year."

Jasper used the term *women* for the sake of civility, but he thought *leeches* was more apropos. None of those women had cared about his brother. They had proved as much as soon as Jasper put them to the test.

Felix blew out an exasperated breath. "I was seventeen! If you can't be a fool in love at seventeen, when can you?"

Jasper strode over to the wash basin. He happened to believe that one should never be a fool, not at any time, nor under any circumstances. But he doubted Felix would appreciate him saying as much.

"So," he asked as he peeled off the shirt he had traveled in that morning, "who is it this time? Another actress? A member of the ballet corps? Or, my personal favorite, a long-lost Russian princess?"

Felix appeared in the mirror behind Jasper's shoulder. He was glowering but refused to rise to his brother's bait. "She is a fellow guest of Lord and Lady Milthorpe. Her name is Pippa. Pippa Weatherby."

If Felix had just met the chit, Jasper would like to know why the hell he was already referring to her as *Pippa*.

But then, he recalled what was familiar about *Pippa's* last name. "Weatherby? Wait—she's not one of those Weatherby Wallflowers, is she?"

Felix laughed. "She's not a wallflower at all. She's the most beautiful woman I've ever seen. Honestly, Jasp, I just met all four Weatherby sisters, and they're actually quite handsome. It's obviously just a stupid nickname someone made up to sell newspapers."

"I was not asking to ascertain if she's pretty. I'm asking because those Weatherby Wallflowers are penniless and grasping. I would wager that the only reason they're at this house party is to try to trick some man into marrying them."

Felix crossed his arms. "Is that not the very reason *you're* at this house party? To find a bride?"

"That's different," Jasper said, accepting a fresh towel from Stephens and drying off his torso.

Standing next to his brother in the mirror, Jasper was struck by how differently they looked. Whereas Jasper was stocky and swarthy, with dark brown hair he kept clipped short and a good sprinkling of hair upon his chest, Felix was lithe and fair and wore his light brown hair in a fashionably windswept cut. The only trait the brothers had in common was their brown eyes, which they had inherited from their father the duke.

The reason they looked so little alike was because they had different mothers. For his first bride, the sixth Duke of Norwood had chosen a scion of the aristocracy. Gwendolyn Cavendish was the daughter of one duke and had the blood of two more flowing through her veins. She had been raised from birth for the role of duchess and had performed her duties with an impeccable sense of dignity.

But she had been carried off by a fever that had swept the house when Jasper had been just six years old. His father had remarried quickly, this time to the daughter of a vicar whose main qualification to the role of duchess seemed to be that she was extremely beautiful.

But Jasper hadn't resented his stepmother. She had always been kind to him, and he had been pleased to get a little brother out of the arrangement. He was seven years older than Felix, so his role had always been more of a respected guide than a pure playmate.

But then, when Jasper had been sixteen and Felix nine, the duke and duchess had both died when their carriage overturned. Jasper had hurried home from Eton to find his little brother alone and disconsolate.

He had insisted that Felix come with him back to Eton.

Nine was a bit earlier than most boys started, but Jasper hadn't known what else to do. He didn't like the idea of his brother being raised by servants, and, as his father and stepmother had both been only children, there wasn't even one aunt or uncle who could take him in. The brothers were the only family they each had left, and they were going to stick together, damn it.

But Jasper had to admit that this series of events had lent a paternal quality to what should have been a fraternal relationship and that Felix did not always appreciate Jasper's efforts to guide him. He wished things could be simpler with his brother. Felix was his only family, and Jasper loved his brother more than any other person on the face of this earth.

But that meant he wanted to protect him. It had gutted Felix when he found out that all of those women had thrown him over the second they found out that he wouldn't come into his fortune for another eight years, and that they had all accepted the hundred pounds Jasper had dangled before them like a carrot in exchange for going away.

Jasper never wanted to see his brother in that state ever again. Better for Felix to be annoyed with him for a week than heartbroken and miserable for a lifetime. And if he had to play the villain in order to protect his brother from greater wounds, Jasper was ready and willing to assume the role.

Felix was still regarding him skeptically in the mirror. "So, it's different when *you* come to a house party hoping to find a wife, but when the Weatherby sisters do the exact same thing..."

"I have something to offer," Jasper muttered, pulling the shirt Stephens handed him over his head.

"And Pippa does, too," Felix said, his voice becoming rhapsodic. "We have so much in common! I fell into conversation with her *so easily.*"

Jasper resisted the urge to roll his eyes. This hardly counted as an accomplishment. Felix fell easily into conversation with every single person he met, whether they were a duke or a dustman.

"She's not merely beautiful," Felix continued. "She's kind. Genuinely kind. And she's as passionate about animals as I am! Well…" He laughed. "Mostly she's passionate about cats. But when I told her about the plight of carriage horses in London, she sounded very concerned. And more than that…" Felix paused, biting his lip. "When I told her about my hopes for the S.P.C.A., she was impressed. I'm certain she was. And, Jasp, that's what I've always wanted! Someone who doesn't just see me as the son of a duke who's going to come into a little bit of money in a few years. Someone who likes me for, well. *Me.*"

He could see that Felix truly meant it. And—God—he *hated* to be the one to always put a damper on his brother's hopes and dreams.

But it needed to be said.

Jasper tried to make his voice gentle as he asked, "And how long have you known this girl?"

Felix raised a hand in acknowledgment. "A half-hour. It's true."

"Felix…" Jasper groaned.

"Look, it's not as if I've proposed. If she turns out to be awful, there's no harm done. But I have a feeling about Pippa."

Jasper tried to choose his words carefully. "I'm sure she's very beautiful. But she's a Weatherby Wallflower, which means she's desperate to snare a husband—*any* husband. We should assume the worst."

Felix waved this off. "She told me about all of that. Didn't try to hide a thing. She even told me very matter-of-factly that she's probably going to have to marry Lord Oglesby."

Felix laughed. "Paradoxically, it actually made me like her better, because she so clearly wasn't trying to lay some trap. I'm telling you, Pippa is an open book."

"Hmm," Jasper said as Stephens went to work on his cravat.

"Just give her a chance," Felix said. "That's all I ask."

"All right," Jasper said begrudgingly. He cast a speaking gaze toward his brother's dusty boots. "Shouldn't you be getting cleaned up? Dinner starts in a half hour."

"There's one more thing." Felix raked a hand through his wavy hair, suddenly looking nervous. "You know how my friends and I have been trying to get our organization off the ground."

"Yes?" Jasper said, shrugging into his coat.

"There are a few associated expenses. Expenses that, out of the men in the group, I am in the best position to cover. So, I'd like to ask you to release a small portion of my inheritance."

Jasper cut his eyes to Felix in the mirror. Why was it that his brother always seemed to attract "friends" who needed his money? "How much?"

Felix swallowed thickly. "Only a thousand pounds—"

"A *thousand pounds*?" Jasper barked, whirling around to face his brother.

"It's only a small fraction of my bequest!" Felix protested.

"It's a bloody fortune to most people," Jasper countered. "What do these *friends* of yours need a thousand pounds for, anyway?"

"Mostly legal fees. The animal welfare laws that are currently in place have no teeth if we can't pay an investigator to gather evidence and a barrister to press charges. People need to see that we are enacting consequences for abusing an animal. Once people see the good work we're doing, they'll be inspired to join. We just have to make a start."

"And why can't these lawyers work pro bono, if it's such a good cause?" Jasper countered.

Felix gave him an exasperated look. "I suppose we could ask, but we could probably only prosecute ten percent of the cases we could otherwise pursue. And these animals can't wait. They need our help *now*."

"Hmmm." Jasper turned back to the mirror, straightening his coat. "You said it was mainly for legal fees. What other expenses do these 'friends' of yours expect you to cover?"

"The rest of the money would go toward fundraising. We'll make it back tenfold! But in order to organize, say, a charity sermon, you need to print handbills, you need to put an ad in the paper, you need a venue and a few refreshments. That sort of thing." Felix cleared his throat. "So. Will you release the funds to me now?"

Jasper sighed as he turned to face his brother. "A thousand pounds is a tremendous sum of money."

"I know that, but—"

Jasper ploughed over his brother's protests. "It does not speak well of your friends that they would ask it of you."

Felix's brow was creased. "You don't understand. I'm younger than most of the men in the group and less experienced. But this is a way I can help! This is how I can be involved, how I can—"

Jasper shook his head. "I fear you have fallen in with a fast set, Felix. A fast set who is all too eager to spend your money."

Felix's mouth fell open. "Did you just refer to *William Wilberforce*, Richard Martin, and Arthur Broome—*Reverend* Arthur Broome, I might add—as a *fast set*?"

Jasper shifted back and forth. He had forgotten that Wilberforce was involved.

Still…

"You cannot deny, Felix, that whenever I have released some of your inheritance to you, you have been cavalier with the funds."

Felix cast his gaze toward the heavens. "Again, I was seventeen years old!"

"You bought a rock, Felix! A very plain, very unextraordinary rock. For *three hundred pounds!*"

Felix held his hands out in front of him, placatingly. "I honestly thought it was an ostrich egg."

"It was not an ostrich egg!" Jasper snapped. "It was a rock! And even considering the *remote* possibility that it *was* an ostrich egg, why in all of God's green goodness did you need to buy it?"

Felix scowled. "The man selling it had only the smallest paddock. I wanted to give the ostrich sufficient room to run around, to have a good life—"

"You are too soft-hearted," Jasper snapped. "You get all worked up over imaginary ostriches and alleged Russian princesses, and you cannot see when people are taking advantage of you."

"Again, brother, I was seventeen!"

Jasper shook his head. "Well, you weren't seventeen during the unfortunate moose incident."

Felix lifted his chin. "That was merely a slight misadventure—"

"You could have died!" Jasper snapped. "And you were the subject of a cartoon. It is still available for sale over at Ackerman's Repository."

"I thought the mother moose had abandoned those calves," Felix protested. "I was only trying to help! Besides, I escaped up a tree—"

"Where you remained for the next two days." Jasper rubbed his forehead. "I don't know what I was thinking, letting you go to Norway. I suppose I should be glad you only antagonized a mother moose. It could have been a polar bear."

"Yes, well, I was only nineteen when that one happened. Not that much older. And I have learned from my mistakes, Jasper." At Jasper's skeptical look, he insisted, "I have! But you will never afford me the opportunity to prove it."

"I am only looking out for your best interests," Jasper began.

"Did it ever occur to you that I might know more about my best interests than you?" Felix snapped. "That I should have some say in my own life?"

Jasper hated to see his brother upset. "Now, calm down—"

"I won't calm down! I will come into my majority eleven months from now. Then, I'll be able to spend whatever I want and marry whomever I want as well. And, if you would look at my current requests with unprejudiced eyes, you would see that they are reasonable. But you won't! You made up your mind years ago that I'm the family idiot and anything I want must be inherently a bad idea."

The words tore at Jasper's heart. Did Felix truly believe that? Could he not see that Jasper had only ever tried to protect him?

"That's not true," Jasper said. "I don't think you're an idiot. I *care* about you, Felix. You're my *brother*. I only want to protect you from making these mistakes—"

"Living life on my own terms is not a mistake," Felix snapped. "I am allowed to want different things from what you want. And just because I refuse to be mistrustful of everyone I meet does not make my judgment bad or my choices *mistakes*."

"Felix," Jasper said, reaching for his brother's arm.

Felix shook him off. "As you yourself pointed out, I need to dress for dinner. Do excuse me, brother."

Jasper watched sadly as his brother stormed out the door. Sighing, he turned to find Stephens cleaning up the shaving things, studiously avoiding his employer's eye.

"It's for his own good," Jasper said.

"Of course, Your Grace," Stephens agreed. He kept his eyes fixed on the floor as he filed out of the room.

Jasper turned to look at the mastiffs. Benedick was asleep.

Beatrice, on the other hand, rose from her place on the mat, turned so that her back was to him, and lay back down, effectively giving her master the canine version of the cut direct.

Even his dogs thought he was an arse.

Sighing, Jasper went in search of someone who might appreciate his company.

CHAPTER 4

Considering how little time the Weatherby sisters had to dress for dinner, Eleanor thought they looked remarkably well as they descended the staircase of Lady Milthorpe's country house.

To be sure, Clarissa had managed to find the one and only dirt-colored dress in the stack of bright silks their hostess had sent over, and Kate's blue gown matched not only her eyes but her mood.

But Pippa looked remarkably pretty in a mint-green dress that Lady Milthorpe's daughter had worn a few seasons ago. And Eleanor thought she looked entirely presentable in a gown of raspberry silk.

As she had been doing for the last half hour, Pippa was chattering about Felix St. James. "I thought him *very* kind and *very* handsome. Did you not think him handsome, Kate?"

"Hmm?" Kate asked, blinking in a way that suggested she had not been attending.

"Very handsome," Eleanor agreed for the sake of placating her sister.

"That's what I thought as well!" Pippa said. "In fact, now

that I think on it, he might be the most handsome man I have ever seen."

"Which isn't saying much," Clarissa noted, "as there were only two eligible men in all of Boroughbridge."

"Pippa." Eleanor drew her sister to a halt just shy of the landing where the grand staircase split into two branches, one leading to the west wing, where their bedrooms were located, and the other to the east. Dropping her voice to a whisper, she said, "Lord Felix treated us all very kindly this afternoon. But I want you to consider the possibility that this was a mark of his gallantry and good manners, rather than an indication of a deeper regard, especially after so short an acquaintance."

"Gallant—that's just the word for him," Pippa mused.

"Additionally, as Lord Felix himself mentioned, he will not come into his majority for another year. He therefore does not have control of his fortune. He is also too young to marry without his brother's permission." Eleanor took her sister's hand and squeezed it. "I do not want you to be disappointed, dear, if, for one reason or another, he does not pursue a deeper connection."

"Oh, gracious, no!" Pippa exclaimed. "Indeed, I had never imagined that so fine a gentleman as *him* would have any interest in the likes of me. Truly, I was not even contemplating it."

Eleanor pressed her sister's hand. "You are wise to proceed cautiously."

"Yes, I have no expectations, none at all, where Lord Felix is concerned."

Reassured, Eleanor turned to continue their progress down the stairs.

"But, as I was saying," Pippa continued, "I cannot think of a single man of my acquaintance who is more handsome than Lord Felix. Do you not agree, Clarissa?"

Eleanor groaned as Pippa chattered on. Her sister might not be lying when she said she harbored no expectations. But it seemed she had developed hopes, whether she was ready to admit to them or not.

"What do you think, Eleanor?"

"Very handsome, yes," Eleanor said absentmindedly.

While this was not by any means a lie, Eleanor had to own that Lord Felix's particular brand of handsomeness was not much to her personal taste. Her preference was for a rugged sort of masculinity, as opposed to boyish good looks. Not that any man would ever look at her twice, but if she were given her choice, she would much prefer...

She glanced up at the sound of booted feet on the stairs opposite them, the ones leading to the east wing.

She would much prefer...

She would much prefer someone *precisely* like the man coming toward her right now.

He was tall and big-boned, with broad shoulders and a chest thick with muscles. His evening clothes were immaculate. Eleanor didn't know enough about fashion to say if they were cut to the latest style, but they certainly looked expensive. He wore his dark hair cropped short, and although he was freshly shaved, you could still see a dark shadow on his imposing jawline. His nose was prominent, too, but unlike Eleanor's, it somehow made him look imperious rather than unsightly. His brown eyes were alert, scanning the foyer, missing nothing.

Beside her, Pippa gasped, snapping Eleanor back to attention.

Felix had appeared at the top of the stairs. As he jogged down, the dark-haired man reached for his arm. "Felix, wait."

"Leave me alone, Jasper," Felix muttered, shaking him off. He hurried over to where the four Weatherby sisters were standing. "Miss Philippa," he said, smiling at Pippa as he bowed over her hand.

Eleanor's gaze shifted back to the man she now knew must be Felix's brother, the Duke of Norwood.

She found him scowling at the sight of his brother, head tipped down solicitously toward Pippa. He seemed to sense her gaze because, for a split second, his eyes met hers.

He wrinkled his nose in distaste as he passed her on the stairs.

Eleanor drew in a shaky breath. Well, she knew precisely how Jasper St. James felt about his brother forging an acquaintance with the Weatherby Wallflowers. Not that his disdain came as any surprise. She had known this would be an uphill battle.

And besides, Eleanor was accustomed to the world's derision. If Jasper St. James despised her, he was in good company.

Felix had offered one arm to Pippa and another to Kate. As they made their way down the stairs, he said, "Miss Philippa, this afternoon you mentioned owning three cats. I believe you said their names were Pepper, Ollie, and Crumpet. Won't you tell me more about them?"

This, of course, was the perfect question, and Pippa responded eagerly. Felix was more than attentive, hanging on her every answer and asking interested questions that kept the conversation flowing. Not that any effort was required. Pippa could talk about cats for hours. But Felix seemed genuinely interested in what she had to say.

Perhaps he really was interested in the youngest Weatherby sister. Moments ago, Eleanor had been warning her sister not to get her hopes up.

But in the face of this encouragement, she decided to adopt a different strategy. She hated to think of sacrificing her youngest sister to Lord Oglesby.

But maybe she wouldn't have to. Maybe Pippa could instead forge a happier sort of connection.

Eleanor decided right then and there that she was going to do everything within her power to promote a match between Pippa and Felix.

Based on the way Felix's brother had scowled at them, he would probably do all he could to prevent the match. Well, let him try. Jasper St. James might be a duke, but he had never faced off against the likes of Eleanor Weatherby. Desperate times called for desperate measures, and nobody was more desperate than the Weatherby Wallflowers. Eleanor would stop at nothing to make sure Pippa won not only security but happiness.

If Jasper St. James thought he could stand in her way, good luck to him.

He was going to need it.

CHAPTER 5

*J*asper watched with distaste as his brother spent the next half-hour conversing exclusively with those Weatherby Wallflowers.

Jasper could guess easily enough which one was *Pippa*, as Felix scarcely took his eyes off the chit. His brother hung on her every word and did not make the slightest attempt to converse with any of the other guests. His attentions, and his interest, could not have been more marked.

He had to own that she was as pretty as Felix had said. That didn't change the fact that she likely saw nothing more in his brother than the hefty inheritance he would come into on his twenty-fifth birthday. All Jasper wanted was for his brother to find a wife who would truly care for him, who would be his life mate and partner. Not some fortune huntress who would bleed Felix dry and leave him heartbroken.

Surely that wasn't too much to ask.

From across the crimson and gold parlor where the guests had gathered before dinner, Jasper observed the four Weatherby sisters. Felix had also been correct in his assessment that they were all passably handsome. To be sure, other than Pippa, they weren't likely to attract much male attention, but that wasn't on account of their looks. The one in the bronze dress kept her shoulders hunched and her chin ducked and wore such a ferocious scowl that it would take a brave man to ask her for so much as the time. The one in the blue gown, on the other hand, stared sightlessly across the room with an expression of disinterested melancholy.

The last sister concerned him the most. She looked to be the oldest of the four, not that she was what you would call old. She had medium-brown hair shot through with streaks of gold and a Roman nose that actually lent her a bit of an aristocratic air—ironic, considering she didn't have a drop of blue blood in her veins. She was taller and more sturdily built than her three sisters, but not in an unattractive way. He had never much cared for waifish women. Jasper was a huge, hulking sort of man, and he much preferred a bedpartner he didn't have to worry about snapping in two.

Not that Jasper was thinking of taking one of the Weatherby Wallflowers to bed. Good God, where had *that* thought come from?

But the main thing that concerned Jasper about the oldest Weatherby sister was her eyes. He couldn't tell their color from across the room. But he could discern the fierce intelligence radiating from them.

Yes, the oldest sister was the one he needed to worry about. Unless he was very much mistaken, she would make a formidable foe.

Scowling at the four Weatherby sisters, he crossed the room to where his host, Lady Milthorpe, was conversing in hushed tones with the butler. Once the butler excused himself, Jasper bowed over her hand. "Lady Milthorpe, it is lovely, as always, to see you."

The countess gave a fond smile. She was still an attractive

woman, for all that her own children were grown, with a pleasantly plump figure and curling hair that was a mix of blonde and grey. "Likewise, Your Grace."

Jasper dropped his voice low. "Have the particular guests we discussed arrived?"

"They have."

Having decided that the time had come for him to marry, Jasper had asked Lady Milthorpe, who was practically an aunt to him, having been his mother's dearest friend, to help him find the next Duchess of Norwood. She had sent him a list of candidates with an outline of both their best attributes and those that might cause him to hesitate. Jasper had chosen two—Lady Josephine Paulet, daughter of the Marquess of Peveral, and Lady Francesca FitzSimon, daughter of the Duke of Wroxley.

"That is Lady Josephine," Lady Milthorpe said, gesturing subtly with her fan to a young lady in a white dress. She had a mane of dark, glossy curls and was presently engaged in conversation with three besotted-looking young gentlemen.

"And that is Lady Francesca," the countess said, indicating a petite, fair-haired young lady in a pink dress, who was standing in the corner with a woman who looked to be her mother.

Jasper felt a pang of disappointment. The two young ladies were fashionably thin and wan... which was not what he liked at all. Their wrists would look comically small next to his.

God, he was going be sleeping with one of these women for the rest of his life, and he would have to be constantly on his guard to make sure he wasn't too rough with her. Would he never be able to relax and actually enjoy himself in bed?

What an unworthy thought. Lady Josephine and Lady Francesca had been selected for their breeding, their accomplishments, and their readiness to step into the role of duchess. These were far more important qualities to consider than bed sport.

"You will be seated next to Lady Josephine at dinner tonight," Lady Milthorpe explained, "and I will make sure you are able to spend some time with Lady Francesca tomorrow."

"Perfect," Jasper murmured. "Thank you for arranging things."

The woman who was the closest thing he had to a mother nodded. "You're most welcome."

"One more thing." Jasper subtly inclined his head toward the far side of the room. "I take it that is Miss Philippa Weatherby who is engaged in conversation with my brother at present?"

"That is correct." Lady Milthorpe frowned, studying his expression. "I know what you must be thinking. But Pippa is a lovely girl."

Jasper arched a single brow. "Is she?"

"She is," Lady Milthorpe said firmly.

"Hmm." Jasper narrowed his eyes as Felix and Pippa chuckled over some private joke. "Am I correct in assuming that the three ladies surrounding them are the other Misses Weatherby?"

"You are. The one in the blue dress is Katherine. The one in the bronze is Clarissa. And the one in pink is Eleanor."

A woman in a dark blue gown was hovering nearby, obviously hoping for a moment of their hostess's time. Jasper bowed over Lady Milthorpe's hand. "Thank you, my lady. You have told me precisely what I wanted to know."

He headed across the room to greet the earl. So, the name of the wallflower in the raspberry gown was Eleanor Weatherby.

It was important to know the name of his enemy.

As he accepted a brandy from a passing footman, Jasper glowered across the room at her.

CHAPTER 6

Ten minutes later, the butler announced that dinner was served. Lady Milthorpe introduced Jasper to Lady Josephine, and he offered her his arm.

They were seated near the head of the table, which was unsurprising, given their rank. As they made their way to that end of the dining room, Jasper noticed a place card bearing his brother's name about halfway down the table. He was seated between Mrs. Cartwright and Lady Duncombe.

Good. His brother would benefit from passing a couple of hours in the company of someone other than that Weatherby chit.

A flash of raspberry silk caught his eye. Eleanor Weatherby stood near the far end of the table, scrutinizing the place cards before her. Jasper could almost see the thoughts flitting behind those intelligent eyes of hers.

She glanced up and down the room, then, quick as a snake, she snatched one of the place cards near the far end of the table...

... and swapped it out with the one at Felix's assigned place.

Jasper stiffened. Why, that brazen little minx!

"Is anything the matter, Your Grace?" Lady Josephine asked in lilting, sophisticated tones.

"Not at all," Jasper said. He hastily pulled out her chair, but his gaze did not stray from the far end of the table.

Felix strolled into the room, Philippa Weatherby on his arm. Seeing his assigned seat, he smiled broadly. "Well, this is a bit of a chance, isn't it?" He held out a chair for Miss Philippa, then settled into the seat next to her.

Eleanor Weatherby was peering around, no doubt trying to ascertain if she had been caught. When her gaze reached the top of the table, she locked eyes with him and froze.

Jasper gave her his most imperious ducal glower.

For a second, she did not move, and no wonder. Jasper had made grown men cry with the very look he was leveling at her right now.

Not Eleanor Weatherby. Boldly holding his gaze, she lifted her chin, and then?

The impudent miss had the temerity to smirk at him! Her eyes all but dared him to say something to Lady Milthorpe, which, of course, he was not going to do. The only thing worse than Felix sitting next to Philippa Weatherby for the duration of dinner would be Jasper kicking up a fuss about it.

Eleanor Weatherby seemed to be enjoying his steaming fury, because her lips twisted upward. Tossing a triumphant grin over her shoulder, she sauntered around the table to assume her seat.

Smoldering with rage, Jasper settled into his own chair.

Soon, the guests had all found their seats. Struggling to keep his feelings in check, he offered Lady Josephine some of the white soup in the tureen in front of him, which she accepted.

"Tell me, Your Grace," she began, taking up her spoon, "do you enjoy the theater?"

Jasper perked up a bit. This seemed like a promising overture. He was a great fan of the theater, in particular, the works of Shakespeare. "I do. What is your opinion of it, Lady Josephine?"

She gave him a dazzling smile. "Oh, I absolutely *adore* the theatre!"

Jasper leaned toward her as he took up his own spoon. "And what do you think about the works of Shakespeare?"

"*Shakespeare?*" She gave an incredulous laugh. "I prefer something a bit more fashionable than those stodgy old plays!"

Jasper struggled not to let his disappointment show on his face. "I see. What plays do you prefer?"

She went on to rhapsodize about some of the plays she had seen in London during the Season. Out of her five favorite plays, Jasper had seen three of them, and although they had been passable enough for an evening's entertainment, they were ultimately forgettable. He didn't think any of them could hold a candle to *Macbeth* or *The Winter's Tale.*

But he attempted to be cordial and said nothing of it to Lady Josephine.

Their conversation turned from the theater to the Season more generally. For Lady Josephine, this seemed to have consisted primarily of various balls and routs.

"Did you attend Thomas Hope's rout in June?" she asked.

"I did not. Parliament was in session that evening." As most members of both the House of Lords and House of Commons were men of fashion who kept the *ton's* hours, parliamentary debate began late in the afternoon and often stretched into the evening.

"Oh!" Lady Josephine looked startled. "Was there a particularly important measure up for a vote?"

Jasper shook his head. "No, just routine business."

She gave a trilling laugh. "Surely you could have skipped just one evening in order to attend an event so significant as Thomas Hope's annual rout!"

Jasper grunted. He considered his service in the House of Lords to be a sacred charge. If it was in session, he was going to be there, and he certainly wasn't going to neglect his duty to attend some party. But he could hardly contradict Lady Josephine without coming off as a great arse.

As the dinner wore on, it became increasingly clear that the primary attractions Lady Josephine felt to becoming his wife would be gaining the title of duchess and having the St. James family fortune at her disposal. She was sophisticated and seemed clever enough, but Jasper did not detect any great depths.

Not that he was writing her off entirely. Lady Josephine was still well-bred and ready to step into the role of duchess. And after all, the reason he had his pick of brides was because of his title and fortune. To hold the fact that these were attractions against a woman would be to ignore the way of the world.

Yet he did not want those to be the *only* reasons his future bride wanted to marry him, and Jasper found himself hoping that Lady Francesca would prove a better match.

Raised voices from the far end of the table caught his attention. Jasper recognized Lucas Robertson, an old schoolmate of Felix's, and his sister, Anna-Maria, at the center of the hubbub.

Jasper couldn't help but scowl. He'd always thought Lucas Robertson was a bad influence on his brother. He also suspected that the sister, Anna-Maria, had her eye on Felix, or, more accurately, Felix's fortune. He shouldn't be surprised that they were here, given that they lived nearby, but he wished Lady Milthorpe could have contrived an excuse to keep them off the guest list.

The Weatherby sister in the brown dress, Clarissa, was glaring poison at Anna-Maria. "Yes, this is a borrowed dress. No, we've never had asparagus before, nor did we have a season in London, as I'm sure you're well aware. Now, if you've exhausted your supply of snide remarks, I would appreciate it if you would let my sisters and I eat our dinner in peace."

"My gracious!" Anna-Maria Robertson chuckled. "Lady Milthorpe has always been known for her charitable nature. Only now do I understand just how well her reputation is deserved."

Clarissa started to respond, but her sister, Eleanor, spoke first. "Clarissa." Her voice was a rich alto that hit Jasper in the gut. She only spoke her sister's name, but she managed to imbue that single word with an unmistakable note of authority.

"But, Eleanor—" Clarissa protested.

Eleanor silenced her younger sister with a look. "*We* would never mar our hostess's gathering by being disagreeable."

The younger Weatherby sister slouched in her seat but said no more.

Beside her, Anna-Maria preened, seeming to have missed the fact that she was the true target of Eleanor's rebuke.

Smirking, she turned to Felix, but her face fell when she found his expression stony.

Such an expression was unlike his brother. Jasper took it that Anna-Maria must've been needling the youngest Miss Weatherby for some time before her sister snapped.

Anna-Maria's cheeks grew ruddy as Felix pointedly turned to Philippa and engaged her in conversation.

Jasper's gaze traveled to Eleanor. He could scarcely believe he was thinking such a thing, but he could not help but admire the deftness with which she had handled the confrontation, and also how effectively she had reined in her sister.

Would that he could be half so effective at managing Felix.

But, judging by the glowers Anna-Maria and her brother were now directing at Philippa Weatherby, who was obliviously chatting with his brother, Jasper fancied he was no longer the only guest counting the Weatherby sisters as his enemy.

CHAPTER 7

Felix was not at breakfast the following morning when the four sisters went downstairs, but Baron Oglesby, who had arrived late the previous evening, was. Eleanor obtained an introduction from their hostess and made a point of sitting at the same end of the table as the baron. Although Felix seemed quite taken with Pippa, their situation was dire enough that they could not afford to put all their eggs in one basket.

Mindful of Pippa's remark that all four sisters needed to make a good-faith effort to charm Lord Oglesby, Eleanor tried to be warm and affable, and she attempted to nudge Clarissa and Kate into doing the same. But she was honestly unsurprised that the baron seemed the most partial to Pippa.

The planned entertainment for that morning was a walk to the new folly Lord Milthorpe had recently constructed. After changing into their worn half-boots, Eleanor and her sisters headed for the front lawn.

The autumn morning dawned crisp with a sky free of clouds. Eleanor was enjoying the cool breeze on her face when Pippa cried, "Felix is here!" and went scurrying across the damp grass.

Felix was indeed there, and he was not alone—he was throwing a stick for the two largest dogs Eleanor had ever seen. They were mastiffs with dun fur and squished black faces that gave them a perpetually sorrowful expression, although their wagging tails and bouncing gait suggested that they were having the time of their lives chasing the stick.

Felix brightened at Pippa's approach. "Miss Philippa!" he said for the benefit of the guests within hearing range. "Good morning."

Pippa paused as one of the dogs came loping up. "Are they friendly?"

"They are," Felix reassured her. "I know they look a bit terrifying. But they're tremendously good-natured and actually quite affectionate."

Pippa stuck out a hand, and the male came over to sniff it. "Who is this gorgeous fellow?" she asked, scratching him behind the ears.

"This is Benny, and the female is Bea. Or, as my brother Jasper would tell you, Benedick and Beatrice."

Eleanor started. "You named your dogs after characters from Shakespeare?" Eleanor adored Shakespeare. She had read his complete plays and knew many passages by heart. *Much Ado About Nothing*, in which Beatrice and Benedick featured, was a particular favorite.

"I didn't. My brother, Jasper, did. They're his dogs, I just like to borrow them sometimes."

"I can see why," Pippa said. Both mastiffs had taken to her immediately, and Beatrice was licking her face, which Pippa did not seem to mind a whit. "They're adorable! Would they let me throw the stick for them?"

"They would like nothing better," Felix reassured her, handing her the stick.

Eleanor settled back a discreet distance with Clarissa and Kate. The only ones who seemed to enjoy Pippa's company more than Felix were Beatrice and Benedick, who were frolicking like puppies in spite of being larger than the pony who pulled their former neighbor Mrs. Ramsay around Boroughbridge in a little cart.

A sharp whistle pierced the crisp morning air. Both dogs looked up, then went bounding off toward the house.

Eleanor turned and saw the Duke of Norwood descending the steps. He had donned a coat of olive-green tweed in a nod to their country setting, pairing it with a waistcoat of burnt umber wool that picked up the subtle check of the fabric. The rustic garments made him look even more hardy and vigorous, and when the two giant dogs fell into step by his side, Eleanor felt a great lump rise in her throat.

Oh, this was awful! The man detested her. The glower he had leveled at her in the dining room last night had left her without a single doubt on that front.

It would not do at all to find him attractive.

Speaking of glowers, he was directing another one at the Weatherby sisters. "Felix!" he snapped. "Come!"

Felix gave an easy grin. "He seems to have mistaken me for one of the mastiffs."

Pippa giggled, and even Clarissa cracked a smile. Kate, who was staring off toward the woods, did not seem to have heard, although Eleanor was pleased to see that she had brought along her sketchpad. Other than making a series of paintings of Pepper, Ollie, and Crumpet so Pippa would have something to remember her beloved cats by, Eleanor had not seen her sister draw or paint since the news of their father's betrayal had broken.

"Felix! I need to speak with you."

Felix rolled his eyes. "Coming, brother."

Lady Milthorpe clapped her hands. "I believe everyone has assembled. If you would be so kind as to follow me, I will show you the way to the folly."

Eleanor fell into step with her sisters as they followed Lady Milthorpe toward the woods. As they approached the edge of the trees, Eleanor admired a gorgeous old maple whose leaves were turning from yellow to orange. When their party startled a herd of fallow deer that went loping off across the meadow, Kate straightened and watched their retreat with a flicker of interest. It might not seem like much, but it was the most animated Eleanor had seen her sister in weeks, and it made her heart give a hopeful squeeze.

She could see the St. James brothers a little way ahead with the mastiffs trotting at their heels. By all appearances, they were arguing in hushed whispers.

Just then, the duke turned his head and his eyes locked with Eleanor's. His lip curled and his eyes narrowed.

She responded with a smug smile.

His scowl deepened, and he turned back to his brother, who looked distinctly annoyed.

After a pleasant ten-minute walk, they caught sight of the folly. It had been designed to look like the remnants of a ruined abbey and was situated at the far end of a little clearing just as it melded into the woods. Everyone oohed and aahed over the picturesque sight.

Their hosts had spread some woolen blankets out upon the grass. Kate marched up to one on the far side of the clearing, took a seat with her back to the folly, and flipped open her sketchpad.

"Kate, dear," Eleanor began, taking a seat behind her, "the folly is that way."

Kate nodded silently toward a spruce tree on the edge of the clearing. It took Eleanor a moment to spot the red kite perched upon a branch. She glanced at Kate's pad and saw that she had already sketched the raptor's outline and was just starting to capture its keen gaze.

Pippa and Clarissa settled beside them on the blanket. Most of the guests had wandered over to explore the folly—all, in fact, save Felix and the duke, who were arguing on the edge of the clearing.

It seemed that Felix had had enough. "Oh, leave me be, will you?" he snapped at his brother. He proceeded to stride across the clearing, stopping at the edge of their blanket. "Miss Philippa," he said, holding out a hand, "could I interest you in having a look around the folly with me?"

Pippa looked hopefully at Eleanor, who nodded. "It's fine, dear. There are plenty of other people about."

Smiling brightly, Pippa accepted Felix's hand and stood. Eleanor watched as they strolled toward the faux abbey, heads tilted toward one another.

A shadow fell over their blanket. Eleanor glanced up to see the Duke of Norwood looming above her, his face creased into a dark scowl. "Miss Weatherby," he said through a clenched jaw, "might I have the pleasure of your company?"

He said the word *pleasure* in such a tone to suggest that it would, in fact, be pleasure's opposite. Frankly, Eleanor was surprised he had approached her at all, as they had not been properly introduced.

She lifted her chin. Never mind that. They had taken each other's measure, and she wasn't the least bit surprised he had gone to the trouble to find out her name. She wasn't going to crumple before Jasper St. James, and the sooner he learned as much, the better.

She pushed up from the blanket and attempted to infuse her voice with as much malice as his. "The *pleasure* will all be mine, Your Grace."

He did not offer his arm so much as seize her wrist in an iron grip. Eleanor tossed her head back and tried to look carefree as he all but dragged her across the meadow. She marveled at his size, which she was experiencing up close for the first time. She wasn't a small woman, either in height or frame, but she felt positively petite standing next to Jasper St. James.

Once they reached the edge of the trees, he rounded on her. "Just what are you playing at?"

"Playing at? I have no idea what you mean. A moment ago, I *was* enjoying the fine view." She flicked her gaze down to his boots and back up to his face, curling her nostrils as if the present view suffered by comparison. Which, of course, was a lie, but she would gladly take on the sin for the sake of annoying him.

It did annoy him, if the way his brow lowered was any indication. "I saw you last night," he hissed. "I saw you switch my brother's place card."

She tossed her head. "Yes, well, he was seated next to Lady Duncombe, who all but bathes in *Eau de Occitanie.* Perhaps I was trying to help preserve his appetite."

"And perhaps," he snapped, "you were trying to promote a match between him and your sister!"

She lifted her chin. "And why would that pose a problem? Are you suggesting, sir, that there is anything wrong with my sister?"

"You know very well that there is! My brother is the son of a duke, and your sister is one of those Weatherby W—"

He cut himself off, seeming to realize the extreme rudeness of what he had almost said.

Eleanor was not prepared to let him off so easily.

She took one step closer, then another. "Go ahead," she said, eyes locked upon his. "*Say it.*"

CHAPTER 8

*J*asper swallowed thickly as he regarded Eleanor Weatherby in the dappled shade of the trees.

She was… not what he had expected.

He'd thought she would be shrewish and shrill. Instead, this penniless spinster radiated the confidence of a queen. Jasper was a large man, and he knew most people found him intimidating even without considering the fact that he was a duke.

But Eleanor Weatherby looked about as intimidated as a lioness squaring off with a fieldmouse. Jasper hadn't felt like a mouse since… well, ever. He'd weighed ten pounds on the day he was born and had a deep bellow for a cry. He was given to understand that he'd been an imposing specimen even as an infant.

Yet when she had stalked up to him just now, he'd had to stop himself from taking a step back.

It was *unheard of.*

"*Say it,*" she repeated, her hazel eyes sparking, daring him to do just that.

He lifted his chin. "I will not."

"Hmph." She smirked up at him. "Then I'll say it, because we both know what you were thinking." She leaned in even closer, and it struck Jasper that if he lowered his chin mere inches, his lips would brush hers…

"You were going to call my sister a Weatherby Wallflower!" She jabbed him in the chest two times to punctuate the insult.

"I was," Jasper acknowledged with a tilt of his head. "It was ill-mannered of me, and I apologize."

Her expression was strangely triumphant, considering he had insulted her just as much as her sister. "You may keep your apologies. We both know you meant it. You would never countenance your brother marrying so far beneath him."

"What I would not countenance," he growled, "is my brother marrying someone who cares nothing for him and only for his money!"

She narrowed her eyes. "How *dare* you! You don't even know my sister. You may say any awful thing about me, but Pippa is the kindest, most caring girl in the world, and I will not stand by while you cast aspersions against her!"

"And yet, according to Rupert Dupree, the lot of you care for nothing but ensnaring a rich husband." He arched a sardonic brow. "And now she has miraculously developed a deep and abiding affection for my brother in less than twenty-four hours. Such a coincidence!"

"Rupert Dupree is a liar and a cad!" she shot back. "I know their acquaintance has been short, but Pippa's feelings for your brother are sincere. Would you spend but five minutes in conversation with her, you would see that. But you won't. You made your mind up about us Weatherby Wallflowers before you spoke a word to any of us!"

"If I made up my mind quickly, it is because I have seen your ilk so many times before!" he snapped.

Based on the fire that flared in her eyes, he half-expected her to slap him.

What she did instead was much worse.

She *laughed* at him.

"No, Your Grace," she said, her smile triumphant. "You have never seen *my* ilk."

She spun on her heel and strode off across the meadow, not once looking back at him.

Jasper found that he was breathing hard. Why, that infuriating woman! He was half-tempted to undress her—

Dress her down. He had meant *dress her down.*

Well… He watched her hips sway saucily as she made her way across the clearing. They were the kind of hips that gave a man something to grab onto.

Oh, all right. Possibly both.

Halfway across the meadow, Beatrice came loping up to her, a large stick in her mouth. Miss Weatherby stopped to scratch his dog behind the ears, a genuine smile stealing across her face. Beatrice dropped the stick at her feet and looked up hopefully. Jasper knew that stick would be a sticky mess. No dog could rival an English mastiff when it came to drooling.

But Miss Weatherby surprised him by picking up the stick without the slightest hesitation and hurling it across the meadow.

He had to admit, she had an entirely adequate throwing arm. He watched as she repeated the maneuver three times, after which Beatrice was ready for a rest, as such big dogs did tend to tire themselves out easily.

He watched his dog follow Miss Weatherby to the blanket where her sisters were sitting and plop down right in the middle of them. Benedick promptly trotted over and joined her.

Bloody annoying wench—she'd even stolen his dogs.

Gritting his teeth, he went off to look at the ruins while he tried to restore himself to good humor.

~

Jasper managed to calm down in time for the walk back to the house, which was fortunate as his hostess approached him with Lady Francesca FitzSimon in tow.

Introductions were made and Jasper bowed over her hand. His initial impression of Lady Francesca was that she was petite, but she seemed even smaller and frailer up close. She didn't even come up to his shoulder, and her tiny hand disappeared into his meaty paw.

"I thought perhaps you might like to walk together," Lady Milthorpe said.

"I should like nothing better," Jasper said solemnly.

He offered her his arm. She was short enough that she had to reach up at an awkward angle to accept it. He almost suggested they each walk on their own, as it looked like it would be uncomfortable on her shoulder for any period of time, but he couldn't think of a way to phrase the suggestion that didn't sound ungentlemanly.

They fell into step. Jasper had to shorten his stride significantly to match hers. Lady Francesca kept her eyes downcast, and he noticed that her lower lip was trembling.

Something occurred to him. "Are you afraid of dogs?" He gestured to Beatrice and Benedick, who had come to his whistle a moment before. "They're quite tame, but I can have my brother call them if they make you nervous."

"No, I love dogs." As if to test this, Benedick came up and sniffed her hand. The massive dog probably outweighed her by ten stone, but the corners of Lady Francesca's mouth turned up and she scratched his neck.

"I see," Jasper said. So, if Lady Francesca wasn't afraid of the mastiffs, it followed that the thing that had frightened her was… him.

Delightful.

Benedick bounded ahead, and they walked in awkward silence for a moment. Jasper sifted through his brain for some item of conversation. "Their names are Beatrice and Benedick. The dogs," he clarified at her confused look.

"After the characters from *Much Ado About Nothing*?" she asked.

"Precisely." She still wasn't looking at him, but this seemed to be as much of a conversational opening as he was likely to get. "Do you enjoy Shakespeare, then?"

"Very much so," she replied softly.

"And what is your favorite Shakespearean play?"

She bit her lip. "A difficult question, when I like so many of them so well. But perhaps I'll say *The Tempest*."

Jasper almost sagged with relief as they fell into a conversation about Shakespeare. He knew that young ladies were often coached to parrot the interests of a gentleman they hoped to attract. He did not think that was the case here, however. Lady Francesca had a thorough knowledge of every play they discussed and could quote liberally from most of them. Her opinions were carefully considered, and she almost seemed to be enjoying the conversation.

Jasper said almost because every few minutes, just when he thought she was warming to him, Lady Francesca would look up at him. Her face would go pale, she would shudder, and the conversation would come staggering to a halt.

Thanks to Lady Francesca's short stride, they fell a bit behind the group. Somehow, the topic veered into politics. Again, Jasper found Lady Francesca's opinions to be sound and sensible.

As they came up to the house, Jasper mused that, intellectually, they were a good match. Lady Francesca was clearly intelligent, and they shared a number of common interests.

To be sure, she seemed terrified of him, but she would likely come around as she got to know him.

Yes, Lady Francesca was now his leading candidate to become the next Duchess of Norwood. It was a pity he wasn't much attracted to her, but again, there were more important qualities to consider.

Jasper tried to summon up some excitement about having found his future bride as he took the mastiffs upstairs for their nap.

He was not particularly successful in this regard.

CHAPTER 9

That afternoon, while the Weatherby sisters were gathered in Eleanor's bedroom, Kate did something unusual.

She spoke.

"I was thinking I might go out to the barn and sketch the kittens," she said. "Would anyone like to join me?"

Pippa looked up from her journal, in which she had been scribbling furiously for the last half hour. "I would! Just let me finish this thought."

Eleanor looked up from her stack of correspondence. She was fielding letters from the many distant relations to whom she had reached out for help. Most of the responses were demurrals, but an elderly great-aunt who lived in Edinburgh had offered to let them stay with her. Eleanor knew that Aunt Agatha lived in a cramped pair of rooms and could barely afford to feed herself. Still, it was better than being without a roof over their heads, and she appreciated the offer tremendously.

Eleanor could sleep on the floor. It wouldn't be enjoyable, but she could do it. All they needed was to buy enough time for a couple of the sisters to find paid positions. If all went well, perhaps they could move Aunt Agatha into a better situation after a few months.

"I have a guess as to what you're writing about," Eleanor said, voice teasing. "Or should I say, about whom."

"And your guess is probably correct," Pippa said good-naturedly.

Clarissa, who had been reading a book next to the window, looked up. "I overheard something this morning I think you should know about, Pippa."

"Oh?" Pippa asked, continuing to write. "What's that?"

"It was that Anna-Maria Robertson."

Pippa looked up, frowning. "Which one is Miss Robertson?"

"She's the one Clarissa was squabbling with at dinner," Eleanor said. "I take it Miss Robertson made a number of disagreeable remarks."

"Ah, yes," Pippa said. "What about her?"

Clarissa leaned forward. "On the way back, I was walking closely enough that I overheard her conversation with her brother. It would seem that Miss Robertson has set her cap for Felix. Suffice it to say, she is not pleased by the attentions he has been showing to you, Pip."

Eleanor shrugged a philosophical shoulder. "It doesn't surprise me that Lord Felix would have captured the fancy of Miss Robertson. He's as good-natured as he is handsome, and by all accounts he will be coming into a respectable fortune. I'm sure half the young ladies of his acquaintance must sigh over him."

"But this is no mere whim," Clarissa cautioned. "After Miss Robertson complained to her brother, he asked her if she wanted him to 'do something about it.' Pippa needs to be on her guard."

"Those were the exact words he used?" Eleanor asked.

"That he would 'do something about it?'" At Clarissa's nod, Eleanor continued, "That isn't necessarily nefarious. He probably just means that he will create an opportunity to thrust his sister into Lord Felix's path so they might have the chance to talk. It's scheming, to be sure, but ultimately not so different from what matchmaking mothers do every day."

Clarissa shook her head. "That's not what he meant. Mark my words—their intentions are malicious."

"Dear," Eleanor said, "do you think your disagreement with Miss Robertson over dinner could be coloring your opinion of her and her brother?"

Clarissa lifted her chin. "Not in the slightest."

Eleanor attempted to shift the conversation. "How on earth did you get close enough to overhear all of that, anyway?"

"It's her gowns," Kate offered. "She blends into her surroundings. Much as the barn owl has its speckled feathers and the fawn its spots, Clarissa is a master of concealment in her dirt-colored dresses."

Eleanor felt her heart squeeze. That was the first lighthearted remark she had heard Kate make since their father's announcement. How she hoped her sister was starting to mend.

Even Clarissa was smiling. "Precisely right, and that's why you won't catch me in some insipid gown of red or blue."

"I'm not sure you'll be able to stick to that, Claire," Pippa said. "Lady Milthorpe is planning at least one dance, and I don't think any of the ballgowns were brown."

"Not so!" Clarissa's eyes sparkled with a wicked gleam. "I found one at the bottom of the stack in a lovely shade of sepia."

Her three sisters groaned.

Pippa snapped her journal closed. "Done! Let me grab my bonnet and we can head down to the barn, Kate."

"Bring your journal," Kate suggested as they headed for the door. "I'll make a few sketches of the kittens in there. That way you can look at them as often as you like."

"Oh, would you, Kate?" Pippa asked as they trailed down the hall.

Eleanor sighed as she regarded the stack of letters that were still to be answered. "I should probably go with them. They're still young enough to need a chaperone."

"I'll do it," Clarissa offered. "I'm every bit as firmly on the shelf as you, and I daresay just as effective at frightening off untoward suitors."

"I would appreciate that," Eleanor said, taking up another letter. "Try not to come to blows," she added as her sister reached the door.

Clarissa cast a wry grin over her shoulder. "I make no promises."

~

Jasper managed to find a chair by the fireplace in the library that was large and sturdy enough that he could sit comfortably without having to worry that the spindly legs would collapse beneath his bulk. He was settling in with a stack of newspapers when Lord Oglesby appeared in the doorway.

"Are those today's papers?" the baron asked, his cane thumping against the Axminster carpet as he crossed the room.

"The ones from London are a couple of days old," Jasper said. "But they arrived this morning, so they're new to us."

"Do you mind if I join you?" the baron asked.

"Please," Jasper said, gesturing to the chair facing his.

They read in companionable silence. After a quarter of an hour had passed, the baron looked up, glancing around the room. "Don't suppose you know where Lord Milthorpe keeps his brandy?"

Jasper rose at once. "I thought I spotted a sideboard over here... surely enough." He pulled the stopper on a decanter and breathed in. "I don't know what vintage this is, but it smells promising. May I pour you one, my lord?"

"If you wouldn't mind," Lord Oglesby replied.

Jasper poured two glasses, handing one to the baron. "Cheers," he said, raising his glass as he settled into his seat.

The baron took a sip and made an appreciative sound. "So, Norwood, I hear you're attending this house party for much the same reason I am—to find a bride."

Jasper froze. He tended to keep his cards close to his chest, and he wondered who might have gone blathering to Lord Oglesby, of all people, about his decision to marry.

The baron chuckled. "Don't look so alarmed. My manservant heard from one of the housemaids that a couple of guests had been added at your request. Don't worry—I'm not interested in Lady Francesca or Lady Josephine. This would be my fourth wife, you know, so I don't have to be all that particular about breeding."

"I suppose not," Jasper muttered, unsure how to respond and wishing for a way to extract himself from this conversation.

"Have my eye on one of those Weatherby girls," the baron continued. "Although that news might not be any more welcome. I hear your brother may be after the same gel. The youngest one, Philippa."

The last thing Jasper wanted to discuss was his brother's rather obvious interest in the completely inappropriate Philippa Weatherby. Deciding he would read the papers another time, he started to make an excuse. "If you'll excuse me, I suddenly recalled—"

Lord Oglesby did not seem to have heard him. "I'll steer

clear of Miss Philippa if your brother is serious about the chit. She's pretty, don't get me wrong, but she's not worth making an enemy of a duke."

Jasper froze halfway out of his chair. Now that he thought on it, this was the perfect opportunity to show Felix that Philippa Weatherby was every bit as grasping as the women who had managed to mesmerize him when he was fresh out of school.

Felix would come into a respectable fortune that would produce an income of around ten thousand a year.

But Lord Oglesby's income was rumored to be around twice that amount, and he was in possession of a title. Comparing the two men from a purely mercenary perspective, there was no competition—the baron was the better catch.

Given the opportunity to marry such a man, Jasper felt certain that any of those grasping Weatherby Wallflowers would throw his brother over without a second's hesitation.

"Actually, my lord," Jasper said, settling back into his seat, "I would not mind in the least if you were to address yourself to the youngest Miss Weatherby. In fact"—he dropped his voice low—"I would consider it to be a favor."

The baron barked out a laugh. "Not too keen on her, are you?"

"Please, do not mistake me. I know nothing material against the young lady. But I am skeptical about the degree of affection she has apparently developed for my brother after a very short acquaintance. I would welcome the opportunity to test the true depth of her regard."

The baron nodded. "Then I will proceed as planned, and perhaps you will get it."

"Good. Very good." Setting down his glass, Jasper was reaching for his discarded newspaper when something occurred to him. "My lord, at the risk of being overly forward, if you should decide to address yourself to Miss Weatherby, would you be willing to let me know what she says?"

"I certainly will."

Jasper bowed his head. "Thank you."

He returned to his paper, feeling more at ease than he had since hearing the name *Philippa Weatherby*.

CHAPTER 10

The entertainment Lady Milthorpe had planned for the following morning was archery. Five targets had been arrayed in the formal gardens behind Milthorpe Manor against a tall wall of hedges. At even intervals along the graveled path, the servants had set up corresponding stations with racks of bows, buckets of arrows, and tables with an assortment of bracers and shooting gloves.

The skies were swirling with dark clouds, ready to burst open at any moment, and only a handful of guests had opted to come out. Felix and Pippa were shooting at the target on the far-left side of the range and having a marvelous time by all appearances, in spite of the weather. Eleanor, Clarissa, and Kate had claimed the target in the very center where they could watch over their youngest sister from a discreet distance.

Clarissa had been filling Eleanor in on what had transpired down at the barn yesterday afternoon. "We hadn't been there ten minutes when who should show up but Felix."

"Felix was there?" At Clarissa's nod, Eleanor continued, "That was lucky."

"So you would think!" Clarissa frowned as the wind picked up her arrow, causing it to go flying into the hedge behind the target. "But guess who followed close on his heels?"

"His brother?" Eleanor guessed.

"Wrong—it was Anna-Maria and Lucas Robertson!"

"Oh, dear. I hope you behaved yourself," Eleanor said.

"She did not," Kate observed.

Clarissa narrowed her eyes at her younger sister. "I did what was necessary under the circumstances."

Eleanor rubbed her brow. "What happened, Kate?"

"Pippa and Felix were down on the floor playing with the kittens, as you would expect," Kate explained. "Well, Miss Robertson didn't want to soil her gown, so she came and stood behind my stool. She was trying to make conversational overtures in order to gain Felix's attention, but he remained absorbed with Pippa and the kittens."

Adjusting for the wind, Eleanor sent an arrow flying toward the target. It landed a few inches from the bull's-eye, but she thought it a decent effort, given the conditions. "Did Miss Robertson grow discouraged and leave, then?"

"No," Clarissa said, "they stayed and made themselves bothersome."

Eleanor cast Kate a skeptical look, but Kate nodded. "They truly did. I had just finished making a few sketches of the kittens in Pippa's journal. I had placed it beneath my stool with my other art supplies. Miss Robertson picked it up and tried to leaf through it."

"I immediately explained that it was not a sketchbook, but a personal journal," Clarissa said. "But instead of giving it back, she tried to make off with it!"

"I thought Clarissa and Miss Robertson were going to come to blows," Kate noted. "They each had one end of the book, and neither would let go. Meanwhile poor Pippa was in distress that Miss Robertson might read it aloud, especially with Felix looking on."

Eleanor snorted. "I'm sure Anna-Maria Robertson didn't stand a chance against Clarissa."

"Unfortunately, you would be wrong," Clarissa noted. "She's surprisingly wiry. And I was wearing cotton gloves, so I couldn't get a good grip."

"But, upon seeing how upset Pippa was, Lord Felix intervened," Kate explained. "He stood up and demanded that Miss Robertson turn the book over. Once she did, he handed it to Pippa unopened."

"That was gallant of him," Eleanor observed.

"Yes," Clarissa agreed, "and he didn't look very impressed with Miss Robertson's behavior. She left in a sulk five minutes later and took her brother with her. So at least we were soon rid of her. But I'm telling you, Eleanor—that woman is trouble."

Eleanor couldn't disagree. "Well, Felix looks as besotted with Pippa as ever."

They surreptitiously glanced toward the far end of the garden. Pippa loosed an arrow which flew wide. Felix laid down his own bow and took up a fresh arrow. Coming up behind Pippa, he placed his own hands over hers on the bow. Her back was to his front, and although he allowed a respectable gap between them, he was all but holding her in his arms. It was difficult to say who looked more delighted by this development—Pippa, or Felix.

"Felix!" barked a deep voice coming from the direction of the house. "Come here now!"

Eleanor sighed. It was not difficult at all to say who was the least delighted by Felix and Pippa's near embrace.

The Duke of Norwood.

She turned her head, and, surely enough, there was Jasper St. James, jogging down the four stone steps that led into the gardens. This time, he had on a charcoal grey tailcoat paired with a burgundy waistcoat. As always, he looked absurdly virile in spite of his fine clothes, as if he were on his way to strangle a lion or wrestle a hydra or perform some other Herculean task.

The duke bore down upon his brother with his long-legged stride. Unless Eleanor was mistaken, Felix was growing weary of his brother barking orders at him. His jaw was clenched, and he was studiously ignoring his brother's repeated commands to come away.

Finally, the duke reached his quarry. "Felix!" he snapped. "Did you not hear me—"

"Miss Weatherby," Felix interjected, "would you permit me to present my brother, the Duke of Norwood? Brother, this is Miss Philippa Weatherby."

Pippa sank into a very proper curtsy. The duke cringed, seeming to realize his own boorishness. "Miss Weatherby," he said, bowing stiffly over her hand. "A pleasure."

He didn't infuse his voice with much sincerity, but Pippa did not seem to take offense. "Do you enjoy archery, Your Grace?"

"I do," he said in a clipped voice. "Why do you ask?"

Pippa's eyes creased with befuddlement. "Oh, I—I thought that might be the reason you were here. At the archery range."

The duke seemed to notice the presence of an archery range for the first time. "Oh, er—yes. Of course."

"Won't you join us?" Pippa asked politely.

"Oh, yes," Felix said, voice dripping with sarcasm. "How we should *love* to have you."

Narrowing his eyes at his brother, the duke took up a bow.

Clearing her throat and giving her sisters a significant look, Eleanor did the same. They needed to make some pretense of enjoying the activity at hand, rather than standing there openly eavesdropping. Clarissa in particular made a poor effort of it, not even taking her eyes off the spectacle unfolding to their left long enough to make her shot. Her arrow went flying into the hedge, ten feet wide of the target.

"At least look where you're shooting," Eleanor hissed. "You're going to kill someone!"

Clarissa rolled her eyes. "It's not as if anyone's over there trimming the verge."

An ominous rumble came from the sky overhead. The De Courcey sisters, who had been making use of the target on the far right, laid down their bows and headed up toward the house. Glancing around, Eleanor saw that the Weatherby sisters and the St. James brothers were the only ones left in the garden.

As Kate made a great show of selecting an arrow, Eleanor watched the activity on the far range out of the corner of her eye. The duke drew back the bowstring and sent an arrow flying directly into the center of the bullseye. It hit the target with such force that the arrow buried itself in the baled straw halfway up its shaft.

Pippa and Felix had been standing together, selecting their next arrows. Scowling, the duke wedged himself between them, forcing his brother to take a step back. Eleanor had never seen the affable Felix look so annoyed.

Pippa merely smiled. "I had the pleasure of meeting your dogs the other day. Beatrice and Benedick are delightful."

Eleanor watched with increasing annoyance as this pattern played out again and again. Felix would attempt to speak to Pippa. His brother would shoulder him out of the way.

Pippa managed to ignore the duke's boorish behavior and

make polite conversation. But Felix was becoming increasingly annoyed.

Finally, Felix could take no more. "Apologies, Miss Weatherby. I fear I am not feeling my most sociable this morning." He directed a glower at his brother. "I will return to the house and hopefully speak with you this afternoon when I am in a better humor."

The duke's smile was triumphant, and Eleanor saw red. Why, that villain! It vexed Eleanor to see him get his way through such repugnant behavior.

The duke turned toward the rack of bows, setting his own weapon down, clearly meaning to follow his brother back to the house. Annoyed, Eleanor yanked an arrow from the bucket, then muttered a curse when she saw she had grabbed a bird bolt, an arrow with a broad, blunted tip, often used by children first learning to shoot a bow.

Suddenly the wind kicked up, sending the tails of the duke's coat fluttering to the side and presenting Eleanor with an irresistible target.

Before she had time to think better of it, she nocked the bird bolt in her bow and launched it at Jasper St. James's impressively taut derrière.

CHAPTER 11

The arrow struck true.

Everything froze, save for Eleanor's heart, which was racing like a hare with a fox on its heels. The duke's shoulders, which had gone rigid, were drawn up to his ears.

Slowly, he turned.

To say that his expression was murderous would be the grossest sort of understatement, the equivalent of saying that it rained occasionally on the shores of Lake Windermere, or that the Irish did not entirely enjoy British rule.

Refusing to be cowed, Eleanor met his gaze and held it.

All at once, six-and-a-half feet of irate duke came barreling down the graveled path toward her. Beside her, Clarissa was openly cackling. Eleanor suspected Felix was doing the same. Although he had clapped a hand over his mouth, his shoulders were shaking uncontrollably, and there were tears streaming down his cheeks.

Kate grabbed her arm. "Run. Run. You need to run."

She would probably regret it, but Eleanor was not the running sort. She lifted her chin and assumed an insouciant expression. She wouldn't have thought it possible, but this caused the fury in the duke's eyes to flare even hotter.

She was bracing herself to be mowed down when he seized her upper arm and proceeded to haul her toward the far end of the archery range. Eleanor stumbled but managed to keep her feet, mostly because he was all but carrying her.

She wasn't sure where she expected him to take her, but she assumed it would be someplace private where he could shout at her until her hair blew free of its pins.

Instead, he stopped at the staging area for the far-right target, the one that had recently been abandoned by the De Courcey sisters.

"What are you doing?" Eleanor hissed, yanking her arm free from his grip. Behind him, she could see her three sisters and Felix huddled together against the wind, watching them in open fascination.

He removed a bow from the rack, then turned to her with a malicious smile. "Helping you improve your aim."

Eleanor tossed her head. "My aim is excellent."

"Oh?" he asked, selecting an arrow from the bucket with the grace of a lion. "It didn't seem excellent a moment ago."

She took two strides forward and leaned into him, refusing to be cowed. "I *always* hit my target."

"Hmm." He looked distinctly unimpressed. "Let's see, shall we?"

With surprising speed for so large a man, he spun her to face the target and came up behind her in one fluid motion. Eleanor wasn't sure how he did it, but somehow, he got her hands into position on the bow beneath his.

She had on a single shooting glove, but it left her fingertips bare, and he didn't have any gloves on at all! The feeling of his big, warm, strong hands covering hers felt slightly indecent... but mostly wonderful. And even worse, he had assumed the same position Felix and Pippa had adopted earlier, with Eleanor's back to Jasper's front and his arms encircling her. Unlike gentle Felix, Jasper did not bother to leave a decorous eight inches between their bodies. No, Eleanor could feel the brush of his coat against the back of her spencer, could sense the heat of him radiating around her.

Oh, but this was the worst part. Because Eleanor, who had never been held by a man before, and had expected to go to her grave without ever having done so, was being held by the most virile, most handsome man she had ever seen. And the most terrible thing of all was how *right* it felt. Everywhere else she went, she was too tall and unfashionably stocky.

But standing this close to Jasper St. James, for the first time in her life, Eleanor didn't feel overlarge and ungainly. She felt *perfect*.

Perfect for him.

But of course, this was nothing but a cruel trick that the universe was playing upon her. Jasper St. James detested her. He was holding her *as a joke*. She would never feel his arms around her again, and, when she looked back upon this moment, her memories would be tarnished by the knowledge that, in spite of the overwhelming feelings coursing through her, the moment hadn't been real, not in any of the ways that counted.

He nocked an arrow and forced her to draw back the bowstring. His voice in her ear was as dark as midnight and caused gooseflesh to break out across her arms and neck. "You see, Miss Weatherby, when you shoot an arrow, you aim it at the target. The *target*," he emphasized as he loosed the arrow.

Her voice when it emerged was breathy. "And what if I did?"

Jasper couldn't decide if taking Eleanor Weatherby in his arms had been a brilliant idea or a terrible one.

Not that it had been much of an *idea*. The closest thing he'd had to a coherent thought after the minx had shot him in the arse was, *I'll show her*.

What he was going to show her, precisely, he still hadn't a clue. One thing he was determined *not* to show her was the cockstand that had sprung up the second he pulled her into his arms. Which made it rather imperative that he carry on with this poorly thought-out plan and keep her in front of him, lest his brother and her sisters get quite the eyeful.

But the point was, he hadn't realized he was going to stop before the fifth target and yank her into his arms until he was doing it. And now he would have to deal with the consequences of his decision.

The first consequence was discovering how perfect Eleanor Weatherby felt in his arms. He was accustomed to going through life feeling like a great hulking brute, too large for door frames, spindly Chippendale chairs, and most of his dancing partners.

But standing with Eleanor Weatherby in his arms, he felt just right. She came up to his nose, meaning he could smell the clean white soap she used. He must be losing his mind, because in that moment, he would have sworn it smelled better than the expensive perfumes worn by the most fashionable ladies of the *ton*. From this angle, he had an enticing view of both her hips, which looked to be just the right size for his hands, and her trembling bosom. Even her arms were the perfect length so that she fit within his embrace like a puzzle piece, handcrafted to nest perfectly with him.

Shocking discoveries, all. But the situation's saving grace, the thing that allowed him to retain the upper hand, was Eleanor's reaction to him. The unflappable wallflower was suddenly flushed and trembling. At last, Jasper had managed to put her off balance.

Although... truth be told, he was feeling a bit disoriented himself. Eleanor Weatherby had a strange effect on him.

He shook himself. This would not do. Drawing back the arrow, he said, "I believe you are mistaken, Miss Weatherby. You see, the target is *over there*."

He loosed the arrow and breathed a sigh of relief upon seeing that it had flown true, because his hands were none too steady.

"And what if I found a more attractive target?" Eleanor asked breathlessly. This made things a thousand times worse, because it wasn't a terrified sort of breathlessness, or an I've-been-running sort of breathlessness.

It was an *aroused* sort of breathlessness. Jasper would know. He was experiencing the same feeling himself.

And the knowledge that Eleanor Weatherby wasn't as indifferent to him as her insouciant glare and nose-in-the-air posture would suggest only fanned the flames currently bursting to life beneath the falls of his trousers.

Some devilish impulse had him reaching across her body to retrieve another arrow from the bucket behind her, so that she was entirely enveloped in his arms. The back of his forearm brushed the underside of her breasts, which were pleasingly full, and he felt her shudder against him.

He was unable to suppress the husky growl in his voice. "You find it attractive, do you?"

She smirked at him over her shoulder and gave him a little nod as if to say, *well played*. Jasper's chest puffed out at the thought that he had finally impressed her.

"Perhaps *attractive* is not the right word. An irresistible target? Oh, dear—I fear that would go to your head as well. Let us say, a *deserving* target."

He nocked the arrow and together they drew back the bowstring. "Think very carefully, Miss Weatherby. Do you truly wish to suggest that you intentionally targeted my backside?"

As he loosed the arrow, she retorted, "Perhaps I was trying to assist you, by calling attention to the body part whose name you were emulating."

Jasper scowled as the arrow bounced off the rim of the target. "Did you just call me an—"

Fortunately, a deafening rumble emerged from the sky just as he said the word *arse*, because Jasper had never cursed in front of a lady and hadn't meant to start.

It seemed that Miss Weatherby understood his meaning well enough, because as soon as the rumbling died down, she shrugged. "If the shoe fits, Your Grace. Or, in this case, the trousers."

Jasper could not believe her gall. He had never been treated with such insolence, never once in his life! "Why, I ought to bend you over and—"

He cut himself off before he could finish that thought. Because giving Eleanor Weatherby a swat on the bottom had been the farthest thought from his mind.

Oh, no—when he pictured her bent over before him, it wasn't his hand he was using to pound her…

She turned in his arms so they were facing each other. Her lips were inches from his. All he would have to do was tilt his head down a fraction, and…

"Bend me over and what?" she asked breathlessly, sounding insufficiently outraged and far too interested for his peace of mind.

Jasper was losing what few shreds of sanity he had left. This had been the worst plan he had ever come up with. He had no exit strategy. They had four curious onlookers standing just thirty feet away, he was sporting a raging cockstand, and the only suggestion his brain could produce was to haul her behind the hedgerow so he could ruck up her skirts and fall on her like a rutting animal. Which he absolutely could not do.

No matter how appealing it sounded.

Now he had no way to get out of this ridiculous situation that was entirely of his own making.

What he needed was a miracle.

A sudden flash of light illuminated the gardens followed by a sharp crack, and the heavens answered Jasper's unspoken prayers by opening up and dumping approximately nine hundred gallons of ice-cold water down the front of his trousers.

CHAPTER 12

At least the sudden downpour took care of the situation in Jasper's trousers.

It didn't dampen his attraction to Eleanor Weatherby an iota. They stood there, frozen, inches apart, as the rain soaked them to the skin.

God only knew how long they would have stood there smoldering at each other had her sister, Clarissa, not come running up to grab her arm. "Quick, Eleanor! We've got to get back to the house."

He watched her blink back to awareness, then allow her sister to lead her up the short flight of stairs that led to the upper gardens.

"Come on, Jasp!" Felix shouted over the rain as he jogged by. He had peeled his coat off and was holding it over Miss Philippa in an attempt to keep her dry.

Shaking himself, Jasper followed.

They had ascended the final six steps that led to the portico, out of the driving rain at last, when Miss Philippa stopped short with a gasp. She pointed across the manicured sweep of lawn to the east. "Look! Lightning must have struck the barn!"

Jasper pushed his dripping hair back from his forehead. Surely enough, flames were rising from the thatched roof of the old barn, just visible over a copse of trees.

"The kittens!" Pippa shouted, starting forward.

Eleanor snagged her arm, yanking her to a halt. "You are *not* running inside a burning building after some kittens!"

Pippa's anguish was obviously not feigned. She fought against her sister's grip, desperate to escape. "We can't leave them! The poor little things!"

She was wild in her distress, but her sister was larger and stronger, and every bit as determined to save her sister as Pippa was to rescue those kittens. Eleanor wrapped an arm around her waist and dragged her inexorably toward the house. "They'll be all right."

"But what if they're not?" Pippa wailed.

Suddenly Felix was there, bowing over Pippa's hand. "Please, do not distress yourself. I'll get them out. I swear it."

It took a moment for Jasper to register his brother's words. By the time he realized what Felix intended, his brother was already halfway down the steps.

"Felix!" he roared. "Stop right now!"

His brother sprinted across the upper garden, ignoring him.

For a split second, he caught Eleanor Weatherby's eye. She had her arms wrapped around her youngest sister's waist, holding her firmly in place as Pippa struggled and shouted after Felix, looking more distraught than ever. For once, instead of vitriol, Eleanor looked at him with sympathy in her eyes, sympathy and understanding.

But he didn't have time to ponder that now. Cursing, Jasper charged down the stone steps in desperate pursuit of his brother.

Jasper might be stronger than Felix.

But his brother was decidedly faster.

Jasper ran as hard as he'd ever run in his life, but he didn't manage to gain an inch on Felix as they sprinted through the rain. He was honestly lucky to keep him in his sight.

Fortunately, as they neared the barn, Jasper's panic abated, because the rain seemed to have put out the fire.

He staggered into the barn's clearing and found his brother studying the smoldering building. "God damn it, Felix," Jasper gasped, panting with his hands on his thighs. "Scared me… to death."

Felix gestured to the back end of the building. "There's a large hole in the roof. It's probably flooding inside. We need to get the kittens out and bring them up to the house."

"Wait." Jasper grabbed his brother's arm. "The building will be unstable. You shouldn't go in there."

Felix shook him off, looking annoyed. "I'm not an idiot, Jasp. I'll avoid the damaged section. I doubt the kittens are back there, anyway, as that's where all the water is pouring in."

"Hang on." At Felix's glare, Jasper held up both hands. "I'll go with you."

Felix grunted but didn't protest as Jasper followed him. Felix pulled open the door and they stepped inside out of the driving rain.

It took a moment for his eyes to adjust to the dim interior. Surely enough, the lightning strike had burned a hole in the thatched roof that was a good eight feet across, and water was pouring in. The dirt floor in the back half of the barn had turned into a muddy pond. Jasper couldn't see signs of any kittens.

"Are you sure they're here?" Jasper asked.

"Shh." Felix grabbed his sleeve. "Do you hear that?"

Jasper couldn't hear anything above the sound of raindrops hammering down on the flooded barn floor. "Hear what?"

Felix tugged him toward a pile of hay in the front corner. It took him a minute, but Jasper eventually picked out the sound his brother had detected—a truly piteous mewling.

Felix began sifting around in the hay. "Here we are!" he cried, fishing a soggy, slate-grey kitten from the pile and handing her to Jasper. "You take Lavender."

"Lavender?" Jasper asked, confused, as he accepted the kitten. "What do you mean—"

"And here's Wellington," Felix added, thrusting a squiggling ball of sodden black and white fur into Jasper's other hand. "That just leaves Sheba and Midnight..."

It took a few minutes, but Felix was able to find the other two cats. "Right. Back to the house."

"Are you sure we should take them to the house?" Jasper asked as they hurried to the door. The rain had slowed from a torrential downpour but continued falling steadily. Frowning, Jasper tucked the two tiny kittens inside his coat. "Lady Milthorpe might not want them inside. Perhaps we should take them to the stables."

"We'll ask her ladyship and certainly take them to the stables if she prefers. But Pippa will want to reassure herself that they're all right."

Jasper rolled his eyes. "You just want the credit for having rescued them."

Felix flashed him a half-smile, which was a significant improvement over the glowers he'd been sending Jasper's way for the past few days. "You know I would've rescued them regardless. But I certainly wouldn't mind if Pippa thought well of me."

Jasper didn't know what to say. His instinct was to

reassure his brother that any woman with an ounce of sense would think well of him. But he didn't trust Philippa Weatherby, nor did he wish to promote the match, so he settled for grunting.

They made their way up to the house through a steady drizzle. As soon as the back door opened, Jasper heard the distraught voice of the youngest Miss Weatherby coming from the foyer at the front of the house.

"What if something happens to him? I'll never forgive myself. How I wish I had never suggested it!"

Felix perked up at her words. Waving off the footman's offer to take the kittens, he hurried toward the sound of Pippa's voice. Jasper followed, dripping on the marble tiles with every step.

"There, there, Pippa, dear," her eldest sister said. "Lord Felix is a sensible man. I am sure he will proceed with caution."

"Besides," Clarissa Weatherby added, "I suspect the rain has put the fire out. Had the entire building gone up, there would be a tremendous amount of smoke."

Rounding the central staircase, Jasper saw the youngest Miss Weatherby, slightly damp herself and wringing her hands as she paced the foyer. "How I hope you're right! Still, I cannot be at peace until I—*Felix!*" she cried, sprinting across the tiled floor as she spotted them. "Thank God you're all right!"

"We're soaked, but none the worse for wear." Smiling, Felix held out the two sodden kittens for her inspection. "And look who we found."

Ignoring the kittens, Miss Philippa clung to Felix's arm, pressing her forehead against his wrist. "I was so scared," she said in a voice that shook.

Felix looked tremendously pleased, his smile tender as he said, "Everything is all right."

Miss Philippa nodded, as if she did not trust herself to speak.

Jasper scowled. She certainly put on a good act of appearing concerned for his brother's welfare.

But he still was not convinced that it was more than an act.

The grey and white tabby cat chose that moment to give a piteous mewl. Starting, Miss Philippa seemed to notice the kittens for the first time. "Oh—Sheba, you poor thing!" She took the kitten from Felix, snuggling it against her chest. "Don't you worry. We're going to take the best care of you!" She paused to stroke the black cat Felix held in his other hand. "Were you able to find Lavender and Wellington?"

"Jasper has them," Felix said, nodding in his direction. "Thank goodness he came along. I would've had quite the time trying to carry four unhappy kittens through a rainstorm."

Miss Philippa's smile was tremulous. "Thank you, Your Grace."

Jasper was saved from having to respond by Lady Milthorpe, who came rushing into the room. "Your Grace, Lord Felix! I am so relieved you were unharmed."

Felix bowed. "Thank you, my lady. We are perfectly well." He held out Midnight. "Would you prefer that we take the kittens over to the stables?"

Midnight mewled piteously, right on cue, and Lady Milthorpe's face melted. "Oh, the poor little things! It won't hurt anything to keep them in the house for a few days."

"Oh, thank you, my lady!" Miss Philippa exclaimed.

"We will make sure they're no trouble for you," Felix said. "We'll take them up to Jasper's rooms, as he has a full suite. They'll have plenty of room to frolic around the sitting room."

"Wait. What?" Jasper said in the same breath Miss Philippa said, "What an excellent suggestion!"

The party was already trooping up the stairs. Jasper jogged a few steps to catch up to his brother. "Felix," he hissed, "we can't put these kittens in my sitting room!"

"Certainly, we can," Felix countered. "I'll come over and take care of them. Shut the door if you don't want to deal with them. You won't even know that they're there."

"I believe you have forgotten about the two gigantic dogs currently occupying the sitting room," Jasper muttered.

"Benny and Bea?" Felix snorted. "They're sweethearts. Wouldn't hurt a fly."

"They might not, but they've never been around kittens before," Jasper countered. "If they decide they don't like them, they could eat them in one bite."

Felix shrugged. "To be sure, we'll introduce them and see how it goes. If the mastiffs seem skittish, we can take the kittens to my room."

Their motley party paraded into Jasper's sitting room. Benedick and Beatrice, who had been napping on their mats beneath the window, sat up at the influx of visitors. Benedick in particular was eyeing the kittens warily.

"Here," Felix said, strolling up to the dogs with Midnight extended in front of him, "let's see how this goes."

He set Midnight down on Beatrice's burgundy corduroy pad. Beatrice drew back, an alarmed expression on her squished black face.

Midnight showed no fear of the dog who was easily one hundred times his weight. Mewling, he took two tottering steps across the corduroy cushion, then promptly fell over.

Beatrice whimpered in distress. With a gentleness that belied her huge size, she took Midnight up by the scruff of his neck and carried him onto the pad. Laying down, she set him down within the circle of her crossed paws.

Meanwhile, Miss Philippa was presenting Sheba to Benedick, who was cowering against the wall. Felix scooped Lavender and Wellington out of Jasper's hands, so he went to comfort his dog.

"It's all right, old boy," Jasper said, squatting down and laying a hand on the back of Benedick's head. "It's just some kittens. They can't hurt the likes of you."

Benedick shot him a look that said he was unconvinced. Jasper gave him a comforting pat on the head and stood.

He hated to leave the mastiffs to the kittens' tender mercies, but considering the degree to which he was dripping upon Lady Milthorpe's carpet, a change of clothing seemed imperative. He retreated to his bedchamber, where Stephens had already laid out a fresh suit for him.

His valet had him stripped, dried, and changed in the space of five minutes. Jasper hurried back into his sitting room to see how poor Beatrice and Benedick were faring.

Beatrice was now keeping watch over both Midnight and Lavender. Lavender had wedged herself almost underneath the huge dog's chest and fallen asleep. Midnight was batting at Beatrice's nose, an affront she was bearing with no apparent annoyance.

Poor Benedick looked to be faring less well. Sheba had discovered his tail and was romping after it upon the mat. His attempts to move it out of the way only made the game more delightful and encouraged Sheba to pounce. Meanwhile, Wellington had climbed up on Benedick's back and was actively exploring this strange, tan surface. Attempting to scale the folds of the big dog's neck, Wellington lost his balance and started to tumble but managed to grab onto a floppy dark ear for purchase. Benedick turned his head in surprise, but made no move to dislodge the kitten, and his expression was one of apprehension rather than annoyance.

"Well," Felix said, pushing up to his feet. Someone had brought him a towel, but he was still soaked to the skin. "Now that the kittens are settled, I'd best go and get cleaned up myself."

The Weatherby sisters also rose and made for the door, likely conscious that Jasper, unlike Felix, did not enjoy their company, and also perhaps of the impropriety of their being in his rooms at all, even if it was just the sitting room.

On her way out the door, Miss Philippa turned and gave him a bright smile. "Thank you, Your Grace, for letting the kittens stay here, and for helping to rescue them from the barn."

Jasper grunted an acknowledgement, and the next thing he knew, he found himself alone with Beatrice, Benedick, and the four frolicsome kittens.

He glanced over and saw that Wellington had managed to climb on top of Benedick's head, where he was sitting, completely at ease. The mastiff gave his owner a pleading look.

Jasper sat cross-legged on the floor and rubbed his dog's back. "I'm not sure how we got here either, old boy. I blame those Weatherby Wallflowers."

Benedick whined in agreement, and Jasper settled in to watch over the kittens that were apparently taking up residence in his rooms.

CHAPTER 13

*T*he rain let up, but only in the sense that it went from a deluge to a steady shower. Lady Milthorpe set up an impromptu card party in the green parlor. The Weatherby sisters didn't have even pennies to lose at whist, and so Eleanor and her sisters passed the afternoon with books borrowed from the house's library.

The rain continued unabated the following morning, so Lady Milthorpe announced that they would amuse themselves by enacting scenes from Shakespeare. While the servants began constructing a makeshift stage in the ballroom, the guests gathered to select their scenes.

Eleanor happened to know that the Duke of Norwood was attending this house party with the purpose of finding a bride. The other guests had been speculating about which young lady would be his choice since the day they had arrived at Milthorpe Manor. She also knew that the young lady who had emerged as the leading contender, Lady Francesca FitzSimon, was very fond of Shakespeare. She assumed that the duke was as well, considering he had named his dogs after a pair of famous Shakespearean lovers.

She therefore expected Lady Francesca to seize the opportunity to perform a romantic scene with her suitor.

But Lady Francesca surprised her. Clarissa was leafing through a copy of *Twelfth Night*. "Here's a funny scene between Viola and Olivia. Would you stage it with me, Eleanor?"

Eleanor sighed. "Much as I love *Twelfth Night*, I'd probably better keep an eye on Pippa."

"How about you, Kate?" Clarissa asked.

A look of alarm crossed Kate's face. "I'm not one for the stage. But I would love to paint some backdrops," she added, casting a nervous glance at Lady Milthorpe.

Their hostess took no offense. "That would be lovely, dear. Come, let's see what paints we can find."

"I'd like to do it with you," Lady Francesca said shyly. "I assume you're referring to the scene where Viola is sent to woo Olivia on Orsino's behalf?"

"The very one," Clarissa confirmed.

"That's one of my favorite scenes," Lady Francesca confessed. "Would you rather play Viola or Olivia?"

"I feel like you would make a more convincing Olivia than I would..." Clarissa noted as the two of them retreated to a far corner of the ballroom, heads bent together.

Pippa and Felix were likewise considering the suggested manuscripts. "How about this one?" Pippa asked, showing him a passage from *The Taming of the Shrew*.

Felix smiled fondly at Pippa. "I'll do whatever scene you prefer, but I must warn you, Miss Philippa—no one could ever find you convincing in the role of a shrew."

Pippa's cheeks were flushed. "It's kind of you to say so. But I think this scene would be, er, diverting."

Suspicious, Eleanor peered over her sister's shoulder. Surely enough, Pippa had selected Act 2, Scene 1. Although the characters they would portray, Petruchio and Katharina, were ostensibly arguing, it was one of the most flirtatious scenes in all of Shakespeare.

Not that she objected to her sister taking part. Eleanor had a suspicion that the sweet-tempered pair would render the scene about as spicy as blancmange.

A shadow fell over the table, followed by a familiar scent of birch and leather. It appeared that the Duke of Norwood shared in Eleanor's suspicions.

Narrowing his eyes, the duke inserted himself between Felix and Pippa. "This happens to be one of my favorite scenes. Why don't I enact it with Miss Philippa?"

"Because I have already said *I* wanted to do it," Felix said tightly.

"You don't even like Shakespeare," the duke countered. "Have you already forgotten how bitterly you complained when I secured a box at the Surrey to see *Timon of Athens* last month? You wanted to see *Tom and Jerry*," he added with a derisive sneer.

Felix's cheeks turned ruddy. "And I would still rather see *Tom and Jerry*! The play you picked was *awful*. We wasted three hours watching the story of a man so stupid that he squandered his entire fortune on extravagant banquets, then attempted to murder all his former friends before dying in the wilderness with a bitter epitaph on his lips. What, precisely, was there to enjoy?"

"*Timon of Athens* is rarely staged," the duke snapped. "It was a tremendous opportunity to see a work that is intellectually challenging, not some mindless entertainment."

Poor Felix was shaking with humiliation.

Eleanor had had enough. She rounded on the duke. "I agree with Lord Felix. There is a reason *Timon of Athens* is so rarely staged."

"Is that so?" The duke regarded her with open contempt. "I suppose you are going to enlighten us?"

Eleanor stepped forward, meeting him glare for glare. "I should be glad to. It is arguably Shakespeare's worst work. It reads like a first draft. He did not take the time to correct obvious discrepancies throughout the text, and there are large sections of prose that are only half-versified. I believe that the bard himself agreed that it was not up to his usual standard and abandoned the work."

The duke gave a disbelieving laugh. "A rather astonishing assertion."

Eleanor leaned in, refusing to back down. "Go back and look at the text. I daresay you will see what I mean. And I also challenge you to show me any evidence that the play was staged during Shakespeare's lifetime. I believe that he set the play aside, never intending for it to see the light of day, for all the reasons your brother cited. It is miserable to read, a three-hour analysis of misanthropy—"

"It echoes many of the same themes as *King Lear*!" the duke snapped, looming over her. "Timon is an idealist whose downfall holds a mirror up to the world's avarice!"

"Timon's character is disjointed to the point of straining credulity," Eleanor countered. "He goes from being guileless and altruistic to being misanthropic and vituperative in the course of one scene. It is unrealistic!"

"It is an unflinching critique of human frailty!" the duke roared.

"It is so unfacile in its execution as to border on satire!" she shot back.

The duke leaned in. "You would dare to criticize Shakespeare?" he asked, voice low and full of venom.

She didn't waver an inch. "Be honest, Your Grace. Are you really upset that I am criticizing Shakespeare? Or that I am criticizing you?"

He gave a harsh exhale, and she felt his breath upon her lips. Eleanor suddenly became aware that they were breathing down each other's necks to the point that mere inches separated their lips, and that everyone in the room was staring at them with rapt fascination.

Shuddering, she took a step back. "And moreover, there is nothing wrong with wanting to see a comedy. Shakespeare himself wrote a number of them."

Felix shot her a grateful look. "That's right. Comedies such as *The Taming of the Shrew*, which I am looking forward to performing with Miss Philippa."

"Oh, no, you're not," the duke said, snatching the manuscript from his brother's fingers. "I will be playing the role of Petruchio with Miss Philippa. You will just have to choose something else."

"I won't," Felix snapped. "You find something else!"

"This is a very long scene and Petruchio has more than half of the lines," the duke noted. "Do you really think you'll be able to memorize all of this?"

Felix flinched.

Pippa gasped.

Eleanor glared daggers at the duke. Really, that was below the belt. To be sure, memorizing so many lines in one day would be a challenge, but these were amateur productions. There would probably be flubbed lines in every single scene that was put on, and no one would mind in the slightest.

Felix's gaze was fixed upon the floor. "Forgive me, Miss Weatherby," he said, voice shaking with some combination of humiliation and rage. "I find I am not in the mood for Shakespeare after all." He bowed stiffly over Pippa's hand. "Do excuse me."

Pippa squeezed his hand. "I understand, and I hope I will see you at luncheon."

His expression softened a trifle. He nodded, then spun on his heel and started to cross the ballroom, shoulders stiff.

The duke looked more annoyed than regretful. "Felix. Felix, wait."

But Felix did not so much as pause. He swept out of the ballroom with an almost palpable sense of wounded dignity.

Eleanor, Pippa, and the duke stood together in awkward silence. After a moment, Pippa offered the duke a tiny smile. "Well, let's begin, shall we?"

CHAPTER 14

*P*hilippa Weatherby was every bit as awful as Jasper had assumed she would be.

But, unfortunately for him, she was not awful in the way he had anticipated.

She was awful in that he was determined to dislike her, and the annoying chit was nigh impossible to hate.

Their rehearsal got off to an awkward start. Jasper wondered if he had perhaps gone a bit too far in his efforts to prevent Felix from pairing with Miss Philippa. His last remark, in particular, in which he questioned whether Felix had the wherewithal to memorize so many lines, had perhaps been a bit harsh. But what was he supposed to do—just sit back and allow his brother to go hurtling down the path to destruction?

Jasper was looking out for Felix's best interests. One day, his brother would thank him for saving him from making an imprudent match.

The eldest Miss Weatherby, who had retreated to a chair along the edge of the ballroom, did not seem to share in his opinion, based on the way she was glaring at him with her arms crossed.

Not that he cared a fig for what Eleanor Weatherby thought of him.

Miss Philippa offered him a tiny smile. "Shall we start with your speech, Your Grace?"

"Indeed." Jasper launched into Petruchio's soliloquy, in which he revealed his plans for wooing Katharina. Fortunately for him, the scene happened to be one of his favorites, and he already had it memorized, so rehearsing it did not require much concentration.

Although… it might have been nice to have something to focus on, other than Eleanor Weatherby's judgmental glower.

Resisting the urge to snarl at her, he returned his attention to Miss Philippa. In truth, she did not make a very good Katharina. The role called for not only vim and vigor but also vinegar, and although Miss Philippa was bright and lively, she was about as acidic as a glass of milk. Never had the words, *Let him that moved you hither remove you hence* been spoken so fondly. Somehow, she even made the line in which she called him an *ass* sound like a compliment.

She did warm to him a bit as they continued to rehearse, and when the servants brought in tea after about an hour, she cheerfully poured him a cup, then settled into the chair beside him.

"I have been enjoying your dogs, Your Grace," she began. "Have you always kept mastiffs?"

Jasper couldn't help but admire the artful way she had steered the conversation toward one of their few safe topics. "Not always. Growing up, my father would not permit Felix and I to have dogs, no matter how much we begged. Acquiring a pair of mastiffs was one of the first things I did upon inheriting the dukedom."

"Was that Beatrice and Benedick, then?" she asked, taking a sip from her cup.

"It was not. I came into the title some fifteen years ago, so Beatrice and Benedick are my second pair."

"Oh!" Miss Philippa looked startled. "I did not realize you inherited when you were so young. Why, Lord Felix must have been just a boy!"

"He was." Jasper found himself leaning forward. The youngest Miss Weatherby was surprisingly easy to talk to. "He was only nine. I was little more than a boy myself, at sixteen."

"So young," she said softly. "Your brother told me that his parents had died in a carriage accident years ago and that you were all the family he has. But I hadn't understood just how young you both were."

Jasper gave her a curious look. "I'm surprised you didn't know. Needless to say, it has been the subject of quite a lot of gossip over the years."

Miss Philippa waved this off. "Oh, I haven't heard any of the latest gossip. You cannot imagine what a provincial creature I am. Before this house party, I'd scarcely left our little village in Yorkshire." She gave a self-deprecating smile that made it difficult for Jasper to loathe her as he wished. "I've spent my entire life holed up in the countryside with my cats."

"Ah," Jasper said, unsure how to respond. He took a sip of his tea.

"So," she asked brightly, "what made you decide on mastiffs specifically?"

"Honestly, Felix was the one who wanted mastiffs," Jasper confessed. "He'd always wanted a great big dog. And I was so desperate to find anything that would make him smile again, I would've bought him a rhinoceros had he asked for it."

Jasper cleared his throat. *Why* had he added that last part?

He hadn't meant to share anything so personal with one of these Weatherby Wallflowers.

Although… as he regarded Miss Philippa cheerfully sipping her tea and conversing with him so politely in spite of his boorish behavior that morning, it seemed particularly unkind to employ such a derisive nickname toward her, even if he didn't speak it aloud.

Get hold of yourself, Jasper. It's all an act.

"I'm curious," she said. "You say that the mastiffs were for Felix. Yet I've very much formed the impression that they're your dogs, not his."

"Beatrice and Benedick are, yes," Jasper agreed. "That first pair, Bruno and Maxine, were both of ours, in equal measure. But it happened that Bruno passed while Felix was at Oxford. That was when we brought in the puppies to keep Maxine company. I, of course, was at home by then, so I was able to spend significantly more time with Beatrice and Benedick during their formative years. So perhaps it is unsurprising that I am the one they bonded with."

Miss Philippa laughed. "That's like me and my cats. In theory, they belonged to all of us. In practice, however, I spent more time with them than my three sisters combined."

"Felix has mentioned how fond you are of your cats. I'm sure you'll be glad to see them upon your return to Yorkshire."

Her face fell, and Jasper sensed at once that he had said the wrong thing. "Miss Philippa?" he asked cautiously. "What is the matter?"

She attempted a smile, but it was obviously forced. "I'm sorry. It's just—I had to leave my cats behind."

Jasper bit back a sharp response. He had suspected all along that Philippa Weatherby was a silly sort of girl. This proved it. She did not even have the mental fortitude to go without seeing her cats for two weeks. "Take heart, Miss Weatherby. You will see them again soon."

She made a bleak sound. "I won't. We can't go back to Boroughbridge, on account of my father selling the house."

"I see. But surely, once you are established in your new home, you will be able to bring your cats to join you."

She gave a humorless chuckle. "We haven't got a new home."

Jasper frowned. That didn't make any sense. "Where is your father?" he barked.

"He'll be on the ship by now."

"The ship?" Mr. Weatherby might be the one on a ship, but Jasper felt like the one at sea. "What ship? What are you talking about?"

"Oh!" She looked up, surprised. "I thought your brother would have told you. Our father sold our house so he could purchase passage on an around-the-world voyage. He's a naturalist, you see."

Jasper did not see, not at all. He shook his head, hoping to clear it. "Your father sold your house in order to go and sail around the world?"

"That's correct."

"But where are the four of you to live?" he snapped.

He immediately felt bad about using such a harsh tone. His ire was directed at the absent Mr. Weatherby, who appeared to be suffering from some sort of severe moral deficiency.

Fortunately, Miss Philippa did not appear to take any offense. "That's what we're trying to figure out right now."

Jasper still could not seem to wrap his head around the notion that this man had abandoned his four daughters. "Do you have family, or—"

"Only a great-aunt who is even more impoverished than we are."

"Perhaps friends who will take you in?"

"None to speak of," Miss Weatherby replied. Oddly, she sounded far less concerned about this dire turn of events than she did about the prospect of never seeing her cats again.

"But that's despicable!" Jasper exclaimed.

"Mmm, it is, isn't it?" Miss Weatherby waved this off. "But we're quite used to it. Our father has always been terribly selfish."

For the life of him, Jasper could not understand how she was so nonchalant about it. A man was supposed to look after his family! How could this Weatherby fellow stand to face himself in the mirror each morning?

Jasper would have walked barefoot across a scorching desert rather than let Felix suffer. He would have swum the English Channel, he would have…

He could have gone on for quite a while in this vein, because there was literally nothing Jasper would not do to protect his brother.

What was *wrong* with this Weatherby fellow? Jasper wished he was here. He had a mind to clout him upside the head.

He sought to make his voice gentle, because none of this was Miss Weatherby's fault. "But how will you survive?"

She laughed. "You would think I would be a bit more concerned, wouldn't you? But that's because you don't know Eleanor as I do. I have absolute confidence in my sister. She'll make sure everything turns out right."

Jasper couldn't imagine how a widely acknowledged spinster with neither money nor connections could bend the world to her will. "But… how is she going to do that?"

Miss Philippa shrugged. "I have no idea! But mark my words, she always does. She has a great deal of practice, you see. She's been doing it for twenty years, after all."

"Twenty years?" Now Jasper was truly confused. He had guessed Eleanor Weatherby was a few years younger than he was.

"Yes, ever since our mother died. Eleanor was just seven—"

"Seven?" Jasper barked. Several heads turned to look at him, including those of Eleanor and Clarissa Weatherby. The subject of their discussion narrowed her eyes at him.

For once, Jasper didn't have the heart to glare back at her.

He turned back to Miss Philippa. "I apologize for my harsh tone. I was merely shocked. Do you mean to tell me that your sister Eleanor has been looking after the three of you since she was seven years old?"

"It sounds implausible, doesn't it? And yet, she has, as well as running my father's household on next to nothing." Miss Philippa smiled fondly as she shook her head. "But Eleanor always finds a way."

Jasper grunted. This was even worse than him starting to like Miss Philippa. The thought of Eleanor Weatherby had him feeling a strange warmth in the center of his chest.

If he didn't know better, he would've called it *admiration*.

No. It was worse than admiration.

She reminded him... of *him*.

Although... no. That wasn't quite right. He had started looking after his brother at age sixteen, with almost limitless resources and the power of a dukedom behind him.

Her task had been immeasurably harder.

Something occurred to him. "I hope you will pardon me for asking an intrusive question, but it sounds like your sister was something of a mother figure to you."

"Yes, I would agree. I still think of her as my sister, but our relationship definitely has a maternal quality."

Jasper considered how he could phrase his question without giving away too much. "Did you ever find yourself pushing back against her direction, as children are sometimes wont to rebel against their parents?"

She bit her lip as she considered the question. "I'm sure there are times when I have. But less than you would think. You see, even when I don't much like what Eleanor is telling me, I know she always has my best interests at heart. Take leaving my cats behind in Yorkshire—as you can imagine, there is no suggestion I could have opposed more strongly. But Eleanor sat me down and explained *why* it had to be that way. We don't even have the resources to look after ourselves! Did I want Pepper, Ollie, and Crumpet to go hungry? Of course not. Plus, moving to a new home can be terribly disorienting for cats, and Pepper is sixteen—too old to learn his way around a new home. Even Ollie and Crumpet could become confused and wander off." She sighed. "As much as I hated it, I knew Eleanor was right. And so, I agreed to leave my cats behind."

Jasper would be the first to admit that he could be mulishly stubborn. But Miss Philippa's words were penetrating even his thick skull. The approach she had just described, of sitting down and explaining your reasoning… that was not what he had done with Felix. He had done… pretty much the opposite. And achieved the opposite result, notably.

A feeling of unease started to creep in. Jasper was only trying to prevent his brother from making a mistake. He was doing it because he loved his brother and didn't want him to make an error that could prove to be both painful and permanent. Felix knew that.

Didn't he?

The more he thought about their earlier confrontation, the more Jasper began to feel ashamed. In truth, he didn't think there was anything wrong with wanting to see *Tom and*

Jerry. And honestly, Felix had a point about *Timon of Athens*. Jasper hadn't much enjoyed the play, either.

Yet he had somehow found himself defending it, simply because he couldn't bear to admit that Eleanor Weatherby had the right of it. Which he knew was ridiculous! *Why* could he not simply have said, *to be sure, it is one of the Bard's lesser works.*

Probably because she was an expert at getting under his skin.

But the larger point was, he had been so desperate to prevent Felix from falling further under Miss Philippa's spell that he had been willing to say *anything* to prevent them from enacting this scene together.

And that was how he had wound up calling his brother an idiot in front of everyone attending the house party.

God, *he* was the idiot. Anyone with eyes could see how wounded Felix had been by his words. Words he didn't even mean! When had he become such a blundering fool?

Now, all he wanted to do was go and find his brother. To apologize, for one. But he also wanted to employ the method described by Miss Philippa, the one Eleanor Weatherby had used to convince her to give up her cats. He needed to explain his concerns, which were legitimate, about a hasty match with Philippa Weatherby.

Although… now that he'd had a chance to converse with Miss Philippa, Jasper had to admit that she was not nearly as bad as he had expected.

Be honest, Jasper. If she were the daughter of an earl, instead of a Weatherby Wallflower, he would have been cautiously pleased about the prospect of Felix courting her. She was quite pretty, she seemed exceptionally kind, and she clearly shared a number of interests with his brother.

Hell, had he met her first, he probably would have contrived an opportunity to introduce her to Felix.

But the fact remained that Philippa Weatherby was not the daughter of an earl. She was a girl caught in a desperate situation, and sometimes desperation made people do unsavory things. There was also the fact that it was not a good idea to marry *anyone* on the strength of a two-week acquaintance.

These were the points he needed to be making to Felix. Not barking and growling and embarrassing his brother in front of three dozen people.

Across the ballroom, Lady Milthorpe clapped her hands. "Shall we resume? Let us rehearse for another hour, and then we shall take a break for luncheon."

But Jasper couldn't go and find his brother, because he was stuck playing Petruchio to Miss Philippa's Katharina.

But he would do it. He would find his brother at first opportunity, and he would apologize.

Feeling slightly better in the wake of this resolution, he offered Miss Philippa his arm.

CHAPTER 15

Once the morning rehearsals concluded, Jasper went looking for his brother. He didn't have to look hard.

Felix was in Jasper's own suite of rooms, sitting on the floor with a kitten in his lap, scratching Beatrice behind her floppy ears.

"Felix! I was just going to go and look for you." Jasper gave an awkward chuckle as he set the book he'd brought with him on an end table. "Didn't expect I'd find you here, of all places."

Felix refused to look at his brother. "I decided to spend my morning with someone who actually appreciates my company." He placed Wellington on the mat next to Beatrice, then stood. "I'll leave."

Jasper stepped in front of the door, holding his hands out placatingly. "Felix, wait."

"Could I get by?" Felix asked shortly, eyes fixed upon the carpet.

It was as bad as he had supposed. His brother wanted nothing to do with him, and who could blame him?

Jasper drew in a breath and braced himself to say two words he rarely uttered. "I'm sorry."

The words came out a bit wobbly. He sounded entirely unlike his usual commanding, ducal self.

But maybe that was what caught Felix's attention, because he actually looked up. His gaze remained wary, but at least he was looking Jasper in the eye. "Come again?"

"I'm so sorry, Felix," Jasper said in a rush. "I shouldn't have said… well, pretty much everything I said to you this morning. I didn't even mean it. I didn't enjoy that stupid play, either."

All at once, Felix's stony façade crumbled. "You *humiliated* me, Jasper!"

"I know." Jasper ran a hand across his face, miserable. "I was *such* an arse."

At least he had found a theme Felix could warm to. "You most certainly were! You all but called me an idiot in front of everyone!"

"I did," Jasper agreed. "I shouldn't have said it. I don't think you're stupid. Of course, you could memorize those lines if you put your mind to it."

Felix crossed his arms. "Well, if you don't think any of those things, then why did you say them?"

"Mostly because of Eleanor Weatherby. She has a way of getting under my skin," Jasper admitted. "She started arguing that *Timon of Athens* was rubbish, and I couldn't bear to let her get the last word in, even though I *agree* that *Timon of Athens* is rubbish. I should have just conceded the point and moved on instead of being so bloody bullheaded." He rubbed an eye with the heel of his hand.

When he looked up, Felix's eyes were sympathetic. "That still doesn't explain why you made that last remark about how I wouldn't be able to memorize the lines."

"I was just so desperate to prevent you from spending the

morning with Philippa Weatherby, I would've said just about anything."

In an instant, Felix was scowling at him again. "Excuse me, brother," he said coldly, attempting to slide around Jasper and reach the door.

Jasper stepped in front of him. "Wait, Felix. *Wait*. We're going to have a civilized conversation about this."

"Oh, are we?" Felix laughed ironically. "That'll be a first for you."

"It will," Jasper acknowledged. "But this time, I can do it, because I spoke to her. I spent all morning with Miss Philippa."

Felix's eyes remained guarded, but Jasper could tell he was also curious. "And?" he asked, arching a single eyebrow.

"She seems like everything you've said," Jasper admitted. "Kind. Cheerful. Good-natured. And she definitely loves cats."

That earned him a laugh. "That she does." Felix's expression became guarded once more. "Then what seems to be the problem?"

"Two weeks, Felix!" Jasper exclaimed. "I wouldn't want you to marry *anyone* on the strength of two weeks' acquaintance! Not the daughter of a duke, not the richest heiress in all of Europe, not a bloody princess. It's just not a good idea."

A soft smile had stolen across his brother's face. "Yet that's the situation I find myself in. She has to marry someone by the end of this house party, or she and her sisters will find themselves without a roof over their heads. If I don't propose, the odds are very high that she'll marry Lord Oglesby. And so, I have to decide."

"I know that now. She explained, and—" Jasper gestured to the sofa and cluster of chairs at the center of the room. "Will you sit with me, so we can discuss it?"

Much to Jasper's surprise, Felix agreed. Jasper poured them each a brandy and took the seat opposite his brother. "I don't like it, Fee," Jasper said, taking a sip of his drink. "This is one of the most important decisions you'll ever make. Marriage is forever, and two weeks just isn't enough time to determine whether two people will suit." Jasper waved a hand, struggling to put words to a sentiment he normally wouldn't express. "I care about you, and I want you to be happy. I desperately do not want you to make a mistake in this."

Remarkably, this maudlin drivel seemed to have been the right thing to say, because Felix was now smiling softly at him, a genuine smile. "And that's why you've been acting like a horse's arse. Because you care about me so much."

"Yes! You have it exactly."

Felix shook his head, but he was grinning. "Well, I'm glad you've finally pulled your head out of your arse. You think I haven't been worried about the exact same thing?" At Jasper's surprised look, Felix continued, "Of course, I have. And I've been wanting to talk it through with my big brother, who knows me better than anyone. Except every time I opened my mouth, you cut me off."

"I'm sorry," Jasper said again. "I need to do a better job of wrapping my head around the notion that you're not nine anymore, or even nineteen."

"That, and suppress your inherent tendency to boss everyone around," Felix noted.

"There's also that," Jasper agreed. He studied his brother. For all his talk of worrying about what he was going to do, Felix looked remarkably relaxed with one booted foot propped up on his knee and an arm outstretched along the top of the burgundy sofa.

"So, what are you going to do?" Jasper asked. "About Miss Philippa."

Felix tapped the side of his glass. "Assuming things continue in their current vein, and I don't discover something about Pippa that changes my mind, I'm probably going to propose." He gave Jasper a speaking look. "That is, if *someone* will allow me to access my fortune a little early. Although I have expectations, I'm not currently in the position to support her."

Jasper winced. He could not *believe* he was about to say this.

But if he didn't get this right, he was fairly certain he was going to ruin his relationship with the person he cared about most in the world.

"If that is your decision," he said slowly, deliberately, "then when the time comes, I will grant you a sum of five thousand pounds to live off of until such time as you come into your full inheritance."

Felix looked pleased and startled in equal measure. "Really? You'll give me an advance on my funds?"

"Not an advance, no."

Felix frowned. "But I thought you said—"

"There's also Addlestone Hall," Jasper said, ploughing over his brother so he could get everything out before the worrying voices in his head got the better of him.

Now Felix looked befuddled, although Jasper knew he was familiar with Addlestone Hall, an unentailed, mid-sized property that was part of the ducal estate. "What about Addlestone Hall? What does Addlestone Hall have to do with—"

"I've long thought Addlestone Hall would be the ideal home for you. It's a good size—not too small, but not so large that it's overly expensive to maintain. It is close enough to London that the journey is not arduous, yet far enough in the country, and with sufficient acreage, that it could support...

well. Whatever menagerie you intend to acquire upon reaching your majority."

Felix's face was crinkled in confusion. "Are you going to rent it to me, then?"

This was sufficient to snap Jasper out of his hasty monologue. "Rent it to you? Gracious, no. It, and the five thousand pounds I mentioned earlier would be my"—he swallowed, then forced his mouth to form the words—"my wedding gift."

Felix stared at him, mouth hanging agape, for five agonizing seconds.

Then he surged to his feet. "You're the best, Jasp!"

Jasper stood as well. "You'd like it, then? Addlestone Hall?"

"Addlestone Hall is perfect," Felix said, clasping both of Jasper's shoulders and squeezing. "I'll be able to go back and forth to London for meetings of the S.P.C.A. But, like you said, I'll also have room to keep a few animals myself."

Jasper squeezed his brother's arm. "God only knows what motley assortment you'll adopt. You'll probably have a regular menagerie by this time next year."

Felix shrugged. "Honestly, I'm not planning on seeking out anything exotic. I'll probably wind up with a herd of worn-out carriage horses."

Jasper grinned. "I'll brag at the club that my brother has the worst cattle in all of Britain."

Felix laughed. "I probably will. Excepting Sharif, of course." Felix was referring to the very beautiful, very expensive Arabian stallion Jasper had purchased for him a few years back. "And I will consider it to be a badge of honor."

"Good. Good. You'll be happy there." Jasper looked away and added, his voice gruff, "That's all I want. I hope you know that."

Felix squeezed his shoulders once more, then let go. "I do."

"Good." Jasper cleared his throat. "Now, don't go rushing into anything. You still have a week to get to know Miss Philippa. I want you to be as sure as you possibly can."

"I agree. And I want you to spend time with her, too. I do value your opinion, Jasp. At least, when you're not trampling all over me."

Jasper nodded tightly. "Of course. I daresay nobody would enjoy that. But I'm determined to do bet—"

From the mats beneath the window, one of the mastiffs gave a plaintive whine. Jasper glanced over and found Benedick looking around. "What is it, old boy?"

Benedick gave a pathetic yowl, which awakened Beatrice from her nap. She sat up, looked around, and woofed in alarm.

Jasper knelt next to his dogs. "What is it, old girl?"

"I think we're missing a kitten," Felix observed.

Surely enough, there were only three tiny fluffballs dispersed across the dogs' beds. Midnight was the kitten who had gone missing. Felix and Jasper began a quick search of the room, but to no avail.

"Blast." Jasper gestured to the door leading out into the hallway. "I didn't shut it all the way. Do you think he got out?"

"Probably so. He's certainly not anywhere else in the room." Felix waved this off. "I'll go and look for him. He can't have gone far."

"Thank you," Jasper said. "I've a couple of things to do before my big performance this afternoon." He gave an exaggerated shudder.

Felix laughed, but then his expression turned serious. "No, Jasper. Thank *you*."

He was halfway down the corridor before Jasper had a

chance to respond, but that was all right. He had finally mended things with his brother.

Feeling better than he had in several days, Jasper returned to the sofa, taking up the book he had brought with him from the ballroom—a copy of *Timon of Athens*. Eleanor Weatherby's assertion that it was an unfinished first draft was utterly outrageous. Jasper prided himself on being something of a scholar when it came to Shakespeare, and he had never heard anyone else make this ridiculous suggestion. He meant to read the play afresh so he would have proper ammunition with which to disprove Miss Weatherby's absurd theory.

An hour later, he had managed to read the first three acts. Much to his horror, he could see what she meant. The verse felt unfinished, full of lazy half-rhymes and passages that didn't *quite* scan.

But more than that... the play felt strangely disjointed, lacking a uniform style from scene to scene. If Jasper hadn't known better, he would have said that several scenes didn't even sound like they were written by Shakespeare—the banqueting scene, for one, and Alcibiades' confrontation with the Senate. He also found much of the humor strangely displeasing. It was abrasive and harsh, without an underlying note of affection to soften it.

Scowling, Jasper tossed the book onto the table. How vexing, that Eleanor Weatherby had been right! She had spotted him taking the copy of *Timon of Athens* from the ballroom. She knew full well he would be reading it right now. He could just picture her smug smile as she asked him what he had thought of the text. How loathsome it would be to have to admit that he had been wrong!

And yet... he could not believe he was thinking this... part of him admired her for her astute observation. Jasper hadn't much liked the play from the first time he read it, had quickly dismissed it as one of Shakespeare's lesser works.

But he had not analyzed the play as adroitly as she had, had not been able to put his finger on precisely what made it inferior.

And so, he was torn between admiration of the fact that Eleanor Weatherby was apparently so very clever and exasperation at the fact that, in this instance, she had been more clever than him.

Jasper ran a hand over his face. He needed to head downstairs and eat something. He needed to keep up his strength for the performances that afternoon.

That, and his impending confrontation with Eleanor Weatherby.

CHAPTER 16

*L*ady Milthorpe had laid out a casual buffet for luncheon, and people were coming and going as they typically did at breakfast. The Weatherby sisters were just finishing up their repast when the St. James brothers strolled in.

Eleanor was surprised to see them together at all, given the duke's abhorrently rude behavior toward his brother that morning. But what was even more shocking was that they appeared to be engaged in affable conversation.

Pippa happened to be up at the sideboard selecting a dessert when they approached. Felix, naturally, greeted her warmly. But much to Eleanor's bafflement, the duke gave Pippa a very cordial half bow and did not show the least sign of displeasure when she and Felix fell into conversation. He stood there filling his plate with roast chicken and cucumber salad with a bemused smile, an expression Eleanor had never imagined he was capable of forming.

He turned and caught her staring. Immediately, his face settled into a ferocious scowl.

Ah—there was the stern duke she knew and despised.

Felix took the seat next to Pippa. The duke took the chair across from his brother, which happened to be next to Lady Francesca FitzSimon. Lady Francesca had been chatting away with Clarissa, the two of them having struck up a friendship while rehearsing their scene from *Twelfth Night*. But as soon as her ostensible suitor sat down next to her, Lady Francesca stiffened and fell silent.

Naturally, Pippa wanted to spend time with Felix, so her three sisters lingered over their tea. Clarissa attempted to continue her conversation with Lady Francesca, but her formerly loquacious companion was rendered silent in the duke's presence. Imagine Eleanor's surprise when the duke, instead, responded to Clarissa's observation about *Twelfth Night*!

Eleanor felt slightly panicked as she watched Clarissa embark upon a conversation with the duke. Clarissa could be extremely acerbic, and the duke was clearly no shrinking violet. But they shared an appreciation for the great Shakespearean comedy, and he even chuckled at some of Clarissa's thinly veiled barbs about Orsino, the duke in the play.

Eleanor peered at them in bafflement. What was going on? The duke was being cordial toward Pippa and even good-humored with Clarissa. Had he decided he liked the Weatherby sisters after all?

He caught Eleanor's eye and his lip curled in distaste.

Eleanor sighed. It would be her lot to be the one Weatherby sister he despised. The most handsome man she'd ever seen, and he hated the very sight of her.

She spent the next half hour conversing quietly with Kate and doing her best to ignore the hulking duke sitting three seats down.

Then it was time for the performances. Eleanor pulled

Pippa aside as they made their way to the ballroom. "Are you nervous?" she whispered.

"Not overly so. I'll probably forget my lines a time or two, but you'll cue me."

"I will," Eleanor confirmed. They had spent a good hour of the break rehearsing Pippa's lines, and although she still tripped up occasionally, Eleanor thought she would acquit herself well enough. "You'll do splendidly, dear."

Pippa didn't look overly nervous. "I'm sure I'll do—oh, dear, what's that sound?"

Eleanor heard it, too, a plaintive mewling coming from the general vicinity of the makeshift stage.

Pippa gathered up her skirts and started to jog. "It sounds like one of the kittens!"

Felix had apparently heard the sound, too, because he was hurrying in the same direction. "I think we just found Midnight, Jasp," he called to his brother.

"Did Midnight get out?" Pippa asked.

They had followed the sound to the back of the stage. Eleanor joined her sister and Felix in bending over to peer beneath the platform. She couldn't see much in the dark space, but a pair of yellow eyes shone back at her.

"The blame lies with me, Miss Philippa," a deep voice rumbled in her ear. "I failed to latch the door properly."

Eleanor tried to suppress a shudder as she straightened. Surely enough, the Duke of Norwood was standing just behind her.

"Never mind that, Jasp," Felix said, peeling off his coat. "I'll have him out of there in a trice."

Handing his coat to his brother, Felix got down on his hands and knees. "Here, kitty kitty!" he called, crawling beneath the stage.

Eleanor wasn't certain if the crowd that gathered to observe Felix's progress made Midnight nervous, or if he was merely being cantankerous. But the kitten refused to budge from his spot in the very far corner of the stage.

Five minutes later, Felix emerged from beneath the stage sans kitten. "I can't quite reach him," he confessed. "He's wedged himself beneath the very bottom step. I can't make my shoulders narrow enough to get back there."

Pippa bent down to inspect the offending step. "I wonder if I could fit."

"Pippa," Eleanor hissed, "do not attempt it. If you will but wait a moment, I'm sure Lady Milthorpe will have a petite housemaid who can go in and retrieve him."

The mewling grew louder. "He sounds distressed!" Pippa cried. Before Eleanor realized her intentions, she gathered her skirts and slipped beneath the stage.

"Pippa!" Eleanor cried to no avail. "What are you—oh, why do I even bother? It's a cat. A company of cavalry elephants couldn't drag her away."

Behind her, she heard the duke give a solitary *humph*. Had the sound come from anyone else, Eleanor would have described it as a chuckle.

But obviously the Duke of Norwood didn't find her amusing in any capacity.

Thank goodness so little light penetrated beneath the stage. Crawling belly-down on the floor was not the most elegant position, and Eleanor worried that, had there been a bit more light, Pippa might be exposing a good deal more than her ankle. But Eleanor could scarcely make out her sister, much less any visible undergarments.

After a nerve-wracking two minutes, a triumphant cry came from beneath the stage. "I have him!" Pippa exclaimed, scooting out.

Eleanor was grateful that her sister had the sense to turn around so that her skirts were trailing after her. As Pippa's head emerged from beneath the stage, Eleanor thought for a moment that she had managed to emerge unscathed.

Then came the sound of fabric rending.

Pippa froze, eyes going wide. Eleanor hastened to kneel beside her. "What is it, dear?" she asked, taking a trembling Midnight from Pippa's hands.

"It's the seam connecting my bodice to my skirts," Pippa whispered. She reached a hand back to feel the damage. "There's a tear of around five inches." She tugged at her skirts. "My dress is still snagged on something. I can't move."

"I have it," Kate whispered. Quick as a snake, she slipped beneath the stage.

Eleanor could have cried. Now she had not one, but two sisters crawling around on the floor, one of whom was now rendered indecent.

Kate was more fortunate in her adventure beneath the stage. She managed to unhook Pippa's skirts swiftly and emerge unscathed. As for the youngest Weatherby sister, Pippa struggled to her feet with pink cheeks, one hand clutching the torn fabric to hold it in place.

Just then, Lady Milthorpe approached, a stack of handwritten programs in her hands. "Are you ready, Pippa dear? You and the duke are leading off the festivities!"

"Oh, dear! I'm afraid I've had a bit of a mishap," Pippa said, gesturing to her torn dress.

Lady Milthorpe's face fell. "Oh, no."

"I'm terribly sorry for damaging the gown!" Pippa said quickly. "You were so kind to lend it to me. I feel horrified that this happened, and—"

Lady Milthorpe laid a comforting hand on Pippa's arm. "It's not that, dear. The tear is right along the seam. We'll sew it up and it will be as good as new."

"Then what is troubling you, my lady?" Eleanor asked.

Lady Milthorpe wrung her stack of programs. "It's just

that I spent the last hour arranging the scenes in the ideal order. We're short on comedies as it is. Without your scene from *The Taming of the Shrew*, the balance will be ruined."

Pippa brightened. "Oh, that's all right. Eleanor can do it."

"She can?" Lady Milthorpe asked hopefully as Eleanor blurted, "I can *what*?"

Pippa waved a hand. "Oh, yes. She was helping me rehearse my lines during the break. She didn't even need to consult the text. She has the whole thing memorized."

Lady Milthorpe brightened. "Perfect!" She seized Eleanor's elbow. "Come, dear. You and the duke will be first to perform."

"I, er..." Eleanor caught the duke's eye. His expression was dark as the thunderclouds outside. "I must beg your pardon, my lady. I need to accompany my sister to her room so she can restore her appearance."

"I can do that," Kate offered. "I'm not needed for any scenes. Besides, out of the four of us, I'm the best with a needle."

Eleanor shot Kate an exasperated look. "His Grace and I have never rehearsed the scene together. I fear it would be far inferior in quality to the other performances."

Lady Milthorpe waved this off. "Oh, that's all right. We're all amateurs here." She herded Eleanor toward the stage. "It will be all the more exciting to see what you two can put together at the spur of the moment!"

Warily, Eleanor looked up at the duke. He looked as if he wanted to strangle her.

Well, Lady Milthorpe was right—that would certainly make for an exciting performance.

Lifting her chin, Eleanor allowed the countess to lead her to her doom.

CHAPTER 17

The audience tittered with anticipation as Jasper and Miss Weatherby took the stage.

Jasper supposed that was his fault. He hadn't been particularly subtle about his dislike for the eldest Weatherby sister.

And now, everyone was expecting a display.

Eleanor Weatherby's eyes were flinty as they took up their positions. They might not have had any time to rehearse, but Jasper was already certain she was going to make a better Katharina than her sister.

Clearing his throat, he launched into Petruchio's speech about how he planned to woo Katharina with false compliments. Right on cue, Eleanor entered, stage right.

"Good morrow, Kate," Jasper said, "for that's your name, I hear."

She glared at him as if he were the most repugnant man on the face of the earth. The perfect Katharina. "Well you have heard," she returned acidly, "but something hard of hearing. They call me Katharine that do talk of me."

They began to bicker, as was called for by the scene.

Eleanor understood every nuance, wringing every drop of poison from each insult. This, in turn, spurred Jasper to new heights. It had honestly been difficult directing Shakespeare's blistering set-downs at Miss Philippa. It had felt unsporting, like kicking a puppy, and so Jasper had never managed to put his heart into it.

But performing the scene with Eleanor was something else entirely. Here was someone who could give as good as she got, someone utterly uncowed by him. She was his intellectual equal, his ideal collaborator, his...

His *partner*.

The thought burst in Jasper's brain like a firecracker, momentarily blinding him. The mere notion was absurd. A Weatherby Wallflower? The rightful partner to a *duke*?

And yet, once established, the notion was strangely difficult to banish from his head. It lingered on the fringes of his brain, distracting him, and that was the most likely explanation for what he did next.

They had come to one of the most risqué sections of the scene, the one in which Katharina demanded that Petruchio remove himself from her presence.

"Let him that moved you hither remove you hence!" Eleanor snapped. "I knew you at the first you were a moveable."

Jasper feigned amusement. "Why, what's a movable?"

Eleanor gave him a withering look. "A joint stool."

"Thou hast hit it," Jasper quipped. "Come, sit on me."

During his rehearsals with Miss Philippa, they had performed the scene the way Jasper usually saw it staged—with Petruchio sinking onto a chair and offering himself to Katharina in a lewd suggestion, which she declined.

But as he uttered those suggestive words, some strange impulse made Jasper grab Eleanor by the hips and pull her into his lap.

He felt her stiffen in shock. Speaking of stiffening, his cock stirred with interest at the feeling of the lush curve of her bottom.

He clenched his jaw. He had to get hold of himself. This was *not* the moment to go springing a cockstand, with the entire house party looking on. His actions were already shocking enough. Out in the audience, he saw dozens of pairs of wide eyes watching him and Eleanor with a combination of astonishment and interest. Felix's jaw was actually hanging agape.

From her perch in his lap, Eleanor managed to summon the presence of mind to utter her next line. "Asses are made to bear, and so are you!"

"Women are made to *bear*, and so are you," he growled in return, squeezing her hips.

The words felt right. Eleanor was made for him, at least, physically. Here was a woman who would not break beneath him in a bed, who could carry his heirs with the same quiet fortitude with which she carried her many burdens.

Gad, this was absurd! Why was he picturing *Eleanor Weatherby* carrying his heirs? In addition to being miles below him in station, she was an obdurate shrew!

Which is precisely what you need, Jasper—someone to clout you upside the head, verbally, if not physically, when you start acting like an overbearing arse.

That was *not* what he needed. He needed a woman of grace and good breeding. One with blue blood and the training to step seamlessly into the role of duchess.

Eleanor could learn all of that nonsense in a week, the annoying little voice in his head responded.

This was ridiculous! He was a duke, and she was a penniless spinster. They had nothing in common.

Oh, come off it. You have everything in common that matters. Look at how she cares for her sisters! You have the same values. She even loves Shakespeare. She's perfect for you, the Katharina to your Petruchio.

Yes, well, even if all that rot were true, she thought that Jasper hated her.

The vexing voice inside his head did not have a quick retort to that one.

They continued Shakespeare's unrelenting banter. As much as he loathed Eleanor, Jasper had to admit that it was a joy to perform the scene with someone who understood it so thoroughly. The repartee grew increasingly suggestive until the text called for Katharina to strike Petruchio. Jasper wondered if Eleanor would seize the excuse to slap him across the face. Instead, she settled for giving him a firm shove to the chest as she rose to her feet.

He could not decide whether it was a good thing or a bad thing that he no longer had her in his lap. Perhaps a bit of both. But this position turned out to be no less dangerous to his peace of mind, as it afforded him a better view of her eyes, which sparked with intelligence.

When they came to the end of the scene, Jasper found it surprisingly easy to deliver his last lines:

"I will marry you.
>   *Now, Kate, I am a husband for your turn,*
>   *For by this light, whereby I see thy beauty—*
>   *Thy beauty that doth make me like thee well—*
>   *Thou must be married to no man but me.*
>   *For I am he am born to tame you, Kate,*
>   *And bring you from a wild Kate to a Kate*
>   *Comfortable as other household Kates.*
>   *Here comes your father. Never make denial;*
>   *I must and will have Katharine to my wife."*

· · ·

Silence descended over the ballroom. Then, all at once, their fellow guests burst into applause.

Some strange impulse had him smiling broadly as he offered Eleanor his hand. She looked at him as if he had taken leave of his senses but placed her fingers in his. Again, he was struck by how well they fit together. Her hand was strong, rather than limp, and her long fingers didn't get swallowed by his meaty paw.

Grinning, he tugged her a step closer. She cast him an annoyed glare out of the corner of her eye, and he had to bite the inside of his cheek to hold in a laugh. Once she had caught her balance, he swept into a bow and she a curtsey while those assembled cheered their appreciation.

Lady Milthorpe bustled onto the stage. "Goodness, Your Grace, Miss Weatherby! That was as good as anything you'd see on Drury Lane. I can scarcely believe that was the first time you've done the scene together!"

"His Grace and I have a good deal of practice at bickering, if nothing else," Eleanor observed.

"I would go so far as to say that you have a natural compatibility!" Lady Milthorpe exclaimed.

"Ire is one of the highest forms of compatibility," Jasper said solemnly. He could almost feel the exasperation radiating from Eleanor as she tried to tug her hand from his, but he held her firm.

He spotted a pair of empty seats in the back row. Jasper escorted Eleanor to them, but as he started to hand her into a chair, she withdrew her hand from his.

Keeping her eyes fixed on the floor, she said, "I beg your pardon, Your Grace. But I should go and check on my sister." She was gone in a flash.

Jasper settled into one of the chairs—the spindly type that always made him feel overlarge and awkward. But it was no use. He could not concentrate on the particularly maudlin rendition of the death of Desdemona taking place on the makeshift stage.

Jasper stood as quietly as he could and slipped from the room. Deciding he needed a few minutes to compose himself, he went in search of an empty room in which to regain his bearings.

CHAPTER 18

*E*leanor stumbled out of the ballroom, hardly seeing where she was going.

Acting out that scene with the Duke of Norwood had been *horrible*, and by horrible, she meant *perfect*.

The reason that was so particularly awful was because for the first time, Eleanor had caught a glimpse of what it felt like to have the regard of an attractive man. To be the one who was pursued, the one who was desired. And not with any attractive man. Oh, no—she'd managed to experience it with the very man she secretly would have chosen above all others.

And it had been nothing but an act. Jasper St. James *despised* her. She knew that. He had made it inescapably clear on a number of occasions.

And yet, as soon as he had begun to recite Shakespeare's flirtatious lines, her poor, stupid heart had tripped over itself. She knew it wasn't real, knew that there was not the slightest possibility that Jasper St. James actually wanted to woo her to his wife. And yet, when she was on stage with him, looking him in the eye while he recited those lines, it had felt that way.

She was not an experienced flirt who could engage in such coquetry and then forget all about it by teatime. She was going to be a wreck for the rest of the house party, blushing and stammering like a sixteen-year-old debutante whenever the duke walked into the room. And she suspected that the memory of enacting that scene with him would send her heart pounding for years hence.

She heard voices from the end of the corridor. She needed to find an unoccupied room in which to compose herself. She laid her hand upon the first knob she came to and pulled open the door.

She stumbled into the music room, which would do well enough. Eleanor slumped onto the piano bench. She tried to take slow, even breaths, hoping it would calm her pounding heart. It didn't work particularly well, but at least no one was there to witness her in her discomfiture.

Unfortunately, her solitude did not last. After a couple of minutes, there were voices in the hall. The door opened, revealing a pair of housemaids who appeared as startled to see her as she was to see them.

"Oh! Beg pardon, miss!" one of them exclaimed.

Eleanor flushed. "Oh, no—it's quite all right. I'll just…"

The maids were already backing out the door. Rising from the bench, Eleanor stumbled toward a door on the far side of the room. She wasn't sure which room it connected to, but perhaps it would prove a bit more private.

She slipped inside what proved to be a tiny room with connecting doors on either end. It had probably once been a powder room dating to the time when powdered wigs had been fashionable, where guests could duck inside to freshen up their coiffures. A couple of cabinets had been installed, and it now appeared to be used to store musical instruments.

She shut the door behind her, pressing a hand against her chest.

Only then did she realize that the little room was already occupied.

Jasper St. James was leaning against the wall, partially obscured between the two cabinets of instruments. He looked different somehow. His face was slack, and he was standing in a shaft of sunlight that had managed to find a gap in the clouds. It made his brown eyes glow almost gold. He looked softer than he usually did, unguarded. Almost boyish.

They regarded each other in silence for seven fraught seconds.

Then they moved with one accord. Her arms slipped around his neck as his hands seized her hips, pulling her flush against him.

And then, his lips descended upon hers.

Eleanor had never been kissed before, but she rather thought it didn't matter. A thousand milquetoast kisses would in no way have prepared her for Jasper St. James. He kissed her like he wanted to devour her, as if he could not decide whether he wanted to seduce her or strangle her. Perhaps both; that was certainly how Eleanor felt about him.

Suddenly he pulled back, breathing hard. One of his big, warm, solid hands came up and framed her face as he studied her.

With a growl, he lifted her off the floor as easily as if she were a doll, settling her with her bottom on the windowsill. It was not wide enough to serve as a seat, but that hardly mattered as he immediately stepped into the vee of her legs, pinning her in place. He started kissing her neck, causing Eleanor to shudder.

"You are," she gasped, clutching fistfuls of his hair, "the most *infuriating* man."

"I, infuriating?" He sealed his lips on the side of her neck and gave a deep pull, causing Eleanor's head to swim and her body to tremble. "*You* are the most vexatious woman I have ever had the displeasure to meet!"

He was kissing his way back up toward her lips. "I *detest* you," she panted.

"And I… *despise*… you!" he said between kisses.

"Yes," she rasped, grinding her hips against the hard ridge beneath the falls of his trousers that was pressed against her core. She had spent all her life in the countryside. It wasn't as if she didn't know what *that* was. "I can feel the full extent of your revulsion."

He snarled as his lips fell on hers again. Eleanor put her hands on his chest, intending to push him off. But her disobedient fingers instead grasped handfuls of his jacket, pulling him closer. Oh, but that motion she had done with her hips had been a mistake! She hadn't realized it would feel so good, and now she couldn't seem to stop herself from rubbing up against him like a cat.

His lips curved into a smile beneath hers. "Oh, yes," he said, grinding that delicious stiffness against her, "I can tell just how much you dislike me."

She cried out, her head lolling back as waves of pleasure washed over her. "Jasper," she gasped. "Jasper, help! Something's happening. I… I don't know… I've never…"

She didn't know why she said that, why she expected the man who had just informed her that he despised her to do anything other than laugh in her face.

But Jasper's hands began stroking tender circles across her back as he continued to rock his hips against her. "It's all right, Eleanor. I'll show you."

If she'd had a single shred of presence of mind, she might have asked, *show me what?* But she simply could not think while he was doing that. She was so far gone, so focused on her craving for the beautiful sensations he was building between her legs, she uttered not a word of protest when he untied her wrap-front gown.

She watched in detached fascination as he reached inside the cups of her stays, lifting her breasts out as far as they would go. He groaned at the sight of her dusky rose nipples, taut and distended, peeking out over the tops of the cups. He began thumbing her nipples and Eleanor jolted so hard she would've tumbled off her tenuous perch on the windowsill had his hips not been relentlessly holding her in place. Oh! She never would have imagined that would feel so good! And it seemed to intensify the pleasurable sensations that were building at the juncture of her thighs.

Suddenly, one of his hands abandoned her throbbing nipple and came up to cover her mouth. Startled, she looked up at him.

He released her mouth as quickly as he'd covered it. "Sorry. But I said your name twice, and you didn't seem to hear. You've got to be quiet, darling."

Darling? Had he just called her darling? Eleanor had no idea what to make of that. Had she been making noise? She supposed she had. Even now, with his reminder fresh in her mind, she couldn't hold in a whimper as he drove her higher and higher.

"Jasper," she gasped. "*Please*. That feels *so good*."

He bucked his hips even faster. "You're going to come for me. Let's see how much you hate me when you're shattering in my arms."

She didn't understand what he meant. All she knew was that he mustn't stop, not if the building should catch fire around them…

His breath was hot in her ear as he growled, "And to think, they call you a wallflower. You have everyone fooled, don't you, Eleanor? If men had any idea that you're like this, you'd have been married at sixteen. There's not a man alive who wouldn't want you in their bed."

Eleanor was sure that was wrong. She'd never had a suitor, not even one. But her tongue felt thick and slow in her mouth, and she couldn't seem to form any words other than, "Please, Jasper! Please! I need... I need..."

"Hush, minx," he whispered. "I know what you need."

Eleanor wasn't so sure, because the next thing he did was remove his marvelous hands from her breasts. She mewled in protest, which made him laugh. He reached down and started drawing up great handfuls of her skirts. Eleanor must have been a shameless wanton, because she allowed him to do so without a word of protest.

Once her skirts were bunched up around her waist, she tried to pull him back to her, but he brushed her hands aside. She trembled as his fingertips traced the inside of her thigh, then jolted as they settled between her legs. He somehow unerringly found the place that was throbbing like a heartbeat for him and began to rub.

Suddenly Eleanor's entire body was trembling. "Jasper," she gasped, clutching his shoulders. "Jasper, I'm... you're... I... Oh, my *God!*"

The bliss was so pure, Eleanor had never imagined that such feelings could exist in this world. She clung to it, never wanting it to end, but it kept building higher and higher until she burst over the crest. Her thighs began shaking violently, her hips bucking up off the windowsill. She clung to Jasper, who was the only thing keeping her from falling to the floor in a trembling heap as wave after wave of pleasure swept through her.

When Eleanor next knew anything, she found herself sitting boneless on the windowsill, her head slumped against Jasper's chest. She stiffened as she realized her situation. She had just behaved in the most wanton manner imaginable, and she had done so with a man who had just openly admitted that he despised her.

What had she been thinking? She could have no expectation that the Duke of Norwood would have a care for her reputation. Much to the contrary, he would probably delight in nothing so much as bringing about the ruination of her, and along with her, her sisters.

A deep voice rumbled in her ear. "You've gone stiff as a board. What can be going on inside your head?"

Eleanor drew back, eyes fixed upon the floor. "I should not have done that."

"Whyever not? You clearly enjoyed it."

"As a woman, that should be the least of my concerns," Eleanor muttered as she tugged her skirts back into place. "I suppose that was precisely what you wanted. Now you'll be able to ruin me, as well as my sisters, in one fell swoop."

His voice contained a note of anger. "That was precisely what I wanted, was it? If you can manage to raise your eyes as high as the falls of my trousers, you'll see that I haven't got quite *everything* I wanted. You'll also see the reason why I kissed you. How low your opinion of me must be, that you think I would stage a seduction for the sole purpose of ruining you!"

"You expect me to believe that you were swept up in desire for an aging spinster?" She gave a bitter laugh. "Even if I were gullible enough to believe that, there is the fact that you just told me you despise me!"

"I do," he reassured her. "But not in the way you think. I despise the fact that you have managed to outmaneuver me where Felix is concerned. I cannot believe you had the gall to shoot me with that bird bolt. And I do not have words to express how vexing it is that you were right about *Timon of Athens* and I was wrong!"

"What?" Startled, Eleanor tore her gaze from the floor.

The duke did indeed look annoyed. "Did you just admit that I was right?"

"I went back and looked at the text before luncheon," he snapped, dark eyebrows slanting in an angry vee. "I must own that you have a point. It does read rather like a first draft. Some of the scenes don't even sound like they were written by Shakespeare."

"The banqueting scene!" Eleanor cried. "And the scene in the Senate."

"Precisely," he said, sounding more annoyed than ever that they were in agreement. "How is it possible that I did not see it before? I feel like such an idiot." He glowered at her. "You are the most exasperating woman I have ever had the misfortune to meet."

There must have been something wrong with Eleanor, because a warm glow had settled over her. He might find her exasperating, but his words also betrayed a grudging admiration.

He leaned forward, looming over her. "In any case, no one will hear about this interlude from me. You have my word of honor. Are you satisfied?"

Suddenly she was conscious of how close he was standing. The air in the tiny chamber seemed to shift, to become charged with latent energy.

Some strange impulse made the words, "Perhaps not entirely satisfied," rise to her lips.

His eyes went from furious to molten in an instant. "Eleanor," he breathed, hands coming to her waist.

She was leaning in, her hands sliding up the firm planes of his chest, her lips yearning toward his, and—

"Looks like she's gone now," came a cheerful voice from the music room.

Eleanor and Jasper froze as another feminine voice

answered her companion in tones Eleanor couldn't quite make out. "Housemaids," Eleanor whispered.

Jasper nodded. "You leave first," he said, nodding toward the far door. "I'll wait a few minutes so we're not seen together."

Eleanor felt something squeeze in the center of her chest. Had he truly meant to ruin her, all he needed to do was open the door to the music room so the maids would discover them together.

Instead, he was letting her escape.

"Thank you, Jasper." Even though she whispered the words, she could hear the emotion in her own voice.

She started to slip past him, but a huge, meaty hand snagged her arm. "We are going to have this out," he hissed in her ear. "You will meet me at the folly at midnight because I am not finished with you."

She swallowed as she nodded. "Very well."

She hurried from the room, wondering what she had just agreed to.

CHAPTER 19

As soon as the door closed behind Eleanor Weatherby, Jasper began yanking open the buttons of his falls with trembling fingers. He felt slightly ridiculous, like a schoolboy with so little control over his body he had to duck around a corner and abuse himself after catching sight of a pretty girl. But right now, he needed to touch his cock, to make himself come. *Desperately*.

He leaned back against the closed door to the music room, confident the maids would not be able to push it open with his bulk against it. He groaned as he took his cock in his hand. He was so engorged, he could feel himself throbbing. Spitting into his palm, he began pumping his hand up and down his own length. His mind was full of images of Eleanor—her dusky rose nipples, peeking out over the cups of her corset. Her full breasts jiggling as he had ground against her. Her nails digging into his scalp as she desperately pulled him closer. And most of all, the dazed, overwhelming pleasure in her eyes as he'd made her come for him.

That's right, Eleanor. You can say you hate me a thousand times, but your body betrays you.

It didn't take him long, as he'd already been at the point of desperation when he started stroking himself. He barely had the wherewithal to yank his handkerchief out of his pocket before his ballocks tightened and he felt that familiar twinge, the one that meant he was passing the point of no return. Then the pleasure washed over him, and he had to clench his jaw to keep from crying out as he spilled and spilled and spilled into his handkerchief.

He slumped against the door, his legs like gelatin and his breath coming in harsh pants. That had been one of the most intense orgasms he'd ever had, which made him wonder—if it was that good even after Eleanor fled the room, how good would it be when he had her naked beneath him?

He meant to find out. Tonight.

After restoring himself to some semblance of a decent appearance, Jasper slipped back into the ballroom and resumed his seat in the back row. He made it in time to watch the last three performances, including the scene from *Twelfth Night* enacted by Clarissa Weatherby and Lady Francesca, which was quite well done.

Sometime during the performances, the rain had finally stopped. The guests gravitated toward the windows to enjoy the spread of cakes the servants had laid out, drawn to the welcome sunlight filtering through the glass.

Felix wandered over. "You were great, Jasp, you and Miss Weatherby both." He rubbed the back of his head. "I daresay much better than Pippa and I would have been."

Jasper spread his hands. "If the scene calls for bickering, then you can't do much better than Miss Weatherby and I." He nodded toward the refreshments. "Would you like some cakes?"

Felix shook his head. "I'm still full from luncheon. Let's check on the kittens."

As they strolled down the hall, Felix said, "I thought the scene between Miss Clarissa Weatherby and Lady Francesca FitzSimon was also well done."

"I did as well," Jasper said. "Lady Francesca is quite knowledgeable when it comes to Shakespeare."

They had reached the stairs, which were deserted. Felix glanced around, then dropped his voice low. "Lady Francesca is one of the young ladies you were considering for your future bride, is she not?"

"She is."

Felix waited a few beats for Jasper to elaborate. When he did not, he said, "And?"

Jasper measured his words carefully. "I was initially hopeful, as Lady Francesca has a number of fine qualities, her love of Shakespeare amongst them. But I have reached the conclusion that we would not suit."

"And why is that?" Felix asked as they turned down the corridor toward Jasper's rooms.

"Honestly? She doesn't like me. When we're together, she trembles the whole time, as if she were a lamb and I a wolf." He shrugged. "We might be well-suited intellectually, but I don't much like the idea of a wife who's terrified of me."

"Oh. That is a shame. What about the other one?" Felix screwed up his face. "What was her name again?"

"Lady Josephine Paulet." Jasper made a slashing motion with his hand. "I've ruled her out. We haven't a thing in common."

"That's too bad."

They had reached Jasper's rooms. Jasper was turning the key when Felix said, "Do you know who you do have a lot in common with, who isn't afraid of you? Eleanor Weatherby."

Jasper fumbled the key as he pulled it from the lock. He

felt his cheeks heating. Little did Felix know what he had been doing with the lady in question not half an hour ago. "Eleanor Weatherby?" He forced a laugh. "We would kill each other within a day."

This was inarguably true. They had already given each other *la petite mort*, as the French were wont to say.

"Don't laugh it off, Jasp," Felix said. "Watching the two of you on stage"—he waved a hand, searching for the right words—"there was something there. A spark, you might say."

A spark that had promptly exploded into a fiery conflagration the second they were alone. Felix was more right than he knew, not that Jasper could admit as much. "We were just acting, Fee."

Felix was studying him in a way Jasper did not much care for. "Are you sure? Because—"

"Benedick, Beatrice," Jasper said, squatting next to his dogs in an attempt to change the subject. "Are you two keeping these kittens in line?"

It really was remarkable how the huge dogs had taken to the kittens. Sheba was back to pouncing at Benedick's tail, along with Wellington and Lavender. But this time, Benedick appeared to be enjoying the game, too, and was swishing his tail eagerly while he watched the kittens frolic.

Midnight appeared to have developed a taste for adventure after his escapade across the house and was trying to sneak off, a plan Beatrice would not condone. Each time he reached the edge of the mat, she would snatch him up by the scruff of the neck and move him back to the center.

Felix chuckled, easily distracted by the animals, as usual. "I admire Bea's diligence. But she's going to have to sleep at some point."

As if on cue, Beatrice yawned. Settling down on her mat, she plunked a gigantic paw across Midnight's back, holding him in place. The kitten mewled in protest, but Beatrice settled her wrinkly head on the mat, ignoring him.

Jasper scratched each dog behind the ears, then took a seat on the sofa.

Jasper's valet, Stephens, strolled into the room. "Does Your Grace wish to take the dogs out now that the rain has stopped? I took the liberty of setting out an older pair of boots, as I imagine the mud will be considerable."

"Thank you, Stephens. If I decide to go out, I will certainly change into them."

Felix settled into the chair opposite Jasper. "Were you able to watch my brother's turn on stage, Stephens?"

Stephens held up the decanter in a silent question. At Jasper's nod, he began filling two glasses. "I was watching from the back of the room, yes."

Felix leaned forward. "And what did you think?"

His valet was giving his brother one of those speaking looks as he handed them each a glass of port. "His Grace's performance was... *illuminating.*"

Felix barked out a laugh. "Jasper was just telling me that things have floundered with the two young ladies he was hoping to court. What do you think, Stephens, are there any other candidates he should consider?"

Jasper swirled his glass. "Be very careful in how you answer that, Stephens."

"As His Grace has alluded, I must think of my employment. I will therefore eschew the most obvious suggestion and mention Miss Emily Stanhope."

Jasper frowned. "Emily Stanhope? Really?"

Stephens shrugged. "She gave a very fine performance from *As You Like It.* Her maid, Polly, has only good things to say about her. And she's quite pretty."

Jasper frowned. "I don't know. She has a button nose. Button noses are insipid, don't you think?"

Felix and Stephens immediately exchanged a suggestive look. Jasper rolled his eyes. Of course, they would interpret this as a tacit endorsement of Miss Weatherby, with her dignified Roman nose.

Jasper stood. "I think I will avail myself of that change of boots, Stephens. I'm sure the mastiffs could use a turn about the garden after being cooped up for a day and a half."

Stephens hastened to fetch the boots, and Felix headed back to his own room. Jasper would enjoy a romp with the dogs, who would not ask annoying questions, allowing him to anticipate his rendezvous with Eleanor in peace.

CHAPTER 20

The rain had ceased, but the path from Milthorpe Manor to the folly was still sodden. Eleanor wore one of her own dresses and tucked the skirts up around her waist. She pulled her petticoats up a few inches, too. Hang propriety; no one was around to see, and she didn't want to have to explain to either her sisters or the laundry maid how her petticoats had come to be ringed in mud.

The clouds shifting in front of the full moon gave the night an ominous feel. Eleanor wrapped her plain grey woolen cloak more tightly about her shoulders and wondered for the thousandth time if this was a good idea. She honestly didn't know what Jasper had planned for tonight. He'd said they were going to "have this out," and that he was "not finished" with her. But what did that mean? She had assumed at the time that he wanted to continue the romantic portion of their interlude, as he had not found his own satisfaction.

But it struck her as the wind tugged at her cloak that the eerie setting—a ruined abbey at midnight!—felt more apropos for a dastardly deed than a romantic rendezvous. Eleanor didn't *think* the duke was going to strangle her.

But with the way he vacillated between kissing her and informing her that he despised her, how could one be entirely sure?

The folly came into view. Suddenly, a great, hulking beast came charging out of the woods. She froze, clutching her cloak, heart flying. Was it a wolf? There weren't any wolves in England. She knew that, but it looked as big as a bear, and—

The beast gave a friendly *woof* and padded up to sniff her hand.

"Benedick!" she gasped. "You gave me quite the fright."

An even larger shape emerged from the shadows, but this one bore a lantern. Eleanor swallowed. She couldn't make out much of the duke's expression in the darkness, but this was it, the moment she would learn Jasper's intentions. Silently, she accepted his proffered hand and allowed him to lead her into the folly.

She staggered to a halt as she came around the corner. A thick woolen blanket had been spread out in the center of the interior. Two more lanterns illuminated the space, washing it in flickering light. Jasper had also brought a bottle of wine and two glasses, a basket she assumed contained food, a handful of cushions, and another blanket.

It certainly looked more like the scene of a seduction than that of a murder.

You would think this would come as a relief, but this realization sent Eleanor's heart racing faster than ever.

Beatrice approached, and Jasper whistled to his dogs. "Go stand guard." The mastiffs trotted off, happy to obey.

Eleanor sat gingerly on the edge of the blanket and started to untie her muddy boots. Now that she was all but certain Jasper's intentions were romantic, she had a decision to make. Having never had a suitor before, she'd never had to seriously consider what liberties she might permit a man to take.

She knew with complete certainty that whatever she and Jasper did here tonight, it would not lead to marriage. He had made his disdain for the Weatherby Wallflowers inescapably clear, and even if he hadn't, she was a thousand miles beneath him in station. The notion that a duke would marry the penniless daughter of an unsuccessful naturalist was risible.

And yet... Eleanor found she did not have to think too hard about whether she wanted to have one night of passion with Jasper St. James. She was never going to marry. No man had ever expressed the slightest interest in her.

This would be her one and only chance to find out what the fuss was all about, and she would get to do it with the most attractive man she'd ever met. It might be a sin, but Eleanor wanted to experience everything Jasper could show her.

Slipping her feet from her half boots, she turned on the blanket to face him. Jasper had removed his boots as well. He looked terribly handsome in the flickering lamplight.

"Would you like some wine?" he asked, gesturing to the bottle.

"Not really," Eleanor answered before she could think better of it, then stiffened. *Why* had she said that? It would have been more natural to accept, even if she was so lightheaded that the last thing she needed was a glass of wine.

But Jasper didn't seem put off. "Good." He surprised her by grabbing her by the arms and hauling her over to him. "I didn't come here for the wine, either."

Then he was kissing her, which had the positive effect of silencing all the nervous thoughts fluttering about her head. It wasn't possible to think about *anything* when Jasper St.

James had his lips on hers, save for things like *gad* and *lud* and *oh my stars* and occasionally even *zonkers*.

Eleanor was so busy not thinking, in fact, that it took her by surprise when Jasper swept her into his lap. She was pressed against his warm, firm chest, and his solid arms went around her, encompassing her entirely. It felt so good to be held by him, to feel cherished for the first time in her life.

She also found that she couldn't stop touching him. The broad planes of his chest and stomach were ridged with muscles she could feel even through his clothing, muscles that flexed and rippled beneath her fingers. Once again, she felt the firm bulge that had sprung up beneath the falls of his trousers. It probably should have alarmed her, but Eleanor felt nothing but excitement at this proof that, through some miracle, this magnificent specimen of the male species desired her as well. Her curious fingers danced low across his stomach, but she wasn't daring enough to touch him there.

Suddenly, Jasper broke off their kiss, drawing back. At first, she thought she had displeased him, but he growled, "*God*, Eleanor," and ripped his coat off with a tremulous sort of desperation. His waistcoat and cravat followed in short order.

Eleanor liked him like this, in nothing but a shirt gaping open at the neck. He looked even more virile, if that was even possible. She could see dark hair curling beneath the thin linen, could even make out the outline of his flat nipples...

A cold rush of air alerted her to the fact that he had opened the ties on her dress. She gasped in surprise, and he paused, giving her a questioning look.

"It's all right," she said between panting breaths. "I was merely startled. But I do want you to... to..."

She couldn't bring herself to say it, but Jasper understood.

Bringing one big hand up to frame her face, he kissed her, and once again, she forgot to be nervous.

He continued fumbling with the fastenings of her clothing. Eleanor had on the practical pair of front-lacing stays she wore every day, which allowed her to get in and out of her dresses by herself. She could feel Jasper picking at the ties as his tongue traced delicious shapes across her lips. Meanwhile, the fact that he wore nothing from the waist up but a thin linen shirt afforded her even better access to his magnificently sculpted chest. The opportunity was so tempting that even Eleanor's innate shyness was quickly overcome by her longing to touch him.

Another rush of cold air marked the moment her stays gave way. Jasper broke off their kiss, pulling back to look at her. Eleanor knew her cheeks were aflame, but she assisted him in pulling her arms free of her sleeves.

She knew her figure was not fashionably delicate. But Jasper did not seem to mind. "My God, Eleanor," he murmured, filling his hands with her breasts. His palms rasped against her nipples, sending sparks shooting through her veins and scrambling her thoughts. The situation did not improve as he kneaded and massaged her, flicking his thumbs over her nipples, and she whimpered with the pleasure of it.

Abruptly, the pleasurable sensations ceased. "I must see you," Jasper said, pushing the mass of her skirts, petticoats, and shift down over her hips.

Eleanor panicked, because Jasper was about to see *all* of her. It hadn't been so bad, having his focus on her breasts. Most men liked full breasts.

But what man liked wide hips and sturdy thighs?

Apparently, the answer was Jasper St. James, because he groaned as the rest of her came into view. "Eleanor," he said reverently, caressing the curve of her waist down to the flare of her bottom. "My God, you're perfect."

"P-perfect?" she squeaked. She gave a self-deprecating chuckle. "I don't know about that. Stout, I will grant you."

"Quit disparaging yourself," Jasper growled, framing her hips. "If there's one thing you should have noticed about me by now, it's that I don't mince words. And when I say you're exactly what I like, I mean it."

Eleanor could scarcely countenance it, but she could see by his face that he was sincere. She had somehow stumbled upon the only man in England who liked her stocky figure!

She didn't have too much time to contemplate her good fortune, because Jasper yanked his shirt up over his head and tossed it aside. She had a brief glimpse of dark hair and brawny muscles before he hauled her naked body up against him.

Every semblance of a coherent thought fled. He was big and firm and warm, and his skin felt indescribably delicious against hers.

She could hear the masculine satisfaction in his voice as he rolled her onto her back. "Like that, do you?"

All she could manage was a whimper. And then the situation immediately became worse, because Jasper *lay down on top of her*, and his weight pinning her to the blanket combined with every inch of his big, beautiful body pressing against hers was incandescently pleasurable.

"Oh, *Jasper*!" she breathed, writhing beneath him. "That feels *so good*!"

He gave a triumphant *humph* in her ear. "I haven't even begun to make you feel good."

Then he was kissing her again and letting his hands roam freely over her naked body. Was it possible to die from an excess of pleasure? If so, Eleanor was in danger of expiring. His hands teased her nipples, stroking and pinching, and she couldn't help but rock her hips against the delicious bulge at the front of his trousers.

"That's it, Eleanor," he breathed. "Take your pleasure on me."

She proceeded to do just that, squirming and touching him everywhere, and rubbing herself against him where she needed it the most. When, after a few minutes, he slid down her body, she mewled in protest.

"Hush, minx," he said, but she could hear the smile in his voice. "You'll like this even better."

He brought his hand to the juncture of her thighs, rubbing that little pearl he had shown her that afternoon with slick fingers, which did go a ways toward relieving her ache. And, even better, he brought his lips to her breasts. When he sucked a nipple into his mouth and gave a good, strong pull, Eleanor felt like there was a string inside her twisting, winding her tighter and tighter.

When she was trembling with need, Jasper abandoned her breasts, sliding lower until he rested on his elbows between her legs. Eleanor was so far gone, she didn't mark his intentions until she felt the warmth of his breath between her thighs.

"Jasper!" she gasped. "What are you... *Oh*. Oh, my *God*!"

His tongue swirling over that little nub was surely the purest form of pleasure to exist in this world. Eleanor knotted her fingers in his hair in case he once again decided to show her "something else" she would like "even better." Because there was *nothing* she would like better than this!

Fortunately, Jasper didn't seem to harbor thoughts of escape. He kept flicking his tongue over that little bud until Eleanor's thighs began to tremble, the pleasure building so high she felt as if she were about to burst. "Jasper!" she cried. "Oh, Jasper—I think I'm going to... I'm... Oh, *Jasper*!"

Her legs began quaking wildly as pleasure overwhelmed

her. She could feel her core pulsing and squeezing as she lay shuddering on the blanket.

Just when the exquisite sensations became too much, Jasper lifted his head. He had the smuggest smile imaginable on his face.

"Ha," he gloated, scooping her into his arms and cradling her head on his shoulder. "I'll wager you don't hate me anymore."

Eleanor waved a hand. "Oh, I definitely still despise you. But please, don't let that come as a discouragement. After you've done that another three dozen times or so, I'm bound to come around."

His deep, rich chuckle rumbled beneath her ear. "I see your strategy."

"Is it working?" she asked weakly.

She felt his lips brush her temple. "You don't need tricks to get me in your bed, Eleanor."

They lay in companionable silence for a few minutes. Once Eleanor's head stopped spinning, she gathered her courage. "You'd probably like to, um…"

He lifted his head, arching a single eyebrow. "Yes?"

"I'm not unwilling." Her cheeks were burning, but she squeezed her eyes shut and said in a rush, "I would like to experience what it's like, and seeing as this is likely to be my only opportunity—"

Jasper snorted. "Your only opportunity?"

"Yes, and I would therefore like to avail myself of it. I would appreciate it if you would take any precautions you can to reduce the chances of conception. Otherwise, you may… er. Proceed."

She rolled onto her back, letting her thighs fall open, and waited for him to climb on top of her.

After a moment, she opened her eyes a sliver and found

him with his head propped up on one elbow, watching her with a bemused smile.

"What seems to be the problem?" she asked.

"I'm not going to take your maidenhead on the cold, hard ground, Eleanor."

"Oh." Her body sagged as tension she hadn't realized was there left in a rush. "But what about your, um..." She gestured vaguely toward his groin.

The corner of his lip twitched. "If you are offering to do something about the extremely uncomfortable cockstand I've been suffering through for the past four days, I would gratefully accept."

"That's exactly what I'm—wait." Eleanor frowned as his words sunk in. "Four days?"

"Mmm." Holding her gaze the whole time, he rubbed himself through his trousers. "I've awoken like this every morning since the day we met, my thoughts full of you. I had to do something to relieve the ache. Shall I show you?"

"Yes." Eleanor sat up. She probably sounded like the worst kind of hussy, but she didn't care. She found the thought of watching Jasper St. James touch himself excruciatingly exciting.

He lay back, settling on one of the cushions he'd brought with him from the house, hands propped behind his head. "Undo the buttons of my falls," he said, voice pitched low.

Eleanor fumbled with the buttons with hands that shook. She marked the way his breath hitched each time her fingers brushed the hardness beneath the fabric.

At last, she managed to undo enough buttons to spread his falls open. As soon as she did, his man-part jutted out. She couldn't help but stare at it in wonderment. It was thicker than she would have thought and nestled in a bed of dark hair.

She didn't get the chance to look long, because Jasper

wrapped his hand around this fascinating appendage and began stroking himself, up and down and up and down. As soon as he started touching himself, his eyes took on a drowsy quality, as if he was lost in a haze of pleasure.

"Could I try that?" Eleanor asked, too excited by what she was witnessing to remember to be shy.

"God, yes. Here." Jasper took her hand and wrapped it around his length, covering it with his own hand. "Touch me like this. *God*, your hands are soft. That feels *incredible*, Eleanor."

Buoyed by these words, Eleanor kept stroking him after he withdrew his hand. She noticed a bead of moisture that had formed right at his tip but wasn't sure if she should touch it. Jasper held no such compunctions. Covering her hand with his, he brought her hand up and swirled it around.

Eleanor was surprised by how slick it was. Jasper groaned as she smoothed it up and down his length.

Jasper let his head loll back, and Eleanor continued her ministrations, enjoying his moans and muttered curses.

After a few minutes, her curiosity got the better of her. "Should I use my mouth on you, the way you did on me?"

He looked up, startled. "Should you use your *mouth*?"

Eleanor flushed. "Is that not something that's done?"

He looked gobsmacked, an unfamiliar expression for Jasper St. James. "No, I mean—it is."

Eleanor peered at him, trying to figure out what the problem was. "Do you not enjoy it, then?"

He laughed, incredulous. "No, I definitely enjoy it."

"Well, in that case." She slid down between his legs, trying to figure out how best to proceed. He had licked her, and it had felt divine, so she decided to try that.

She swirled her tongue around the very tip of his member, as that was where he seemed to be the most sensitive. His entire body jerked in response, and he cursed.

Eleanor could tell it was the good kind of cursing, though. Tamping down a smile, she did it again, and then again.

"*God*, Eleanor!" he panted. "Do you want me to spill in your mouth?"

Lifting her head, she took up the rhythm with her hand. "Is that something you would like?"

His big body was shaking. "Like? *Like?* I would give up my dukedom to have you… to have you…"

He broke off with a groan as Eleanor closed her mouth around him again. After a minute of trembling and moaning, Jasper began barking out orders. "Keep stroking me with your hand. Hold me tighter… tighter… *Yes*, just like that. Now, suck me… Oh, *God*, Eleanor. That's… That's going to make me… Yes. Yes! *Yes!*"

He roared as a pulse of warm liquid filled her mouth. His seed, Eleanor realized. She wasn't sure what to do, so she kept going as best she could, swallowing the milky liquid that filled her mouth.

After a minute his hands came to her head, easing her off. She felt his appendage softening beneath her hands.

He pulled her up and cradled her against him, wrapping his sturdy arms around her. The warmth of his body was a tantalizing contrast to the cool night air. He snagged the extra blanket he'd brought and draped it over both of them, and Eleanor could not remember the last time she had felt this content.

Eleanor was in danger of drifting off into a contented sleep when Jasper's deep voice rumbled beneath her ear. "Isn't this nice? We've managed to go an entire half hour without bickering."

Eleanor smiled against his shoulder. "A minor miracle, to be sure. Luckily for you, I am too gracious to point out that a *certain party* was the instigator of said bickering."

She felt as well as heard him chuckle. "Prepare to be shocked, Miss Weatherby."

"Shouldn't you call me Eleanor, considering our current state of undress?"

"Probably, but there's something appealing about the way *Miss Weatherby* rolls off the tongue, especially when you're being waspish."

She poked him in the ribs. "I, waspish? I was merely returning the treatment I received in kind."

He chuckled. "And that is what is going to shock you, because I agree. I was the boorish one. I made assumptions about your sister that were, in retrospect, unfair."

Eleanor propped her head up on her hand, scarcely able

to countenance what she was hearing. "Then… you are no longer opposed to a potential match between your brother and my sister?"

"I still don't like it," he said in a clipped voice. "Not because of any perceived failing on your sister's part. Only because their acquaintance has been too short." He sighed, looking uneasy. "But I will acknowledge that your sister does not appear to be the ruthless fortune huntress I first assumed her to be."

Eleanor snorted, laying her head back on his shoulder. "Pippa is about as ruthless as one of the kittens. Less so, actually. The kittens have claws." She smoothed her palm across his muscular chest. "You're the one who seems to have a taste for ruthless women."

"You're not ruthless," he said immediately.

"I absolutely am. I've had no choice. Someone had to make sure my sisters were taken care of, and believe me, it wasn't going to be my father."

"Pippa was telling me about that. If you will forgive my saying so, your father sounds deplorable."

"He really is," Eleanor mused, taking no offense. "Oh, the stories I could tell you. They would turn your stomach."

"I felt humbled when Pippa told me what you four have been through. I realized our situations are more similar than I'd thought."

"Similar?" Eleanor laughed, incredulous. "How is the situation of one of the richest dukes in England akin to that of four penniless wallflowers?"

"That's fair," he said quickly. "What I meant was, my father and stepmother died when I was sixteen and Felix nine."

"Ah." Eleanor understood in an instant. "And so it fell to you to look after your brother when you were not yet grown yourself."

"Precisely. I felt like such an idiot when I found out about your situation. Because nobody knows what that's like. And then I met the one person who does understand, and I managed to make an enemy of you."

"Are we still enemies?" Eleanor yawned. She was feeling extremely comfortable lying naked with Jasper. Possibly too comfortable. She couldn't allow herself to fall asleep in his arms. The chances of their being caught together were too high. "We have a funny way of showing it."

"I'm not sure what we are," Jasper said sleepily.

"Well, the house party only lasts for another ten days. I don't know that we need to worry about it overly much."

"Mmm," he agreed.

They lay there in companionable silence for a while. When Eleanor caught herself nodding off for the third time, she sighed. "I'd probably better get back to the house before I drift off."

Jasper grunted. "I suppose you're right."

They quickly dressed, then packed up the things Jasper had brought from the house.

Jasper whistled for the dogs, but only Beatrice trotted to his side. "Where's Benedick, old girl?"

Beatrice glanced over her shoulder and whimpered.

They each took a lantern and followed Beatrice twenty paces into the trees. There they found Benedick lying in the underbrush and whining piteously.

"What is it, old boy?" Jasper asked, starting to kneel beside his dog.

Eleanor grabbed his shoulder. "Jasper! Watch out!" She raised her lantern, illuminating a stinging nettle plant at his feet.

Jasper cursed, then came around to Benedick's other side. "Is this what you've stepped in, old boy?" He knelt down and began inspecting the big dog all over. "I believe he's been stung on three out of his four paws. All the nettles are out, though. Come on, Benedick. Can you stand?"

Benedick lumbered to his feet, then immediately plopped back onto the ground. He made a woeful sound.

"Should we go back to the house?" Eleanor asked. "Perhaps we could find a wheelbarrow."

Jasper shook his head. "A wheelbarrow would only get mired in this mud. I'm going to have to carry him."

"Carry him!" Eleanor exclaimed. "But he has to weigh…"

"More than two hundred pounds," Jasper supplied. "There's nothing for it, though. The only way over is through. Come here, you big galoot."

Eleanor watched as Jasper attempted to lift his giant dog. Honestly, he made a better effort of it than she would have thought. He got the mastiff up to the level of his stomach, his cheeks turning scarlet with exertion, before sinking back down to the muddy ground.

He muttered a curse, breathing hard.

Eleanor set her lantern down and grabbed Benedick's muddy haunches. "Here, you take his front half, and I'll take his feet. I came out here without a lantern. We can make it back to the house by moonlight."

Jasper's gaze snapped to her. "Did you just offer to help me carry my muddy dog back to the house?"

Eleanor looked up, surprised by his tone. "Of course. Not that I'd stand a chance of lifting him alone, but perhaps together we can manage."

He was staring at her as if she'd taken leave of her senses. "There is not another woman in my acquaintance who would have offered to do that," he said slowly.

Eleanor felt her cheeks flush. *Perfect.* She had brought into sharp relief just how burly and unfeminine she was.

She drew herself up. She refused to feel insulted by the likes of Jasper St. James. "Well, then what do you propose?"

He was still staring at her, his expression inscrutable. "I think," he said slowly, "I can manage him, if I can just get him up over my shoulders. If you can help me get him into position, I will attempt to do the rest."

"Fine," Eleanor muttered.

They had a rough go of it. It took three tries, and Eleanor didn't understand how Jasper didn't buckle under Benedick's weight. She hadn't appreciated just how massive the big dog was until she was trying to shove his rump up onto Jasper's shoulder.

But they eventually managed to drape him around Jasper's neck. Eleanor gathered up the remnants of the picnic and they set off for the house.

They didn't speak as they made their way along the path. Which was perhaps unsurprising—Jasper was laboring with sixteen stone of dog wrapped around his shoulders. Yet even though there was a reasonable explanation for his silence, Eleanor couldn't help but wonder if Jasper's enthusiasm had also been dampened by her highly unladylike offer to help him carry his dog.

Not that it much mattered. In another ten days, the house party would end, and she would never see Jasper St. James again. Of course, she would be disappointed if it turned out she had ruined everything. But she had already gained more from their acquaintance than she would have ever dreamed possible. She would try to be grateful rather than bitter.

At one point, his foot slipped in the mud and he started to overbalance. Dropping the blankets, Eleanor put both of her hands on Benedick's rump and pushed as hard as she could, and Jasper just managed to keep his feet. Once again, he stared at her, that inscrutable expression on his face.

Eleanor averted her gaze and began gathering up the blankets and cushions. "We should keep moving. The less time you have to bear Benedick's full weight, the better."

When they reached the formal gardens, Eleanor stashed the blanket and baskets behind a hedge. "Will you be all right from here?"

"I can manage."

"Good." Eleanor wrung her hands as she stared at his boots. Goodness, but leave taking was an awkward business. "Well, uh—"

"Will you come to my room tomorrow night?" Jasper asked abruptly.

Eleanor looked up, startled. He was regarding her with that expression he'd been using the last quarter hour, the one she couldn't read.

Well, at least she hadn't put him off entirely. "Y-yes," she stammered. "I would like that. Er… Good night."

She spun on her heel and prepared to sneak back into the house. Had she thought she would feel less anxious at the conclusion of her midnight rendezvous with Jasper?

It appeared that her state of nervous anticipation would be lasting for at least another twenty-four hours.

CHAPTER 22

Jasper watched Eleanor scurry through a side door to Milthorpe Manor, seemingly unaware that the planet had just shifted off its axis.

Two weeks ago, if someone had told him that he would choose his future duchess because she offered to help him carry a muddy dog through the woods, he would have told them they were cracked.

But in the moment that Eleanor Weatherby offered to do just that, Jasper had realized something. Ever since his father died when he was sixteen, people had looked to him. The expectation was that Jasper, as the duke, would solve everyone else's problems.

No one spared a second's thought to who would help solve his.

Then Eleanor Weatherby had come along and offered to help him carry his dog, of all the ridiculous tasks.

But in that moment, he understood with sudden clarity that if he married Eleanor, he would not be alone anymore, quietly going about the business of helping everyone else while no one gave a second's thought to whether *he* needed any help. Eleanor did not have it in her to sit back and leave an unpleasant task to someone else.

She would, for lack of a better term, help him lift the dog.

Which sounded slightly ridiculous. But it was true. Perhaps a better way to phrase it would be, when life cast troubles across his path, which life was bound to do at one time or another, Eleanor Weatherby would be a steadfast partner and helpmate.

Up until that moment, Jasper had not considered that this was something he should be looking for in his wife. Farmers and blacksmiths desired a wife who would serve as their helpmate. Jasper had been focused on the qualities prized by the aristocracy—breeding, beauty, wealth, and refinement.

But now that he thought on it, all of those traits paled in comparison to having a wife who would support him unwaveringly through difficult times.

The more he considered the idea, the more he liked it. Which was absurd! A mere twelve hours ago, they had been discussing how much they detested one another. While kissing, to be sure, but still.

But for someone he ostensibly hated, he liked an awful lot of things about Eleanor Weatherby. He liked her clever mind and her interest in Shakespeare. He liked the fact that she wasn't cowed by him. Hell, he was coming to realize that he needed someone to tell him when he was acting like a great arse. Just look at how much his relationship with Felix had improved since he had conceded that she might have a point.

And he had certainly liked making love with her. As he had suspected, Eleanor was in possession of some very fine curves. Her passionate responsiveness and eagerness to give as well as receive pleasure were everything he wanted in a bed partner.

But on top of all that, it was such a relief to make love with a woman without having to ask, *Am I crushing you?*

every two minutes, and the answer usually being *Yes*. Eleanor had specifically *liked* the feeling of his weight on her.

She would like the rest of it, too. He would make sure it was good for her.

She was simply his *partner*. Temperamentally. Intellectually. And physically as well. In every particular, they fit together like lock and key.

In fact, now that he had allowed himself to imagine life with Eleanor by his side, the thought of marrying any other woman of his acquaintance felt like a tragedy. Because they were meant to be together, for all that he was a duke and she was a Weatherby Wallflower.

Felix was never going to let him hear the end of this. But it would be worth putting up with his brother's needling.

Because he would have Eleanor.

Thus resolved, he staggered up the steps of the back portico, feeling light in spite of the extra sixteen stone of dog he carried across his shoulders.

In spite of staying up late rubbing salve on Benedick's injured paws, Jasper found that he tossed and turned in his bed and got little sleep. As dawn broke through the window, he decided he might as well rise early and head down to breakfast.

When he arrived, he saw that most of the guests were still abed. In fact, only one other person was present—Lady Francesca FitzSimon, who was standing at the sideboard, filling her plate.

They both froze at the sight of one another. Was there anything as awkward as standing before the woman you were ostensibly courting, after she had watched you haul another woman into your lap and all but seduce each other on stage? Jasper certainly couldn't think of anything.

Jasper cleared his throat. "Lady Francesca, good morning."

"Good morning," she whispered, her eyes suggesting that there wasn't anything good about it. Jasper wondered if her stilted response stemmed from displeasure at his flirtatious scene with Eleanor, or if she merely hated him.

"I hope you don't mind if I join you."

"Of course not!" she cried, in spite of looking alarmed at that very prospect.

Jasper was careful as he filled his plate not to stand too close to Lady Francesca, or to give her any other cause for alarm. Once he had selected his breakfast, he took the seat across from her, not because he imagined that she wished to converse, but because to sit at the far end of the table felt rude.

As he accepted a cup of coffee from one of the footmen, Jasper cast about for a safe topic of conversation. "I enjoyed the scene you put on with Miss Clarissa Weatherby yester—"

"May I speak frankly, Your Grace?" Lady Francesca interrupted as soon as the footman withdrew.

"Please do," Jasper said, startled.

She spoke in a rushed whisper. "My mother informed me that your purpose in coming here was to select a bride. She also told me that I was one of several candidates."

Jasper rocked back in his chair. Lady Francesca had not been mincing words when she said she wished to speak frankly. "Your mother spoke correctly."

"My mother wishes very much for me to be a duchess..."

She trailed off. Jasper tried to make his voice understanding as he said, "I sense that the word that is coming next will be *but*."

Lady Francesca's eyes were anguished. "I pray you will

not take this as a personal slight, Your Grace. The thing is, I am the third of three sisters."

"Oh?" Jasper frowned as he buttered his toast. "I had somehow formed the impression that you were the only daughter in your family."

"I can easily see why you might have thought as much. My sisters were quite a bit older than I am, and both married more than ten years ago."

Jasper frowned. "Were, Lady Francesca?"

She nodded, then drew in a breath as if steeling herself. "They both died in childbirth."

He almost dropped his toast. "I… I am so terribly sorry."

"Thank you," she replied in a clipped voice. "Like most of my family, my sisters were extremely petite in their stature."

All at once, Jasper understood why Lady Francesca found the prospect of marriage to him terrifying. "And you are worried that you would share in their fate."

"Please understand that I have no complaints when it comes to your character. But…" She trailed off, eyes pleading.

Jasper inclined his head in agreement. "It is an eminently reasonable concern. If I may speak with equal candor, had I known that about your sisters, I would not have included you in my list of candidates. I was a ten-pound baby, you see."

She shuddered visibly. "A ten-pound baby. My gracious!"

He gave a weak chuckle. "Indeed. I therefore agree that, although you have many qualities that I very much admire, not least of which are your keen intellect and your appreciation of Shakespeare, our stars, as the Bard would say, are crossed."

"Precisely!" She bit her lip and her expression became serious, as if she were choosing her words carefully. "I don't know that I shall ever marry, but if I do… Well, suffice it to say, I hope that it would be to someone who looks quite different from you. But my mother would never permit me to decline your proposal, were you to issue one."

Jasper took no offense. "You may rest assured, Lady Francesca, that I will not."

She looked palpably relieved. "Thank you so much for understanding, Your Grace."

After that, they fell into conversation quite naturally. Lady Francesca truly was clever, and knowledgeable about Shakespeare as well, and Jasper enjoyed her commentary on the scenes they had witnessed yesterday.

She cast him an arch look as she stirred her tea. "I thought you and Miss Weatherby made a splendid Petruchio and Katharina."

Jasper strove to keep his features neutral. "We do excel at arguing."

She narrowed her eyes at him. He could tell she was having none of it. "I felt there was more to it than that."

"Did you?" He tried to feign innocence, but the corner of his mouth was twitching.

"I did." She leaned forward, eyes sparkling as she said, "And we both know how that particular play ends, Your Grace."

"I cannot imagine what you are suggesting," Jasper said, a grin breaking out over his face.

And that was the moment the four Weatherby sisters walked into the breakfast room.

CHAPTER 23

*E*leanor stopped so short upon walking into the breakfast room that Kate had to grab her shoulders to stop herself from ploughing into her back.

She had spent the better part of last night tossing and turning, trying to parse what Jasper had meant by the cryptic statements that had ended the night. He had seemed taken aback by her offer to help him carry Benedick, a reminder, no doubt, of how brawny and unladylike she was. Yet he had still asked her to come to his bed tonight.

What did it all mean?

The sight of him smiling flirtatiously at Lady Francesca FitzSimon, a far more fitting candidate for the position of Duchess of Norwood and one of the young ladies Eleanor knew Jasper was considering for his bride, brought into sharp relief what last night had *not* meant.

He might want to dally with someone like Eleanor. But it didn't mean anything, and it did not preclude him from continuing his search for a bride.

To be fair, he did smile at her once he noticed her presence. "Miss Weatherby," he said, rising from his seat. He nodded to each of her sisters in turn. "Miss Weatherby, Miss Weatherby, Miss… Perhaps it would be better for me to simply say *Miss Weatherbies* so you will have time to eat your breakfasts before the sun goes down."

Pippa giggled and Jasper cast her a smile. Eleanor peered at him cautiously. Perhaps he had meant it when he said that Pippa had made a good impression, and he would not stand in his brother's way were he to wish to form an alliance with her.

"May I help you to prepare a plate?" Jasper asked. Ostensibly, he could have been speaking to any of the Weatherby sisters, but he was looking at Eleanor. He leaned forward confidingly. "The kippers are particularly good this morning."

"Do you think the kittens would like some?" Pippa asked, oblivious to the tension radiating from her eldest sister.

"I feel quite confident that they would," Jasper said. "Here, let us set some aside to bring them once you have had a chance to eat."

Taking up a plate, Eleanor reminded herself that Jasper had made her no promises. That he was perfectly within his rights to continue his pursuit of Lady Francesca.

Even if it *hurt*.

She felt rather than saw Jasper sidle up to her. "Are you well this morning?" he murmured.

"Perfectly well," she whispered tightly, keeping her eyes fixed upon her plate. "Thank you."

"Good." He fell silent, as if to give her the chance to elaborate. When she did not, he said, "I believe Lady Milthorpe has apple picking planned for this morning."

"That will be delightful," Eleanor said, not raising her eyes from the platter of poached eggs. "It appears we will have fine weather for it."

"Eleanor," he whispered. His hand suddenly covered hers on the handle of the serving spoon.

Eleanor glanced around, alarmed, but everyone else was seated at the table and seemed to be paying them no mind. She glanced up at him, eyes wide.

His brow was creased, and his eyes were full of concern. "Are you certain everything is all right?"

She swallowed. None of this was Jasper's fault. He had never suggested that their affair would be anything more than a temporary interlude. She had gone into their liaison with her eyes wide open.

The only problem was that she had no experience when it came to having an affair, be it of the heart or the body. In retrospect, it had been foolish to imagine she could become involved physically with Jasper without losing her heart in the process. And the exquisite pain she had felt upon seeing him laughing with Lady Francesca indicated that she was farther gone than she had realized.

Their relationship, if you could call it that, had been doomed from the start. She had never imagined they would have a future beyond this house party.

She was still determined to snatch whatever moments with Jasper that she could. But those moments would now be bittersweet.

"Everything is fine," she murmured. "Truly. Go and sit before someone notices something."

He studied her for another beat, then nodded. He resumed his seat across the table from Lady Francesca, who was engaged in conversation with Clarissa. Pippa had taken the seat to the duke's left, but the one to his right remained open.

Eleanor knew better than to fall into that trap. She took the seat next to Pippa and did not look over to see if this made Jasper frown.

*J*asper and Beatrice arrived late to the apple picking. Benedick was improving rapidly thanks to the salve supplied by Lady Milthorpe's housekeeper, and he was standing well enough that Jasper had considered bringing him. But after looking over his dog, he determined Benedick was still in some discomfort and probably didn't need to be walking around on sore paws for the better part of the morning. Jasper finally decided to leave the big mastiff in the dubiously tender care of the kittens and jogged down the stairs with Beatrice trotting after him.

He strode toward the orchard at a rapid clip, and Beatrice whined in complaint. The mastiffs liked to romp occasionally, but such big dogs weren't built for running long distances. Patting Beatrice's wrinkly head, he slowed his stride.

He was anxious to speak with Eleanor. Her stilted behavior at breakfast made it clear that she was now regretting the intimacies they had shared last night.

He hoped he could offer her some reassurances on that

front. The passage of eight hours had done nothing to dim his conviction that Eleanor Weatherby was the woman he was meant to marry. Still, he thought he should heed the advice he had recently given to Felix and slow down. No matter how perfect she seemed for him, their acquaintance was a short one. He would be wise to hold off his proposal until the end of the house party and focus on spending time with Eleanor to see if they were truly as compatible as he hoped.

Arriving at the orchard, he saw that Lady Milthorpe's guests had already spread out. Jasper looked around but saw no sign of any of the Weatherby sisters.

Fortunately, he had Beatrice. "Find Felix, old girl."

Beatrice was all too happy to search for one of her favorite people and promptly turned to the left. Surely enough, they soon found Felix, surrounded by all four Weatherby sisters, as well as Lady Francesca, who was chatting with Clarissa.

Pippa noticed them first. "Beatrice!" she exclaimed, squatting down to scratch the droopy-eyed dog behind the ears. "Are you going to pick apples with us this morning?"

"She informed me on the walk up that she mostly plans on napping beneath a tree," Jasper said.

"After a couple of hours of picking apples, I just might join her," Pippa said.

Jasper snagged a basket. Catching Eleanor's eye, he smiled. "Shall we?"

Her brows descended, and her lips flattened into a thin, straight line. Jasper couldn't parse precisely what was going on behind those hazel eyes, but he could read the displeasure radiating from them well enough.

If anyone else noticed Eleanor's disquiet, they said nothing of it. Pippa and Felix were already strolling off, arm-in-arm, with Beatrice trotting at their heels. Clarissa was up on a ladder, dropping apples into a basket held by Lady Francesca while they prattled away.

Jasper glanced around, looking for the final Weatherby sister.

Eleanor spotted her first. "Kate!" she called toward a slight figure in a pale blue dress who was attempting to slip behind a tree. "Won't you join us?"

Kate narrowed her eyes at her sister as she emerged from her hiding place. "I thought I would sketch the proceedings," she said, brandishing a sketchpad and roll of pencils.

"I think you should pick apples," Eleanor said through clenched teeth. "Lady Milthorpe has gone to a great deal of trouble to plan this entertainment."

"Which is why I thought she might appreciate a sketch to commemorate the occasion," Kate replied, already scurrying away.

"Kate!" Eleanor snapped. "Kate, come back here!"

Jasper seized her hand, placing it on his arm and clapping his own hand on top so she couldn't escape. "Let's see what apples are over here, Miss Weatherby," he said as he towed her into the far reaches of the orchard.

Once they were out of earshot of the other guests, Jasper released her. She glared up at him, eyes sparking. "What are you doing?"

"Trying to figure out what the hell is wrong. You've been acting strangely all morning."

"I haven't been acting strangely at all. I'm trying to help you!"

"Help me?" Jasper peered down at her, dumbfounded. "How are you helping me by pretending I don't exist?"

Abruptly, the anger left her face, leaving only sorrow behind. "Look, Jasper—I saw the way you and Lady Francesca were laughing together this morning."

He frowned. "Lady Francesca? What does she have to do with—"

"I know you're courting her," she said, cutting him off. "That she's the leading candidate to be your future duchess. There's been a fair amount of gossip about it." She wrung her hands. "I'm trying not to ruin things for you."

Jasper bit back a groan. If only she knew whom he was really considering for the role of Duchess of Norwood. "Eleanor, I'm not going to marry Lady Francesca."

She held her hands out in front of her, taking a step back. "It's all right. Really, it is. She would be perfect for your"—she squeezed her eyes shut, as if the word was difficult to say—"your bride. She's well-bred. And pretty. And extremely knowledgeable about Shakespeare." She was looking everywhere but at him. "I like her. I really do. She's nice. And she's not snobbish. She's struck up quite the friendship with Clarissa."

"Eleanor. Look at me."

She did not comply but continued in a rush, "And this morning, it seemed like you were finally developing a rapport—"

"Would you care to know *why* we were finally developing a rapport?"

She continued as if she had not heard him. "—and it is truly not my intention to stand in your way. I quite like the idea of you being married to someone like that. A woman of substance and good character, with whom you share some common interests—"

"*Eleanor.*" He seized her by the shoulders. Finally, she lifted her gaze to his.

For all her talk about how happy she was that he was supposedly marrying Lady Francesca, her expression was forlorn.

Paradoxically, this pleased him. Eleanor wasn't as indifferent to him as she liked to pretend.

But it gutted him to see her upset, so he wanted to reassure her with all possible haste.

"The reason you found me chatting companionably with Lady Francesca this morning is because we finally cleared the air."

She frowned. "Cleared the air? What do you mean?"

"She doesn't want to marry me," he said firmly. "She is, in fact, terrified of the prospect. Both of her older sisters died in childbirth. As I am sure you noticed, she is extremely petite, and the thought of marrying a great hulking fellow such as me filled her with dread. But her parents, who would very much like their daughter to be a duchess, would put considerable pressure on her to accept me were I to propose. We only began to develop a rapport, as you put it, after I promised her that I would not issue her an offer of marriage."

A pair of pink splotches appeared on Eleanor's cheeks. "That's... that's... I didn't know that." She cleared her throat. "Well, the gossip was that there was another candidate. Lady Josephine, I believe."

"I eliminated Lady Josephine from consideration almost immediately. She would enjoy being a duchess and spending my money. But we have nothing in common."

The splotches on Eleanor's cheeks turned crimson. Her eyes were fixed upon the grass. "I... I see. Still, I am sure you will resume your search for a bride after the house party is over. You would not want to be seen spending too much time in my company."

Jasper weighed his words. He did want to go slowly, to get to know Eleanor better before issuing a proposal. How to reassure her without making promises when he was not completely sure?

"I will certainly endeavor not to do anything that would tarnish your reputation," he said carefully. "But I awoke this morning excited at the prospect of spending the day with you. Surely it will not hurt anything to spend an hour or two in each other's company, picking apples."

"You're probably right." She nodded tightly, still not looking at him. "Very well. Let's get on with it, then."

"You don't have to look so grim about it," he said, strolling over to a nearby tree. He set the basket down upon the ground and reached for a high branch, pulling it down so Eleanor could reach the fruit.

"I am trying to be circumspect," she said tightly, plucking apples from the branch and dropping them into the basket.

This wasn't working. What he needed was a new approach.

It occurred to him in a flash. "Let us talk of something else, say, Shakespeare. What do you feel is Shakespeare's best play? I think it is *The Two Gentlemen of Verona.*"

She looked at him, horrified. "*The Two Gentlemen of Verona?* That is quite possibly Shakespeare's worst play! It is incohesive, incoherent, and the ending is—"

She broke off, squinting at him. Jasper was trying to keep a straight face, but not succeeding particularly well.

She threw her hands up in annoyance, but she was smiling. "You were jesting! Of course, you were jesting. *The Two Gentlemen of Verona* is atrocious."

"It really is," he agreed. "Almost as bad as *Timon of Athens.* Tell me, how did you come to the conclusion that Shakespeare started and then abandoned that play? I saw exactly what you meant as soon as I started to read it again. But I am convinced that it never would have occurred to me on my own."

They filled one basket with apples while eagerly discussing Shakespeare. They argued passionately over which was the Bard's best tragedy—*Hamlet* or *King Lear*—but neither of them seemed bothered by the disagreement. They continued to debate while Jasper carried the overflowing basket of apples up to the front of the orchard on his shoulder, then headed back with two more empty baskets. They filled these while Eleanor told him about her childhood growing up in Yorkshire, including her father's failings, which were numerous.

"He went looking for a *Pegasus*?" Jasper snapped. "In *Eritrea*?"

"He did," Eleanor confirmed. "That was the year the four of us could only afford meat once a week. If I never see another bowl of porridge, it will be too soon. We ate so much of it that year."

Jasper scowled. "But why did he have to go all the way to Ethiopia? Why could he not economize by being an idiot closer to home?"

"Pliny the Elder wrote about the winged horses of Eritrea," Eleanor explained. "Most people believe the story to be apocryphal. Just not my father. He thought perhaps it could be a turning point in his career."

"Part of me would like to meet your father," he said darkly. "I would have a few things to say to him."

"I'm sure you would. And I haven't even told you about the wyverns yet."

His brows descended. "The *wyverns*?"

"Yes." She looped her arm through his as they moved on to the next tree. "He had to go all the way to Tatarstan to fail to find those…"

Jasper even found himself telling her about the dark days after the deaths of his father and Felix's mother, about how Felix had been distraught, and he hadn't known what to do.

She made a sympathetic sound. "A feeling I know all too well."

He set the basket on the grass so he could pull a branch laden with apples down within her reach. "I know our acquaintance has been short, but I cannot imagine you not knowing what to do. You invariably seem to do the right thing where your sisters are concerned." He made a bleak sound. "Talking to Pippa about your recent situation brought into sharp relief how poorly I had been doing by Felix."

She dropped a pair of apples into the basket. "Believe me, I have made a thousand mistakes where my sisters are concerned. I don't mean to suggest that the mistakes don't matter. But the mere act of showing up, of trying, matters a great deal. You cared enough to bring Felix back to Eton. It might not have been a perfect solution, but the fact that you wanted him with you must've sent a powerful message."

Jasper shrugged. He wasn't quite so quick to absolve himself of his recent behavior. "I can be terribly ham-fisted where Felix is concerned. As you have observed. I just can't bear to see him hurt. To make a mistake."

"I know exactly what you mean, and yet, mistakes are sometimes the only way we learn. Sometimes it's little things. Clarissa never wanted to bring her cloak anywhere when she was a girl. I let her leave it at home once. She was cold, but I never had to nag her again. But sometimes it's harder." She twirled a fallen branch in her fingers, worrying the leaves. "I've known for years that my father would break Kate's heart one day. She didn't see him as clearly as the rest of us. She wanted him to love her so much, she convinced herself that he did. I would try to gently point out the ways his behavior was detrimental to our well-being, but she always contrived an excuse for him. The past three weeks have been the hardest on her, by far."

Jasper cringed. Too well did he know what it felt like when your sibling was heartbroken. "Will she be all right?"

Eleanor gave him a little smile. "I think she will. She's

starting to turn the corner. Besides, she's a Weatherby Wallflower. We're a hardy lot."

She made the remark lightly, but Jasper felt shame sweep over him, that he had once used the disparaging nickname invented by the papers toward Eleanor and her sisters. "I wish I had not called you that, even once. It was horrifically rude of me. I apologize."

Eleanor waved this off. "Believe me, the Weatherby sisters are used to far worse."

"You shouldn't be. None of your problems are of your own making. They were all orchestrated by your father. Now that I have met the four of you, I know how stupid of a nickname it truly is. You are all handsome and talented. I honestly do not believe any of you would have been wallflowers, had you been given the opportunity to come to London for a Season."

"It's Rupert Dupree's fault."

Jasper tilted his head. "That is the part I cannot countenance. I know he wrote a letter, claiming that the four of you were fortune huntresses."

Eleanor snorted. "He did more than that—he jilted Clarissa."

Jasper's brow descended. "He *what?*"

"He jilted her. Lady Milthorpe had somehow arranged for a match between him and Clarissa. He would have none of it, as he made clear in the cruelest, most public manner imaginable." She laughed. "I'm surprised you don't remember. I am given to understand that all of England was talking about it."

Jasper held up his hands. "I'm sure you're right. I don't pay much attention to the gossip rags. I remember hearing the nickname, but obviously not the details behind it. It doesn't make any sense."

Eleanor's gaze was sharp. "What doesn't make any sense?"

"I know Rupert Dupree. We were at school together. He's younger than me but older than Felix. And that doesn't sound like him at all. He might be as dumb as a post, but he doesn't have a mean bone in his body."

Eleanor snorted. "Clarissa has a clipping of the letter. She takes it with her everywhere, like some kind of dark talisman. I'll show it to you, and we'll see if it doesn't change your mind."

"I would like to see it. Not that I disbelieve you. I'm just struggling to square the notion of Rupert doing something like that. If you could have seen how kind he was to Felix when he first came to Eton, and there were so few boys his age…" He raked a hand through his hair. "It's disappointing that the fine young man I knew apparently turned into a cad."

"He certainly did. And I would not recommend mentioning to Clarissa that you're friendly with Rupert Dupree, or Rotten Rupert, as she calls him. She tries to pretend she doesn't care, but his rejection wounded her. I know it did."

"I will bear that in mind."

Across the grove, some movement caught his eye. It was Felix and Pippa. "Look," he murmured.

Peering through the branches, he watched as Pippa and Felix both went to drop an apple in their basket at the same time and almost bumped heads. Pippa pressed a hand to her heart and started to step back, but Felix stepped forward, framing her face. A charmingly awkward dance ensued in which they tried to figure out which way to tilt their heads, and then Felix pressed his lips gently to hers.

He grinned, nudging Eleanor with his elbow. "How about that?"

She was giving him an incredulous look. "Who *are* you?"

He laughed. Jasper wasn't quite sure himself.

But one thing he did know—he liked this version of himself, the man he was under Eleanor's influence—far better than who he'd been at the start of the week.

That was worth mulling over.

He scooped up their basket, which was full. "Come on. Let's bring this to the front."

The apple picking was winding down. At the front of the orchard, they encountered Felix, who couldn't stop grinning, and Pippa, who was bouncing on the balls of her feet. Jasper did his best to keep his features neutral, not wanting to spoil their moment by revealing what he and Eleanor had witnessed.

He found Beatrice sitting with Kate near the entrance. Kate stood as he approached, opening her sketchbook. "I couldn't resist sketching your dog. I hope you don't mind."

Jasper leaned in to look at the sketches. He couldn't help but exclaim, "I say, Miss Katherine—these are outstanding!"

They truly were. She had drawn a dozen different poses, not only of Beatrice sitting and lying, but of her in motion as well. Jasper was no artist, but he did know his dogs, and these looked precisely like Beatrice. More than that, he fancied that Kate had captured Beatrice's personality.

He had assumed that Felix, who didn't have a critical word for anyone, had been exaggerating Kate's talent. Not a whit—she was as good as any artist he might find in London.

Jasper wondered if he could convince Kate to make a formal portrait of the mastiffs. He had the perfect spot for it in his study.

Together, they headed back to the house. Jasper was pleased that he'd been able to discover the cause of Eleanor's earlier reticence and even more pleased by how their conversation had gone. He was more convinced than ever that she was his ideal life partner.

And he would see her again at luncheon, this afternoon, and then, tonight.

When she would come to his bed.

As they walked back to Milthorpe Manor, Jasper had to restrain himself so he wouldn't bounce on the balls of his feet just like Pippa.

CHAPTER 25

"*H*as anyone seen my journal?"

Eleanor glanced up from the letter she was penning. Or, at least, that she was attempting to pen. After spending the better part of the day in Jasper's company, and with his invitation to visit his rooms tonight looming before her, her thoughts were hopelessly frazzled.

I'm not going to take your maidenhead on the hard, cold ground, Eleanor.

Well, they wouldn't be on the hard, cold ground tonight. They would be in a bed. *His* bed. She shuddered at the thought.

It wasn't that Eleanor didn't want to make love with Jasper. She very much did. She was wildly attracted to him, and this would likely be her only chance to experience what went on between a man and a woman.

But surely it was normal to be anxious about such an event. What if, in spite of whatever precautions Jasper took, she conceived? What if the act did not live up to her imaginings? What if *she* did not live up to Jasper's expectations, and he wanted nothing to do with her afterward?

What if she came to regret it?

"Eleanor? Eleanor?"

Blinking, she realized that Pippa had been saying her name, possibly for some time. "I'm sorry, dear. I was woolgathering. What is it?"

Her youngest sister wrung her hands. "Have you seen my journal?"

Eleanor glanced around her bedroom, where the four sisters had gathered before dinner. "I can't say that I have. Did you bring it in here?"

Poor Pippa looked miserable. "Not that I recall, no."

"Where did you last have it, Pip?" Clarissa called from her seat on Eleanor's bed.

"In my bedroom. I wrote in it a little after lunch. I only had a few minutes, but there was something I very much wanted to record..." She trailed off, her gaze taking on a faraway look.

Eleanor strove to keep her features neutral and not make it obvious that she knew all about the happy event to which Pippa referred—her kiss with Felix. "So, you had it after lunch. That wasn't all that long ago. Did you bring it anywhere else?"

"No," Pippa said. "That's the strange part! I spent all afternoon with you four, playing lawn bowls. I certainly didn't bring it there, and I haven't had time to go anywhere else."

"It must be in your room, then," Eleanor said. "Where do you usually set it?"

"On the writing desk in the corner. Except it's not there."

"Perhaps one of the maids moved it while cleaning and forgot to return it to its usual place," Clarissa offered.

Pippa tilted her head, considering. "I don't believe that's

likely. The maids visited my room this morning during the apple picking. I don't think they've been in there since."

Kate, who had been quietly drawing the view outside the window, closed her sketchpad. "Come on, Pip. I'll help you search your room."

"Thank you, Kate. Although I've searched and searched."

"Maybe a fresh set of eyes will help," Kate said as the two of them headed out the door.

Eleanor set aside her letter. Her response was so disjointed that she would probably have to rewrite the whole thing. "I suppose we should dress for dinner," she said to Clarissa.

"There's something I was hoping to discuss with you," Clarissa said. "I was speaking to Lady Francesca today. She has a great-aunt who is in need of a companion. The great-aunt is reportedly sharp-tongued and acerbic and has scared off a couple of companions who were of a weaker constitution. Lady Francesca thinks I would be perfect and wants to recommend me."

Eleanor froze. This was precisely what they had agreed, that all four of the sisters needed to do their utmost to find a means to support themselves. And, although it seemed likely that Pippa would receive a proposal from Felix, their future was by no means secure.

But if Clarissa accepted this position, it would mean that the four sisters who had been together for their entire lives would be separated. Eleanor had known it might come to this, but now that it was happening, she found she was unprepared.

She tried to hold her voice steady, to not betray her qualms. "What do you want to do?"

"I want to accept," Clarissa said with characteristic decisiveness. "Lady Francesca has told me several stories about her great-aunt Winifred, and I think we would rub along splendidly. It's a good opportunity and precisely the sort of position we agreed to look for."

"It is," Eleanor agreed tightly. "We did say that we would all look. Of course, we did. But it would mean you moving to…"

"To Manchester," Clarissa supplied.

"Manchester," Eleanor breathed. "So far!"

Clarissa took the chair Kate had positioned next to the window and brought it over to sit next to Eleanor at the writing desk. "Not so very far from our old home in Boroughbridge."

"That's true. I suppose I'm already assuming the most likely outcome is that Pippa and Felix will wed, and we'll all wind up in London."

"There's the rub, all right. I wouldn't feel comfortable relying on one of my sister's husbands for my daily bread. I mean, I would if I had no other choice. But if it is possible for me to earn my own way, I would very much prefer it."

Eleanor's eyes stung. "Honestly, I feel the exact same way. It's just that the four of us have always been together. I've known theoretically that one day we would go our separate ways. But now that we're on the cusp of it, it's more painful than I had imagined."

Clarissa reached forward and pressed Eleanor's hand. "But we will write. And what will make it bearable will be the fact that we will all be embarking on our own adventures."

"Adventures?" Eleanor snorted. "I'm not sure that serving as the companion to a grouchy curmudgeon of a woman will be an adventure. And I won't even be doing that much. I'll just be the spinster sister, living by the grace of my brother-in-law."

Clarissa's eyes were keen. "I'm convinced that Pippa won't be the only one to marry at the end of this house party."

Eleanor frowned. "Do you mean to tell me that Kate has found a suitor?" She rubbed her brow. "I must be losing my touch, that I didn't even notice—"

"Eleanor!" Clarissa laughed, incredulous. "Do you truly not understand that I was referring to you?"

"M-*me*?" Eleanor was stunned into incoherence. "What do you... You can't possibly... *Me*?"

"Of course, you, you ninny!"

"Clarissa!" Eleanor protested. "I am firmly—*firmly*—on the shelf. I will never marry. I've accepted that. Besides which, I cannot imagine whom you could possibly be contemplating as my potential groom."

"Oh, I don't know—perhaps the man who has spent the entire day dancing attendance on you?"

Eleanor's cheeks felt as if they were aflame. "You cannot possibly be referring to... to..." She couldn't even bring herself to say it.

Clarissa had no such compunctions. "The Duke of Norwood, of course!"

"It will never happen. Never. Not in a thousand years. Not in—"

Clarissa interrupted her ruthlessly. "I can scarcely countenance it, given how close you two were all morning. But is it possible that you have not seen how he looks at you?"

"The very notion is patently ridiculous. Jasper is a *duke*. That means that his wife will be a... a..." Her lips refused to form the word.

"A duchess?" Clarissa supplied. "What of it?"

"I am not duchess material!" Eleanor cried. "Just look at me, Claire!"

"I am looking at you. I see the finest woman I know. I think *Jasper*, as you've apparently taken to calling him, sees the same thing."

Eleanor bit her lip. She should not have slipped and referred to him by his first name.

Clarissa rose to her feet. "In any case, I must be off to don a dirt-colored dinner dress. I'll see you downstairs *Your Grace.*"

"Clarissa!" Eleanor snapped. "You mustn't joke about such things. What if someone were to hear?"

"Oh, all right. I will behave myself. It will go against form, but for you, I will endure it."

"I'll see you at dinner, if I can distinguish you from the wood paneling, that is."

Clarissa smiled as she headed out the door.

Eleanor found that her heart was flying. How alarming, that her sister had perceived a connection between her and Jasper, to the point that she even thought they might marry!

If Clarissa had any idea what Eleanor was planning to do tonight, she would crow in triumph.

Swallowing, Eleanor went to dress for dinner herself, preparing to smile blandly at the man who would be taking her virginity in a few short hours.

CHAPTER 26

Five hours later, Jasper was pacing his sitting room, barefoot and wearing nothing more than a shirt gaping open at the neck and a pair of loose trousers, waiting for Eleanor to arrive.

He was so anxious you would have thought he was a lovesick fifteen-year-old about to lose his own virginity. His fingers itched to pour himself a brandy, except he'd had two brandies after dinner, and he didn't want his head to be fuzzy.

He caught Beatrice staring at him as he passed the mastiffs' corduroy pads. It was probably Jasper's imagination, but he would've sworn her dark eyes were reproachful.

"Don't look at me like that, old girl."

She lay her big black head down on her folded paws but didn't divert her gaze.

Jasper was biting back the impulse to argue with his dog when three taps sounded at the door.

He was across the room in an instant. He grabbed Eleanor's arm, pulling her inside his rooms and locking the door behind her.

He turned to face her in the candlelight. She wore her plain grey wool cloak over... whatever she had chosen to don for their assignation. Her eyes were bright, and she looked flustered, but mostly excited.

"Good evening," she said, her voice breathless.

"Good evening," he returned, his own voice pitched deep.

They stood in awkward silence for a beat before Eleanor grabbed his wrist and towed him toward the connecting door that led to his bedchamber.

Jasper had prepared the room, which was awash in candlelight. He wanted to be able to see Eleanor, to remember this, the first time he made love to the woman he was all but certain would be his wife.

Eleanor untied her cloak and tossed it over a chair. She had on a night rail of plain cream flannel, long-sleeved and without a scrap of ribbon to adorn it. But God help him, Jasper thought she looked a thousand times more appealing in fresh flannel with her hair in a plait, smelling of clean white soap, than the most sophisticated courtesan dripping in silk, lace, and perfume.

Eleanor Weatherby did not need frills and ornaments to render her desirable; she was desirable in and of herself.

She climbed up so she was kneeling on the bed. *His* bed. Jasper staggered to a halt, momentarily stunned by the sight.

"Well?" She held out a hand. "Aren't you coming?"

He hastened to the bed, scooping her up and settling her in his lap. In this position, her head was only an inch lower than his, and the full swell of her bottom had his cock stiffening. She felt perfect in his arms, exactly what he wanted.

While he was busy musing how wonderful it felt to have a lapful of Eleanor, she threaded her fingers into his hair and brought her lips to his. As her nails scraped across his scalp, Jasper felt a surge of arousal straight to his groin.

Last night at the folly, Eleanor had been reticent, which was unsurprising, as yesterday had been her first experience with lovemaking. She had no such qualms tonight. Eager sounds emerged from her lips as she traced the outline of his arms through the thin linen of his shirt. Admiration was plain on her face as she stroked his shoulders, then forged a path down his chest and across his stomach, which had gone as hard as an anvil.

God, she would be the death of him.

He returned the favor, palming her full breasts through the soft flannel of her nightgown. Eleanor responded by hiking her skirts up enough so she could swing a leg over and straddle him. That was his Eleanor, who knew what she wanted and wasn't afraid to seize it with both hands. And even better, that the thing she wanted was *him*. God, he loved this woman.

Wait. Jasper paused in the act of reaching for the tie at the neck of her night rail. He loved her? Was that right? It certainly *felt* right, but he was a careful man. Careful and cautious, the sort who thought these things through, and—

Eleanor chose that moment to grab the hem of his shirt and pull it up over his head, and any hope of coherent thought flew straight out the window.

Now, Jasper knew his burly, hairy chest was not what you would call elegant. But someone seemed to have forgotten to inform Eleanor Weatherby that his tailor despaired of him, because she was making delighted little noises as she explored every inch of his brawny frame with curious fingers. When she swirled her thumbs around his nipples, Jasper's control snapped. Seizing the hem of her night rail, he yanked the bloody garment up over her head, leaving her naked. He groaned. Her figure was even better than what he'd glimpsed in the faint light of the folly, curvy and full in all the right places.

Eleanor glanced up at him, startled…

… for all of two seconds, before she melted into his chest, gasping his name with a voice filled with wonder. He wrapped his arms around her, and she actually cried out in pleasure. He swallowed her cries in a kiss. She was touching him absolutely everywhere, and he was doing the same to her, and Jasper couldn't think of anything that could possibly feel so good.

Well. Perhaps one thing.

His body jerked as he felt her fingers fumbling at the buttons of his falls. He broke off the kiss with a gasping breath. "There's no need to rush."

"*Please*, Jasper. I need to feel you."

Jasper wasn't about to say no to that, so he peeled off his trousers and crawled over her, carefully aligning the underside of his swollen cock with the cradle of her thighs.

"Yes," Eleanor gasped, pulling him close. "I've been dreaming of this ever since last night."

The corner of Jasper's mouth twitched. "You've dreamed of me crushing you?"

"*Yes.*"

The amazing thing was, he could tell that she meant it. The expression on her face was one of perfect contentment. Her fingers traced over his back reverently, as if he were a priceless Greek sculpture.

Jasper felt something cracking in the general vicinity of his heart. He was accustomed to being desired for his title and his fortune.

But, unless he was very much mistaken, which he almost never was, Eleanor had no expectations that she would benefit from his title and fortune. She was naked in his bed tonight because she desired Jasper the man, not Norwood the duke.

A fine distinction, but a devastating one. He felt strangely vulnerable, as if emotions he was always careful to smother were bubbling to the surface.

This woman could break him, he realized with a start.

And yet… she wouldn't. He knew with absolute certainty that she wouldn't.

He could trust Eleanor Weatherby with his heart, an organ many would doubt he possessed.

"Jasper. *Jaaas-per.*" Gentle fingers caressed the side of his head. He blinked out of his stupor to see Eleanor smiling up at him. "What can be going on inside that head of yours?"

I love you. The words popped into his mind without the slightest hesitation. *I want you beside me. Always.*

But he bit them back, because he was trying to follow his own advice and not rush in. "Sorry," he muttered before taking her mouth in a passionate kiss.

Eleanor didn't seem to have any complaints. She kissed him back with joyful enthusiasm, pressing her naked body eagerly against his.

In spite of his lapsed attention, it seemed that her arousal was building nicely. He definitely detected squirming in the general vicinity of her hips.

Jasper rocked against her experimentally. Eleanor rewarded him with a moan.

"You like that, do you?" he asked, giving her a few teasing strokes with the underside of his cock.

"*So much,*" she said, letting her head loll to the side.

Far be it for him not to give Eleanor what she wanted. And so, he rode her. He rode her while she dug her nails into his shoulders, and he rode her while she wrapped her legs around his hips. He rode her when she tossed her head against the pillow, and he rode her when she stammered that it felt "s-so g-g-good."

Finally, he pushed himself up on one arm and started to work his way down her body. She tried to pull him back down, but he swatted her hands away, and her efforts grew halfhearted as she realized his intentions.

He paused on his way down to flick his tongue over each of her nipples, enjoying the way this made her squirm upon the counterpane. But she was already far gone, so he hastened to the spot where she needed him the most.

It didn't take long. He was still swirling his tongue around her center in teasing strokes when she gasped his name and dug her nails into his scalp. Realizing she was close, he began flicking his tongue rhythmically over her pearl.

The results were instantaneous. He felt her thighs go tense around his shoulders, then suddenly, she came apart, legs quaking and breath coming in gasps. "Jasper! Oh, Jasper, that's so good! So very good!"

He kept stroking her, drawing out the last waves of her pleasure, until he felt her stiffen. He then rolled off her, pulling her close with her head on his shoulder.

Eleanor purred as she curled into Jasper's side. As eager as he was to make love with her, it also felt good to have her lying in his arms, and he tried to focus on that, rather than be impatient for his own release.

"I'm sorry," she said after a moment.

He glanced down at her. Her eyes were closed, a drowsy contentment on her face. "Why are you sorry?"

"I know I need to do something for you, too."

He snorted. "Believe me, if we do what we have planned, I will be perfectly happy." He propped his head up on an elbow, studying her. "That is, if you still want to go through with it."

When she opened her eyes, they were bright with excitement. "I do. I want to know what it's like. This will probably be my only chance to find out, after all."

It took a great amount of discipline not to laugh aloud at

such a ridiculous statement. But that would necessitate an explanation, lest she think he was laughing *at* her.

"Very well, then," he said with as much solemnity as he could manage.

He kissed her then, gently, slowly starting to build her back up. He allowed his hands to wander across her chest, keeping his touch light and playful while trying to ignore his cock, which was throbbing painfully.

After a few minutes, his thumb brushed over her nipple, and he felt Eleanor shudder. *Thank God.* He didn't want to rush her, but if he didn't get inside her soon, he was in danger of spilling on the sheets.

It only took him a few minutes to get her squirming on the bed again. He let his hand drift across her stomach. She spread for him at once, and he felt his heart squeeze. How wonderful it would be, to be married to this woman who was as eager for him as he was for her.

He found her wet, which wasn't entirely surprising, as he'd already brought her to climax once. But she was impressively slick, which boded well for their first time. After taking a moment to tease her folds, he slowly slid a finger inside of her.

It went in easily, but of course, his cock was significantly thicker than his finger. Eleanor broke off their kiss with a gasp. "Jasper!"

"How does that feel?" he asked, stroking gently in and out.

She frowned as if in deep concentration. "It… it doesn't feel *bad.*"

He bit back the impulse to grin. "How about this?" he asked, bringing his thumb to the little bundle of nerves at the apex of her thighs and starting to swirl.

She collapsed back on the pillow. "*That* feels *wonderful!*"

"Good." He continued working her with his hand, in the

places both inside and outside her body. She tolerated his finger stretching her but relished his thumb teasing her bud.

When he added a second finger, she stiffened, but only for a moment, as her body stretched to accommodate him.

When she was easily taking both fingers, Jasper withdrew. "It's time."

He reached over to his side table, where he had a sheath ready and waiting in a glass of water. He slipped it on and tied the ribbon while Eleanor watched in open fascination.

Positioning himself between her legs, he took her in his arms as he began to press slowly forward. Jasper felt a vein throb in his temple as he forced himself to take his time. "Is that all right?" he managed to choke out.

Eleanor bit her lip in concentration. "It is. It only hurts a little."

He grimaced. He only had the tip in, and his cock was as heavily made as the rest of him. Threading his arm between their bodies, he gave her a tight smile. "Let's see if this helps."

His fingers found her little nub, and he gently began to stroke. He saw the pleasure come into Eleanor's eyes, giving her something to focus on other than the pain. Flexing his hips, he was able to slide in another inch.

He continued fondling her as if he hadn't a care in the world, in spite of the fact that he was so desperate to thrust into her he could have died of wanting it. Through some miracle, after a few minutes, he found himself fully seated.

"How is it?" he asked.

"It's all right." Eleanor wiggled her hips experimentally. Her hazel eyes were guileless as they found his. "Is that it, then?"

He couldn't help it; he smiled. "No, my darling Eleanor, that is not it."

Still caressing her bud, he slowly withdrew, then slid

forward again. Her mouth fell open into the shape of an O. Jasper might not have been a wide-eyed innocent, but he was in much the same state. She felt divine even through the sheath, wet and tight and deliciously slick.

"Is this all right?" he asked, pulling out and thrusting forward again.

"It is. It doesn't feel the same as when you touch… that other spot. But I like it. I think?" She bit her lip in concentration. "The fullness feels good."

"Can I go a little faster?" he asked, voice tight.

"Yes, Jasper." Her fingers caressed his bare back. "Go ahead."

Thank fuck were the words that shot through his brain. He began thrusting in and out, and damn if it didn't feel better than anything he'd ever experienced before. It wasn't just the pleasure of her passage perfectly caressing his cock with each stroke. It was also the strange tenderness she had stirred up in him. Because this was Eleanor, *his* Eleanor, the woman who was giving herself to him tonight with no expectations of riches, or of a duchess's coronet, but simply because she desired him every bit as much as he desired her.

Being with her like this, seeing her smile up at him as he took her innocence rather destroyed him, truth be told. He had wanted to hold off, to delay his own pleasure until she peaked again. But she felt so perfect in his arms that he felt his climax rushing up to overwhelm him.

"Eleanor!" he gasped, thrusting faster as every muscle in his body went rigid. "God, Eleanor, that's so good! I… I'm going to… *Oh, my God!*"

His big body shook as he came, each pulse of his orgasm so pleasurable he knew nothing else.

Sometime later, he realized he had collapsed upon her. He could feel her fingers, tracing delicate patterns across his back. He cringed, feeling embarrassed to have spent himself in three minutes like a boy.

But when he lifted his head, Eleanor was smiling at him. "Was it good?"

Was it good? Of all the absurd questions. "It was incredible," he answered honestly. "Thank you. There was only one problem."

Her delighted expression melted away. "What was that?"

He was already withdrawing, sliding down the length of her body and pressing her thighs open. "I wanted to make you come again. Let's see if I can remedy that."

He brought his tongue to her nubbin. She was already exquisitely aroused from his previous ministrations and immediately curled her fingers into his hair as she cooed encouragement. He started off with teasing flicks, but she was far enough along that soon he was laving her with the flat of his tongue.

"Jasper!" she gasped. "Oh, Jasper, that's so good! I'm going to… I'm… *Jasper!*"

He felt her throb against his tongue. He kept stroking her as she babbled her pleasure, thighs trembling around his head, and only stopped when she stiffened beneath him.

Smiling, he crawled up the bed and took her in his arms. "There. That's much better."

"I'm certainly not going to argue with that," she muttered, smiling as she snuggled against his chest.

Jasper grinned, too. Now this was perfect contentment. He couldn't recall feeling this happy since…

… possibly ever.

A niggling sensation penetrated his fog of perfect happiness. He had the strange feeling that a serpent was hiding somewhere in his garden of paradise.

That was when he noticed it—something wet, dripping down his thigh.

He glanced down and muttered a curse.

Beside him, Eleanor stiffened. "Is anything the matter?"

Jasper swallowed, his eyes wary as they found her. "It's the sheath. It tore."

CHAPTER 27

*E*leanor blinked up at Jasper, disbelieving.

Why had she thought she could make love with Jasper and escape without consequences? She was a Weatherby Wallflower. She had the most rotten luck in the world.

Jasper was peering down at her, brow creased. "It might have torn afterward, while I was seeing to your pleasure. But even if it tore while I was inside you, you shouldn't trouble yourself. Ultimately, it's not a problem."

Eleanor propped herself up on one elbow, annoyance piercing her sense of panic. "Not a problem? That's easy for you to say! What if I conceive? I will be ruined, my sisters will be ruined, and—"

Jasper sat up on the bed, taking her hands. "That's not what I meant. The reason I said it's not a problem is because... Damn it." He glanced around at the rumpled bedclothes. "I was hoping to make this a little more romantic."

Eleanor had absolutely no idea what he was talking about. "Romantic? I don't expect romance, Jasper. I've always understood that nothing would come of this. You can save the romance for your future duchess."

"You *are* my future duchess!" Jasper snapped. He rubbed an eye with the heel of his hand. "God, I'm making a hash of this."

"What are you talking about?" Eleanor screeched. "I'm not your future duchess! You shouldn't joke about such things!"

"I'm not joking." He squeezed her hands. "That's the reason I said it wasn't a problem that the sheath broke—because I had already decided that you are the one I want for my wife."

Eleanor blinked at him, uncomprehending. "But you *hate* me!"

He shrugged. "It's a degree to love."

Eleanor sat all the way up, yanking her hands from his. "It is not, and you've butchered the quote! Viola tells Olivia that she *pities* her, not hates her. And in the end—"

He waved a hand, dismissive. "Yes, yes, they agree that pity is not a degree to love, after all. See, this is precisely why I want to marry you. Who else will even recognize my obscure Shakespearean references, much less correct them?"

"That is scarcely a foundation for marriage!" Eleanor hissed. "We've just established that you *hate* me—"

"I don't," he said, managing to recapture her flailing hands in his.

Eleanor had never been so confused. "That's not what you said yesterday!"

Jasper was unperturbed. "Yes, but I was wrong. What I hated—quite desperately—was the idea of someone taking advantage of Felix. Which I sincerely believed was what you and your sisters were doing. Once I discovered that I had been mistaken, the supposed hatred I harbored toward you vanished in an instant." His brown eyes bore into hers, appealing and sincere. "I never hated you, Eleanor. Not really. From the moment I first spotted you, I thought you were lovely—"

"*Lovely?*" Eleanor felt a deranged laugh bubbling up inside her. No one had ever thought her lovely, not once in her life. "I'm not lovely!"

"You certainly are. You mustn't give credence to all that Weatherby Wallflowers nonsense. That's nothing but a bunch of rot the gossip columnists made up to sell newspapers. Have you ever been to London?"

Eleanor didn't see what that had to do with anything. "No, but—"

Jasper shook his head. "See, those journalists have never even clapped eyes on you. Felix told me the same thing as soon as he met you—that the four of you were all very handsome."

Eleanor was utterly befuddled. "Felix said that?"

"He did. And the reason I became fixated upon you from the start was that I immediately perceived that you would be a formidable opponent. You were so clearly determined, intelligent—"

"Jasper! This is ridiculous. You *detested* me!"

"I respected you," he countered. "And that respect only grew the more I came to know you. You stood up to me. You were completely uncowed."

"Oh, yes—just what every man desires, a harpy to contradict every word he utters."

Jasper seemed unperturbed. "I, for one, could use someone to tell me when I'm acting like a horse's arse. Especially when it's you, whose good judgment I trust implicitly."

Eleanor laughed, disbelieving. "You have taken leave of your senses!"

"I have not. This is the best and most sensible thing I've

ever done. What do you say, Eleanor? Will you make me the happiest man in all of Christendom?"

"I will not!" she hissed. "Or maybe I will, by refusing you. I'm sure come morning, you will realize your mistake and be glad I decided not to hold you to this ill-considered proposal."

"I will realize no such thing." His expression turned smug, and he somehow managed to look ducal and commanding sitting naked amongst the rumpled bedclothes. "In the morning, I shall make you a proper proposal. And you, Eleanor Weatherby, are going to accept it."

She shot off the bed, snatching her night rail from off the floor. "I will do no such thing!" she snapped as she pulled it over her head.

When the flannel settled into place, she found him leaning back against the headboard, hands behind his head, a smug smile upon his face. *Lud*, but his arms looked gorgeous in that pose...

"Ah," he said, "but you will. Have you forgotten that you and your sisters will find yourselves homeless at the end of this house party? You're obliged to accept any respectable offer of marriage." His eyes gleamed with triumph. "Including mine."

Eleanor's fingers fumbled the ties on her cloak. He was, of course, right. A few short days ago, she would have considered herself lucky to receive the address of Lord Oglesby, a man old enough to be her grandfather. So why was she now filled with trepidation to receive a proposal from Jasper, the man she had pined after from the second she laid eyes on him?

The answer came to her at once. She risked nothing by accepting Lord Oglesby, at least, where her heart was concerned.

With Jasper, on the other hand, her heart was already in

twelve different kinds of peril. She would be devastated when he came to the sad realization that marriage to the likes of her was not what he wanted after all.

"We'll speak in the morning, then," he said as she laid her hand upon the doorknob.

Eleanor fled, for once having nothing in the way of a retort.

CHAPTER 28

$\mathcal{J}$asper got little sleep that night, but at least he managed to think of a more fitting way to propose to Eleanor. He decided he would take her to the part of the gardens where the archery range had been constructed three days ago. He would drop to one knee, professing that this was the spot he had been struck by Cupid's arrow and little had he realized that Cupid's quiver was loaded with bird bolts.

It was a bit trite, but it was the best he could do on three hours' sleep.

Having risen early, Jasper had finished his breakfast before most of the house party had even started. He was therefore pacing the morning room, rehearsing what he was going to say to Eleanor, when a commotion broke out in the breakfast room.

Pippa's voice was the one he heard first. "Give that back! It's mine!"

Anna-Maria Robertson answered. "Tsk, tsk, Miss Philippa. It looks like someone should have been more careful with her things."

"I was careful with it!" Pippa cried. "I don't know how you got hold of my journal, but I insist that you return it right now!"

Jasper was storming down the hallway toward the breakfast room, blood boiling, fully intending to demand that Anna-Maria Robertson return Pippa's journal, when her brother, Lucas, uttered words that stopped him in his tracks. "Here's a telling passage—listen to what Miss Philippa wrote about Lord Felix."

Jasper staggered to a halt just shy of the doorway. Not that he truly believed Pippa would have written something unkind about Felix.

But it didn't hurt to make absolutely sure.

Lucas Robertson continued, "'Everyone says that Felix isn't very clever. I suppose they must be right. In fact, *I'm counting on it.*'"

How his legs carried him through the doorway, Jasper would never know, because, had he been asked, he would have sworn he was at the point of collapse. It could not be true. Philippa Weatherby wasn't like this. She loved his brother! He *knew* she did. She—she *had to.*

Felix would be *crushed* if she didn't.

"It doesn't really say that," Jasper blurted as he crossed the breakfast room in three strides. "Tell me it doesn't really say that!"

Inside, a frantic Pippa was reaching desperately for her journal while Anna-Maria Robertson blocked her at every turn. The other three Weatherby sisters were nowhere to be seen.

Anna-Maria tried to make her expression solemn but couldn't conceal an undercurrent of triumph. "See for yourself, Your Grace."

Her brother pointed to a paragraph at the bottom of the page. Jasper leaned forward, dread churning in his stomach.

Surely enough, the words were precisely what Lucas had just read aloud.

Everyone says that Felix isn't very clever.
I suppose they must be right.
In fact, I'm counting on it.

Desperate for evidence that Pippa had been played false, he flipped through the earlier pages of the journal.

The handwriting was the same.

"No!" Pippa cried. "I didn't mean that the way it sounds!"

Jasper staggered backward. As much as he wanted to believe her, the evidence was right there, written in her own hand.

He had been right all along. Philippa Weatherby had only been interested in his brother for the fortune he was due to inherit.

Damn it all to hell. How Jasper wished he had been wrong!

He stumbled out the door, ignoring Pippa's protestations of innocence. He had to find Felix, had to warn him.

He encountered his brother on the stairs. "Felix!" Jasper gasped. "Lucas and Anna-Maria Robertson… they've somehow got hold of Pippa's journal."

"What?" Felix started jogging around him. "How dare they! Why didn't you stop them, Jasp?"

Jasper seized his brother's arm. "The passage they're reading aloud… It's about you."

Felix froze. His eyes found Jasper's, strangely blank. "About me?"

Jasper swallowed. "It's bad, Fee."

Worry dawned in Felix's eyes. "Pippa wouldn't… She couldn't possibly…"

Jasper tilted his head toward the stairs. "I suppose you need to see for yourself."

Felix rushed down the stairs, Jasper right on his heels. In the breakfast room, Pippa was still trying to retrieve her journal. She cried out as Anna-Maria Robertson blocked her with an elbow to the chest.

Felix rushed to Pippa's side. "What is the meaning of this? Pippa, are you all right, sweetling?"

Pippa seized his hands. "Felix! You mustn't listen to anything they say!"

He frowned. "What do you mean?" he asked, his voice sharpening.

"Let me explain—" Pippa began, but Lucas spoke in a booming voice, drowning her out.

"Listen to this, Lord Felix—'Everyone says that Felix isn't very clever. I suppose they must be right.'"

"*What?*" Felix cried, rounding on Pippa. The raw pain in his brother's eyes was wrenching for Jasper to see. "You think I'm an idiot?"

"I don't! I swear, I don't!"

"Just wait, it gets worse," Lucas continued. "'I suppose they must be right. In fact, I'm counting on it.'"

Felix recoiled. He turned to face Pippa, looking betrayed. "I thought... I thought you cared for me," he whispered.

"I do!" Pippa cried. "I didn't mean that the way it sounds. You must believe me, Felix!"

"Here, Lord Felix," Lucas called. "Come and read for yourself."

Felix tore himself away from Pippa long enough to scan the paragraph for himself. The room had fallen totally silent.

After a moment, he turned to Pippa. His eyes were hard. "How could you?"

"It's not what you think!" Pippa wrung her hands. "They're twisting my words."

"I saw what you wrote!" Felix snapped. "It's written in your hand. You all but called me an idiot!"

"That's not what I meant!" Pippa insisted.

Felix's face remained cold, implacable. "Then what did you mean?"

"I..." Pippa tried to glance at the pages of the journal. "I've filled so many pages over the past few days, I don't remember *precisely* what I wrote—"

Felix snorted. "A likely excuse!"

"—but I have never written anything about you that was anything less than fawning!" She made another desperate grab for the journal. "Let me show you the full passage. I know it will vindicate me—"

"I think I've seen enough!" Felix snapped, turning on his heel.

"No! Felix! Wait!" Pippa cried as Felix strode from the room.

Jasper hurried after his brother. "Felix—wait. Tell me what I can do."

Felix did not slow his stride. "You can leave me alone, Jasper."

"Alone?" Jasper didn't care for that answer. "I don't think that's wise. Right now you need support—"

"Not from you!" Felix snapped. He wheeled around as he reached the bend in the stairs. "You're probably *delighted*. You never thought Pippa liked me for me, because, honestly, who would? Well, congratulations, Jasper! You were right! You were right, and I was wrong. As usual!"

"I wish to God I had been wrong," Jasper said, voice shaking. "Anything that hurts you is the *last* thing I would want. You have to believe me, Fee."

Jasper watched as Felix's flinty facade crumbled, leaving only misery behind. "I do. I do know that. You're the only person I can trust. I thought I could trust Pippa but look how that turned out." He squeezed his eyes shut. "I feel like such an *idiot*, Jasp."

"You're not an idiot," Jasper said in a rush. "You're a good man, a decent man. You didn't deserve that."

Felix ran a hand over his face. "The gossip is going to be *brutal*."

"There won't be a word of gossip," Jasper vowed. "I will make sure of it. Not a breath of this will get out."

"Not a breath of what will get out?" a creaky voice asked from the top of the stairs.

Jasper and Felix looked up in unison. "Lord Oglesby," Jasper said. "Good morning."

The baron made his way to the landing upon which the brothers stood. "What's this commotion all about?" he asked, glancing from Jasper to Felix and back again.

"Nothing," Jasper said with forced lightness. "Nothing at all."

"Oh," the baron replied. "Judging by the doleful look on your face, I thought there might have been some unpleasant business involving your Miss Weatherby."

"She's not my Miss Weatherby," Felix said vehemently. "I want nothing to do with her."

"Oh—I hadn't realized." Lord Oglesby shook his head as if to clear it. "Well, it happens that I proposed to the chit last night. Just as you requested, Your Grace."

Felix's eyes snapped to him, brimming with betrayal, and Jasper felt his heart drop all the way to the pit of his stomach.

Felix turned to face the baron. "What do you mean, just as he requested? Jasper asked you to propose to Pippa?"

"Wait, Felix," Jasper said in a hoarse voice. "Let me explain."

In the same breath, Lord Oglesby replied, "Oh, yes! He suspected Miss Weatherby of having mercenary intentions, so he took me aside and asked me to issue a proposal of my own, just to see what she would say."

"How could you, Jasper!" Felix shouted.

Jasper held out both hands. "It's not what you think—"

"You were never in my corner! All the time you were professing to be so concerned for my future happiness, you were actively working to undermine it!"

"I wasn't!" Jasper cried as an astonished Baron Oglesby looked on. "I swear, I wasn't!"

"First Pippa, and now you," Felix said, voice shaking. "I haven't a friend in the world."

"Felix." Jasper seized his brother's arm. "Felix, *please.*"

Felix shook him off. "Don't touch me! I can't stand the sight of you right now." He turned and fled toward his room.

That was when Jasper noticed Eleanor and her two sisters hurrying down the stairs toward him.

Eleanor frowned as Felix rushed by her, pointedly ignoring her greeting. "Whatever has come over your brother?" she asked as she reached Jasper on the landing.

There was no sense in beating around the bush. "It's Pippa. She and Felix have had a falling out."

"A falling out?" Eleanor frowned. "Over what?"

"Come and see," Jasper said grimly.

As the four of them jogged down the stairs, Jasper explained, "The Robertson siblings seem to have taken Pippa's journal."

"They *what?*" Clarissa snapped.

"They've been reading it aloud," Jasper continued.

"And why did you not stop them at once?" Clarissa demanded.

Eleanor's brow was creased in confusion. "Was Felix embarrassed by Pippa's fawning descriptions of him?"

Jasper gave her a grim look. "It wasn't fawning."

They were rounding the door into the breakfast room. "I have difficulty believing—Clarissa! *Stop!*"

Clarissa stormed up to Anna-Maria Robertson. "Give me my sister's journal, you bitch!"

Clarissa lunged for Anna-Maria's throat, but Eleanor grabbed her around the waist. Anna-Maria flew into hysterics, in spite of the fact that Eleanor had moved quickly enough that Clarissa didn't manage to lay a finger on her. Pippa had collapsed upon the carpet, where she sat sobbing, while Lucas was shouting for someone to control these Weatherby hoydens, and Kate?

Kate seized the opportunity presented by this chaos to sneak around behind Lucas and snatch the journal right out of his hands.

"Give that back!" Lucas shouted.

"Why should she?" Eleanor demanded, as commanding as any duchess. "It's not yours."

Lucas recoiled in the face of her ire. "Well, no, but—"

"But nothing!" Clarissa snapped. "No one has any business reading my sister's private thoughts."

"You probably need to see it," Jasper said, looking at Eleanor.

He could almost see the thoughts churning behind those intelligent eyes. "And why is that?"

Jasper rubbed his brow. "Because you need to understand precisely what Miss Philippa wrote about my brother." He held her gaze steadily. "And why I will be taking Felix's side."

Eleanor frowned at him. Jasper had the sinking feeling that they had just gone right back to where they'd been for most of the house party, back when they'd hated each other.

But he didn't look away, and neither did Eleanor. After a moment, she said, "Pippa, dear. Show me the passage."

Kate helped Pippa up from the floor. "I want to see it, too," Pippa said between sniffles. "I've no memory of writing those words, but I *swear*, I haven't had a single bad thought about Felix, not since the moment I clapped eyes on him. This is all a mistake, a horrible mistake…"

Jasper sincerely doubted it, but he said nothing. The four

Weatherby sisters huddled together while Pippa paged through the book.

While he watched them attempt to relocate the relevant passage, Lord Oglesby stole up beside Jasper. "Might I have a word, Your Grace?"

The baron led him to the hallway outside the breakfast room. "What is it, my lord?" Jasper asked wearily.

"Due to the outburst from your brother, I didn't have the chance to tell you what Miss Philippa said in response to my proposal."

Jasper had a fair idea. "Let me guess—she was delighted at the prospect of becoming a baroness."

"Not at all!" Lord Oglesby cackled. "Turned me down flat. Very politely, mind you. But she explained that she was head-over-heels in love with your brother. I prodded her a bit, as you'd mentioned that you wanted to test her. Mentioned that Lord Felix hasn't yet come into his fortune and isn't yet old enough to marry without your approval. I explained that if she held out for him, she would find herself facing a year of poverty and deprivation. Do you want to know what she said?"

"What?" Jasper asked, dread pooling in his stomach.

"She said that, so long as she was with Lord Felix, she could live in the meanest hovel, and she would count herself the happiest of creatures." The baron jabbed his bony elbow into Jasper's ribs. "She's better than we thought, eh?"

Jasper didn't know what to say. Pippa's refusal of the baron's offer of marriage didn't square with the passage he'd just seen in her journal.

What was going on?

Just then, Eleanor appeared framed in the doorway, eyes sparking fire. "Get in here, you idiot!"

Jasper glowered at her. "If I am an idiot, it is for trusting your sister, who has proved to be nothing but a grasping—"

"The passage was taken out of context!" Eleanor snapped. "Come and see for yourself."

Jasper leaned down and peered at the familiar, damning words:

Everyone says that Felix isn't very clever.
I suppose they must be right.
In fact, I'm counting on it.

But when Eleanor turned the page, the passage continued:

Because, you see, that's exactly what everybody says about me. And, as selfish as it may seem, I despair that if Felix were the sort of man who prized cleverness above every other virtue, he would never consider the likes of me. I think being clever is rated too highly, anyway. I would much rather have a husband who is kind than clever. And no man is kinder than Felix. Sometimes it terrifies me how desperately I love him. I can't imagine what I would do if something were to happen to him. But mostly, my thoughts are bright. We're going to be happy together. I just know that we are. Some things are meant to be, and I am convinced that Felix and I are one of them.

Oh, God. Pippa had expressed herself clumsily, but the words were ultimately of adoration. Which tracked perfectly with what Lord Oglesby had told him and everything he had observed about Pippa.

Jasper had come so far, had made so much progress in the past few days. Yet at the first sign of doubt, he had promptly reverted to old habits.

He glanced up at Eleanor's furious face. "I must find my brother. I will make this right. I swear it."

Eleanor's voice was cold as she said, "See to it that you do."

Before hurrying after Felix, Jasper crossed the breakfast room in three strides. He noted that the Robertson siblings had slunk back to their rooms, which was fortunate for them. They would not wish to face Jasper at this, the peak of his fury.

Pippa sat ensconced between Clarissa and Kate, who were propping her up. She still managed to look pretty, even with her face blotchy and tear streaked.

"Miss Philippa," he said, bowing over her hand. "I apologize for my conduct earlier. I should have known at once that you would never write anything in disparagement of my brother."

Pippa glanced up at him, green eyes miserable. "Does Felix hate me now?"

Jasper chose not to answer that question. "I will find him at once and explain that it was all a misunderstanding. Keep your journal at hand. I will bring him to you if I have to throw him over my shoulder and carry him down the stairs."

That earned him a small, miserable smile. "Thank you, Your Grace."

Jasper rushed out and took the stairs two at a time, hurrying toward Felix's rooms.

CHAPTER 29

The Weatherby sisters gathered in Eleanor's rooms. At first, hope hung in the air that the misunderstanding between Pippa and Felix could be quickly resolved.

After an hour passed, however, it seemed that something was wrong. Eleanor penned a quick note to Lady Milthorpe asking if there were any updates, then rang for a maid to deliver it.

Lady Milthorpe herself appeared at the door some ten minutes later. Eleanor marked their hostess's drawn expression, and the way she was wringing her hands.

"Has Lord Felix been located?" Eleanor asked.

"The household has been all abustle trying to do just that," the countess explained. "We were eventually able to track him to the stables. Apparently, Lord Felix requested that his horse be saddled, then departed with some haste."

"Do you know where he went?" Clarissa asked.

"We do not," Lady Milthorpe replied. "He is likely just working off his frustration in the saddle. He left all his belongings in his room, so we fully expect him to return before supper. Still, his brother, my husband, and a half a dozen grooms have set forth in all directions in an attempt to track him down, so that he can be reassured of the truth of Miss Philippa's affections with all possible haste."

Eleanor smiled tightly. "I suppose there's nothing for it, then, but to wait."

Lady Milthorpe's eyes were sympathetic as they fell on Pippa "I'm afraid so. I will bring you word the moment there is any news."

Eleanor pressed her hand. "Thank you, my lady."

All they could do after that was wait. After another hour, Kate attempted to distract Pippa by fetching Sheba and Wellington from Jasper's rooms. It was a mark of their youngest sister's despondency that even the kittens could not cheer her. Indeed, Pippa scarce seemed to notice them at all.

After the passage of two more hours, servants appeared with a tray for luncheon. Eleanor, Clarissa, and Kate picked at the food. Pippa didn't eat a bite and had to be encouraged to drink the cup of tea Clarissa pressed into her hands.

They didn't receive any news until the shadows outside were starting to grow long, and Jasper's valet, Stephens, knocked upon the door.

He gestured to Benedick and Beatrice, who were wearing their leashes. "I was just taking the mastiffs out for their evening constitutional. I wondered if a little fresh air might do Miss Philippa some good?"

"Thank you," Eleanor replied in hushed tones, "but she hasn't even noticed the kittens. I doubt she can summon the will to move from the bed."

"Ah. Of course."

Stephens was about to take the mastiffs off when Lady Milthorpe appeared.

"What news?" Clarissa asked, hurrying to the door.

The countess looked weary. "Lord Felix was spotted."

"Then he hasn't returned?" Pippa called from her seat on the bed.

"But that's good news, that he's been spotted," Kate said, squeezing Pippa's hand. She paused, taking in the countess's expression. "Isn't it?"

The countess shook her head. "He was spotted leaving Northampton, on the road toward Birmingham."

"Birmingham!" Eleanor exclaimed. "Surely he won't go as far as Birmingham!"

Lady Milthorpe nodded grimly "That seems to be his intention. And if he makes it to Birmingham, he could head absolutely anywhere from there."

Pippa rose from the bed. She was quaking like a leaf in a high wind, and Kate's hand wrapped around her arm seemed to be the only thing holding her upright. "Then... he's not just working out his temper in the saddle."

"It would seem not," Lady Milthorpe confirmed.

"He's leaving," Pippa clarified.

Lady Milthorpe twisted her handkerchief in her hands. "I'm afraid so."

"But his brother will be able to track him," Clarissa said. "Surely, he's had to change horses several times by now. The duke will ask at every inn. They would not loan out a saddle horse without agreeing upon a destination. Otherwise, they couldn't retrieve it. There will be a trail to follow."

Stephens made a bleak sound.

"What is it, Stephens?" Eleanor asked.

The valet spoke reluctantly. "His Grace paid a small fortune for Lord Felix's mount when he came across the block at Tattersall's. His stallion is of Arabian stock, imported from the Middle East."

Eleanor's heart filled with dread. "What are you saying?"

"Such horses are bred to cross deserts. The ones that were not strong enough to do so did not survive to become part of the bloodstock." Stephens' eyes were sorrowful. "Not one horse out of a hundred could carry his rider all the way to Birmingham. But Sharif could probably carry on for a hundred miles at a steady canter without being overly bothered about it."

Pippa's knees gave out, and she sat heavily upon Eleanor's bed.

Stephens bowed his head. "I must see to the dogs. I am so sorry, Miss Philippa."

Lady Milthorpe retreated as well, with the promise that she would send up a supper tray.

Across the room, Clarissa caught Eleanor's eye. Understanding passed between the two sisters.

For the past few days, the Weatherby sisters had been working under the assumption that a proposal from Felix to Pippa would be the event that would pull them back from the brink of destitution.

It now appeared increasingly likely that such a proposal would not be forthcoming, at least, not by the end of the house party. To make matters worse, there had been a dozen captivated witnesses in the breakfast room who had heard what they believed was Pippa mocking her would-be suitor in her journal. It fit very neatly into the narrative of the grasping Weatherby Wallflowers and was bound to cause a fresh fit of gossip in the scandal sheets.

They needed a solution to their predicament, and they needed it now, before the newspapers made mincemeat of what was left of their reputation.

"So," Clarissa began, "if Felix is not going to marry Pippa—"

"Felix will be brought around," Eleanor said, giving Clarissa a speaking look. "It just might take slightly longer than we would like."

"Time we do not have," Clarissa said. "Once the scandal sheets get wind of this—"

"I know." Eleanor rubbed her temple. "Believe me, I know."

From her perch next to Pippa on the bed, Kate said softly, "Did I mishear, or did Lord Oglesby say that he had made Pippa an offer of marriage?"

Clarissa snorted. "An offer she declined. Who knows if he would be willing to renew it after that scene in the breakfast room today?"

Pippa had gone as white as the counterpane. "Besides," Eleanor said, "Pippa is going to resolve things with Felix. She *is*," she said firmly, glaring at Clarissa when she started to speak. "It makes no sense to dangle her before Lord Oglesby when she is on the cusp of a match that will actually make her happy."

The sisters fell silent. Eleanor was trying to muster the courage to tell her sisters that Jasper had proposed last night, if that was the proper term for it. She was still more than halfway convinced that he was going to take the proposal back, especially after the events that transpired that morning.

There was also the distinct possibility that when she saw him, she was going to strangle the great lummox. Of all the idiocy, to believe those horrible Robertson siblings over Pippa, who didn't have a deceptive bone in her body.

She was fully aware that the bridegroom being rendered a corpse would put a distinct damper on the wedding ceremony.

Still, in her current frame of pique, Eleanor could make no guarantees.

Kate squeezed her eyes shut. "Perhaps Lord Oglesby would be willing to consider me instead."

"Or me," Clarissa offered swiftly.

"Really, Claire," Eleanor said, "do you seriously expect

him to consider you after the way you lunged at Anna-Maria Robertson's throat?"

Clarissa waved this off. "He's what, seventy-two years old? How good could his eyesight possibly be?"

"To say nothing of the fact that you called her a bitch," Kate muttered.

"Oh, pish posh," Clarissa said. "I'm sure his hearing is starting to go, too."

"He couldn't possibly be that deaf," Eleanor noted dryly. "You shouted it so loudly they probably heard it all the way back in Boroughbridge."

At this remark, Pippa smiled.

It was a tiny smile, and it didn't reach her eyes.

But it was better than the expression she'd been making all day.

"I appreciated the way you sallied forth to my defense, Claire," Pippa said. "It felt good to have someone stand up for me."

Clarissa shot Eleanor a triumphant look. Eleanor rolled her eyes in response.

"Still," Kate said, "Clarissa isn't wrong. We need to find something to tide us over until Felix can be tracked down. And if that means I have to marry Lord Oglesby—"

"I believe we might have another option," Eleanor said stiffly.

All three of her sisters fell silent, staring at her. Eleanor's cheeks heated, and her tongue felt thick in her mouth.

"And that is?" Kate finally asked.

Eleanor fixed her eyes upon the crown molding behind her sisters' heads. "Yesterday, the Duke of Norwood asked me to marry him—"

"I knew it!" Clarissa shouted in the same instant Kate gasped, "Did he truly?" and Pippa burst into tears.

"Pippa!" Eleanor cried, hurrying over to the bed. She sat

on Pippa's other side and wrapped her arm around her sobbing sister. How could she have made the announcement so callously, without considering how the news of a possible engagement would feel to Pippa, whose own matrimonial hopes had just been dashed?

But, as always, Pippa's heart was better than Eleanor had any right to expect. "I'm sorry, I'm just so happy for you," Pippa clarified, fanning her face. "For my entire life, you have put yourself last in order to look out for us." She beamed through her tears. "If there is anyone on the face of this earth who deserves to be a duchess, it's you."

"Hear, hear!" Clarissa cried.

Kate's gaze was fixed upon Eleanor's face. "And yet, unless I am very much mistaken, you are not unreservedly happy about the duke's proposal."

Eleanor chose her words carefully. "There is the fact that I'm furious with him. None of this mess with Felix would have happened if he hadn't immediately assumed the worst about Pippa."

"And?" Clarissa asked.

Eleanor bristled. "What makes you assume there is an *and*?"

Clarissa smirked at her. "Because I know you."

Eleanor blew a strand of hair out of her face. "And a part of me cannot help but assume that he will withdraw his proposal when he considers the matter in the harsh light of day."

Pippa frowned. "The harsh light of day? Is that to say that he proposed to you at—"

Eleanor felt her cheeks burning. "It's a metaphor! A metaphor!"

Pippa nodded acceptingly. Behind her back, Eleanor caught Clarissa and Kate exchanging a knowing look.

She cleared her throat. "Returning to the matter at hand

—I am skeptical that His Grace truly wishes to marry me. But, our circumstances being what they are, I thought I should mention his proposal, such as it was, as we need to consider every possible avenue of rescue from our financial troubles."

Clarissa waved this off. "Oh, he wants to marry you, all right."

Eleanor started to protest, but she was cut off by Kate, the little traitor. "He looks at you like he wants to *devour* you."

Eleanor frowned. "Two days ago, I was convinced that he hated me."

Clarissa shrugged. "Love, hate—two of the strongest emotions known to man. And apparently, two sides of the same coin."

Kate nodded. "You inspired a strong reaction in him from the very first."

Eleanor, who never felt flustered, was starting to feel flustered. "Yes, well, assuming his proposal has not been withdrawn—"

"Which it hasn't," Clarissa said firmly.

Eleanor narrowed her eyes at her sister—"imagine how Pippa would feel, to find herself trapped in the same household with the man who played an instrumental role in the unfortunate scene that played out this morning."

Pippa looked up from her lap. "Would you like to know what I think?"

"Of course, dear," Eleanor said.

Pippa's voice shook. "I have spent the last four weeks hearing about how I would have to lure a man old enough to be my grandfather to the altar, because that was our only hope. After I met Felix, the focus shifted to him, which was a welcome change. But it still put me under a great deal of pressure to bring him up to scratch."

Eleanor squeezed Pippa's hand. "I'm so sorry, dear."

"It wasn't your fault," Pippa said. "The blame lies solely with Father. But our choice seems to lie between one of us marrying Lord Oglesby, and you marrying a man who, in spite of the mistake he made this morning, clearly adores you, and is perfect for you in every particular. Is there truly a need to debate such a question?"

Eleanor nodded grimly. "You have cut straight to the heart of the matter, Pip. I will attempt to make things right with the duke. Whenever he returns."

She glanced at the darkening window, wondering when that might be.

CHAPTER 30

As he staggered up the steps of Milthorpe Manor in the dark, Jasper mused grimly that he should've been exhausted. He'd spent the last twelve hours in the saddle, scarcely pausing to eat and drink. But he was so wracked with anxiety, he knew that even were he to collapse upon his bed, he would not settle into a restful slumber.

He hadn't been this miserable since the deaths of his father and stepmother fifteen years ago. He had just ruined his relationship with Felix. The thought of his brother out there on the road, feeling humiliated and betrayed, absolutely gutted him. He was desperate to make amends, but before he could prostrate himself at his brother's feet, he had to find him. And that was proving to be a challenge.

He had received an update from Lord Milthorpe's stablemaster when he came in—Felix had last been spotted on the road toward Birmingham. Naturally he was riding Sharif, the Arabian stallion Jasper had spent a bloody fortune on. That was the rub, all right—Sharif could carry Felix all the way to Birmingham and beyond, as easily as most horses took a jaunt in Hyde Park. Just contemplating the number of roads leading out of Birmingham made Jasper's head pound. His brother could be anywhere by now.

He would find Felix. He would make things right. But it appeared that it was going to take significantly longer than Jasper would have liked.

And that was only the first of his problems—he had very likely also ruined things with Eleanor. The only image he seemed to be able to hold in his mind other than Felix's look of betrayal was the fury with which Eleanor had regarded him in the breakfast room. She was right to be furious—he had stood idly by while her sister had been humiliated, falsely accused, and had her privacy violated before more than a dozen witnesses. He had been the opposite of a white knight, and he felt devastated by his own failure.

And he knew it was selfish to worry about his own happiness when he had played a hand in ruining Felix's. But he had not realized how deeply he loved Eleanor, how much he needed her in his life, until the prospect of her refusing to have anything to do with him became such a distinct possibility.

At least he wouldn't have to wait weeks to have it out with Eleanor. He would learn his fate tonight.

The prospect made him feel like he might be ill right there on Lady Milthorpe's carpeted staircase.

Surely enough, as he reached the top of the stairs, Eleanor stepped out of an alcove, chin raised and eyes flinty.

"I know you have been out riding all day," she began. "I am therefore not sure if you have a moment to talk—"

"Yes—please—let's do it now." Jasper brushed a leaf off the cuff of his coat and raked his hands through his hair in an attempt to make himself presentable. "I think there's a sitting room through here," he said, gesturing to a door.

Eleanor led the way into the silver and blue parlor and went to stand by the fireplace. Not wanting to sit while she stood and frankly concerned that he was too filthy for the furniture, Jasper loomed awkwardly next to the sofa.

She fixed her eyes upon the carpet. "The matter I wished to discuss was the proposal of marriage you issued last night," she said in a clipped voice.

"What about it?" Jasper asked, his own voice hoarse.

She squeezed her eyes shut. "I was not sure if you had thought better of it, or if your offer still stands."

Although her voice was as cold as a December morning, hope flared in Jasper's chest. At least she hadn't told him outright that he was the last man she would ever consider marrying, and he should abandon all hopes to the contrary. Eleanor Weatherby was a forthright woman, and if she had determined she was going to throw him over, she would have told him at once.

Wouldn't she?

"It still stands," he said in a rush. "I've been in agony all day, not just about Felix, but out of fear that I had driven you away as well." He paused, struggling to read her expression. "Have I?" he asked softly.

She opened her eyes a slit. Her mouth was pinched, as if she had just drunk a bitter draught. "As you pointed out last night, some of us do not have the luxury of turning down a respectable proposal, even when the man who issued it has behaved in the most disgraceful manner imaginable—"

"I have," Jasper said, rushing forward to seize her hands. "I absolutely have."

"—not merely disgraceful, but mutton-headed—"

"Mutton-headed is just the word," Jasper agreed. "Beef-witted. Duncical, even."

Suddenly her stony reserve cracked, and tears streaked down her cheeks. "Pippa is *despondent*! She has been sobbing upon the bed all day."

"I'm so sorry," Jasper said, voice trembling.

"I don't know what to do for her," Eleanor sniffed, wiping her cheek with the back of her hand. "Not only has she been publicly humiliated, but she is in agony over whether things can be mended with Felix."

"Her reaction is imminently understandable. And it's all my fault."

"Well…" Eleanor glanced up with him, sympathy tempering her pique. "The fault lies primarily with the Robertsons."

"While their conduct was atrocious, I was too quick to rush to judgment. Would that I could somehow go back and demand to inspect the journal more closely! But I thought I knew best, as usual." He shook his head. "I wouldn't blame Pippa if she hates me. But, Eleanor—does this mean you'll marry me?"

Her nose wrinkled as if the prospect were distinctly untasteful, but she nodded. "Yes. I will."

Jasper had hauled her into his arms before she even finished the sentence. He was muddy and smelled of horse, but he couldn't help himself, and besides, this was far from his worst offense on the day. "Thank God. I've been frantic. I was so sure you were going to throw me over. It feels selfish to worry about my own happiness when I've ruined my brother's, but I'll admit I've been doing it."

He pulled back to kiss her but paused when he found her lips in a thin, white line. "Will you ever be able to forgive me?" he whispered.

"It's happening again," she said, voice shaking. "This time, it will be even worse than when Rupert Dupree jilted Clarissa. This will be in all the papers. People will accept without question that Pippa is grasping and malicious. I cannot bear to watch my sisters go through that again, and for something they did not even do!"

He squeezed her hands. "I will not let that happen. I swear it."

She did not seem to have heard. "I am so, so *sick* of being treated like rubbish because of the mistakes of some man! First it was Rupert Dupree, then, it was my father, leaving us penniless and desperate." She swiped a thumb beneath her eyes. "Although in truth, it has always been my father. He never showed an ounce of care for his daughters. But that is not my fault!"

"It's not," Jasper agreed, rubbing her arms. "Of course, it's not."

"That's the worst part—having no ability to improve my lot. Were I allowed to work, I would be the best barrister in all of England!"

"You would be terrifying to behold."

"But I can't," Eleanor said, voice tinged with bitterness. "The only forms of employment considered respectable for a woman pay a pittance. My present misfortunes were all caused by decisions someone else made, and I can do nothing about it. It is insufferable!"

"I'm sure it is," Jasper murmured.

"It is not my fault that I am poor, or that I'm a Weatherby Wallflower! It doesn't make me worse than everyone else! Really, it doesn't have anything to do with me. But no one sees that."

"*I* see it," Jasper insisted. "It's the reason I want to marry you. Because you, Eleanor Weatherby, are more precious than gold."

Her eyes were skeptical when they cut to his face, but then they softened. Jasper hoped she saw sincerity when she looked in his eyes.

"I know I have behaved abominably," he continued. "But I swear, I will make up for it. I will make sure nothing gets out that will cause Pippa embarrassment."

Eleanor looked unconvinced. "How are you going to do that?"

"At the risk of sounding like a ridiculous braggart, I am rather good at being both large and terrifying. And if that fails to put the fear of God into Lucas Robertson, I'll have the mastiffs attack him."

That earned him the tiniest of smiles. "Beatrice and Benedick are about as ferocious as the kittens. They wouldn't hurt a fly."

"Less ferocious, by far. You should see what Midnight did to my boots. But Lucas doesn't know that." He caressed the back of her hands with his thumbs. "I realized something while I was out riding around today. The thought of losing you… it felt like dying. I love you, Eleanor. You're everything I've always wanted in a wife, in a partner."

She started crying again, and Jasper's heart sank.

But then she said, "God help me, I am fairly certain that I love you, too."

He had to kiss her after that, and thank God, she let him. They were both trembling by the time Jasper lifted his head.

"I should be getting back," Eleanor said. "My sisters were fairly confident that you still wanted to marry me. But they are no doubt in a state of some anxiety, wondering if we're going to have a roof over our heads when this house party ends."

Jasper stepped back, retaining her hands. "Please, go and reassure them. They will always have a place in my household."

"Thank you," she whispered. She squeezed his hands one time, and then she was gone.

Jasper headed down the hall toward his rooms. Although one weight had been lifted from his shoulders, he still felt ill when he thought about Felix.

But if there was one thing he had learned through the

many hours he'd spent reading Shakespeare over the years, it was that one should not surrender to some craven scruple of thinking too precisely on the event. The path to solving his problems lay clearly before him, and the solution was action.

It would not be a simple task. He had to track his brother down before he could even start to make things right. There were hundreds—perhaps thousands—of steps he would have to take if he wanted to find his brother.

But if he had to visit every inn in Birmingham, he could do that. If he had to interrogate every innkeeper in England, he could do that, too.

His first task began tomorrow—saving Pippa's reputation. He probably wouldn't get much sleep tonight, but no matter.

He had planning to do. Tomorrow morning, he was going to make a *scene*.

And it was going to be worthy of Shakespeare.

CHAPTER 31

The first thing Jasper did the following morning was to inform Lady Milthorpe that he was going to cause a dreadful disturbance in the breakfast room.

The countess clutched the pearls she wore, but all she said was, "Whatever Your Grace deems necessary."

He took up a position in an alcove in the hallway where he could watch the guests come and go. When Eleanor came down with her sisters, he wanted to offer a greeting, and an apology to Pippa. But he needed the element of surprise on his side, so he stayed hidden in the shadows.

He was a bit surprised when Lucas and Anna-Maria Robertson strode into the room, looking entirely unconcerned that they might face consequences for their actions. Were they more clever, they would have fled the house party yesterday.

Of course, they had underestimated Eleanor and her sisters. They had assumed that no one would stand up for the lowly Weatherby Wallflowers.

They had assumed wrong.

Jasper waited long enough for them to fill their plates, then stormed into the breakfast room.

Lucas froze with a forkful of eggs halfway to his mouth. The expression on Jasper's face must have been terrible to behold because the fork began to tremble in his hand.

Coming to stand directly across from Lucas, Jasper slammed his black leather riding gloves down on the table. Teacups clattered in their saucers and the two dozen guests who had been breaking their fast fell silent.

At the far end of the table, Jasper saw the four Weatherby sisters look up from their plates.

"I assume you know why I'm here," Jasper began, voice full of malice.

Lucas gave a high-pitched laugh. "I'm sure I do not."

Jasper did not beat around the bush. "I'm here to call you out."

"C-call me out?" Lucas squeaked. "Why would you do that?"

Jasper leaned forward, placing both fists on the table. "For attempting to dishonor my future sister-in-law."

Lucas attempted a breezy chuckle. "Given the fact that your brother has run off, I'm not sure Miss Philippa is going to be your sister-in-law after all."

Jasper loomed closer, and Lucas physically recoiled, in spite of the fact that they had a table between them. "I have asked Miss Eleanor Weatherby to be my bride, and she has done me the honor of accepting. Miss Philippa will therefore be my sister by marriage regardless of whom she does or does not marry."

Lucas's face had taken on a greenish tinge. "Surely you jest. Your Grace cannot mean to marry a Weatherby Wal—"

Jasper snarled, and Lucas squealed.

"You will be very careful," Jasper ground out, "in how you

refer to the future Duchess of Norwood. But as I said, I demand satisfaction. Name your second."

Lucas glanced around the room. There were a dozen men present, but not one of them would meet his eye.

"Pistols or swords?" Jasper growled. "How would you prefer to die?"

"I see now that an apology is in order," Lucas said in a rush. "At the time, I believed it to be a lighthearted jest—"

"You believed nothing of the kind," Jasper snapped.

Lucas was blinking rapidly, looking everywhere but at Jasper. "I see now that I have erred and erred severely." He turned to face Pippa. "I apologize, Miss Philippa. My behavior yesterday was, er—"

"Execrable," Jasper supplied.

"Execrable. Yes, exactly," Lucas agreed. "I regret it most sincerely."

Jasper's voice was thick with irony. "Oh, I'm sure you do. But you are missing an important point."

Lucas had the weaselly look of a man who would agree to almost anything to get himself out of his current predicament. "What's that?"

"That you did not merely make a mistake. You *lied*. You took the passage out of context in such a way that it sounded like Miss Weatherby was deriding my brother, when in fact she was praising him. Because that's what you did." Jasper leaned forward, bending his elbows so he loomed in front of Lucas. "Isn't it?"

Lucas swallowed. "It is."

"Not only did you perpetrate a gross invasion of Miss Weatherby's privacy, you made the deplorable and *false* insinuation that my brother is less than intelligent." Jasper narrowed his eyes. "I should call you out for that alone."

Lucas looked like he was going to cry. "I do apologize,

Your Grace, and I would be most willing to apologize to Lord Felix as well."

Jasper straightened. "The best apology you could give him is never to inflict your presence on him again." He gave Anna-Maria Robertson a hard look. "That goes for both of you."

Anna-Maria looked startled. Jasper knew full well she had been motivated by hopes of marrying Felix herself. "But Your Grace—"

"Do not show your faces in London," Jasper said, cutting her off. "I think you will find that every member of decent society would rather cross the street than acknowledge your acquaintance."

The Robertson siblings exchanged a look of horror. They had clearly been banking on the assumption that Jasper would be eager to prevent a match between Pippa and Felix and would therefore overlook the contemptible means by which they drove the happy couple apart.

They had failed to recognize that the tides had turned. Now they would pay the price.

"Not go to London?" Anna-Maria sputtered. "But… for how long must we stay away?"

"For however long my ire lasts," Jasper replied.

Anna-Maria gave a nervous laugh. "And how long might that be?"

Jasper gave her a contemptuous glare. "Who can say, Miss Robertson? All I know is that right now, I am feeling very, very angry."

He caught Eleanor's eye at the end of the table. She was blinking rapidly, and if he didn't know better, he would have said her lower lip was trembling. It was a distinctly un-Eleanor-like expression, one he had never seen on her face before.

He wanted to go to her, to make sure she was all right.

But there was one thing he needed to do first.

Turning so that his gaze swept across the entire room, Jasper said in a voice that carried, "I think it goes without saying that I would be most displeased if word were to get out about this unpleasant incident, which should never have happened in the first place. Very, very, extremely displeased," he added darkly. "Mark my words, if I hear one breath of gossip about Miss Philippa, or about Felix, I will not rest until I discover the source of the slander. And that source will share the same fate as the Robertsons." He paused to allow his words to sink in. "Have I made myself clear?"

A veritable chorus of agreement filled the room.

Glaring at the Robertsons, he jerked his head toward the door. "Go and pack your things. I believe you are both about to recall another engagement. A most urgent one."

Anna-Maria Robertson swiped at her eyes as the two of them hurried from the breakfast room. Jasper did not feel the least bit sorry.

Jasper rocked back on his heels. For the first time all morning, he smiled. The rest of Lady Milthorpe's guests were decent sorts. And they all seemed intelligent enough to understand that no *on dit*, no matter how juicy, was worth risking a duke's displeasure.

Jasper headed to the far end of the table, not bothering to make himself a plate. That could wait.

He needed to check on Eleanor first.

He lowered himself into the chair next to hers. "Are you well?" he murmured.

She did not answer. She was still blinking rapidly, eyes fixed upon her plate.

Jasper turned to Clarissa. "What is it?"

Clarissa poked her sister in the arm. "I think you broke her. She's never once been at a loss for words, not in the twenty-five years I've known her."

It occurred to Jasper belatedly that perhaps one or more of the Weatherby sisters would have preferred that he not make a scene. "I hope you don't mind that I, er..."

"Not at all," Clarissa said, waving her fork. "It was *perfect*." She gazed blissfully into the distance. "I shall never forget the way Anna-Maria's face turned puce. I fancy it will be the happy memory I call up from now on, whenever I'm feeling sad."

Jasper wasn't surprised that Clarissa approved. But she was not the party most directly affected. "Miss Philippa?" he asked.

Pippa lifted her chin. "I, too, did not mind in the least. I can't tell you how many hours I spent tossing and turning last night, imagining all the horrid things they would write about me in the papers." She gave him a smile. "At least now I don't have to worry about that. Thank you, Your Grace."

Air rushed out of Jasper's lungs as he released a breath he hadn't realized he was holding. "That is a relief. Perhaps, as we're to be family soon, you would do me the honor of calling me Jasper."

Clarissa waved a hand. "Oh, all right, Jasper. I only wish you had not sent Lucas and Anna-Maria Robertson off quite so soon. How I should relish the look on their faces when they see that we're all on a first-name basis now."

Jasper grinned. "As enjoyable as that would have been, nothing, I think, is worth tolerating their presence." He turned to Eleanor. "I'm still wondering how you're faring."

She looked at him then, and the expression in her eyes... he thought it might be wonder, but of course, he was a great lummox of a man. What did he know about these things?

"Eleanor?" he asked, trying to make his voice gentle.

Abruptly, she rose from her chair. "Let's go someplace where we can talk."

CHAPTER 32

*E*leanor knew a good place for a private conversation—the little closet next to the music room where she and Jasper had shared their first kiss. She led him there, then closed the door behind them.

A trace of worry creased his brow. "Is everything all right? I hope I did not embarrass you by causing a sce—"

"You stood up for me."

He tilted his head, as if struggling to parse why this had shaken her so profoundly. "Of course, I did."

Eleanor shook her head. "There's no *of course* about it. I've been wracking my brains for the last quarter of an hour, and I do believe that is the first time anyone has ever stood up for me, excepting my sisters. Usually, I am the one who has to stand up for everyone else." She laughed, swiping her thumbs beneath her eyes. "It has rendered me a bit flabbergasted."

He took her hands in his. "Do you know when I realized I wanted to marry you?"

"I've honestly no idea."

He stroked his thumbs across the backs of her hands. "It

was the night we went to the folly, when you offered to help me carry Benedick back to the house."

"Oh," Eleanor said, flushing at the memory. "You gave me a strange look. I felt certain I had appalled you with my unladylike offer."

"Not at all." A shaft of light broke through the clouds and fell on his face. His eyes looked bright. Hopeful. "I realized in that moment that no matter what the future brought, you would always help me, to the best of your ability. And I will always help you, Eleanor. I will *always* stand up for you. You're not alone anymore."

Then she was crying in earnest, but they were the happiest of tears. The weight she had carried alone for the past twenty years, of having to look after her sisters, no longer felt so heavy upon her shoulders.

Not only that, but instead of spending the rest of her life toiling in the household of her father, who had always taken her for granted, she would spend the rest of her life with Jasper. Strong, honorable Jasper, who she could happily talk to for hours on end, and who fiercely defended the people he loved.

Occasionally, a little too fiercely.

But she could help him with that.

"I love you," she said, looping her arms around his neck. "I can't believe I get to marry you. It feels too good to be true."

"And I love you, Eleanor." He put his hands on her hips, pulling her to him. "You were right when you told me I'd never met your ilk before. You are a peerless treasure, and I can honestly say, 'I would not wish any companion in the world but you.'"

"*The Tempest*," Eleanor observed. "A beautiful, and fitting, quote. But I must confess, the passage that springs into my mind is from *Romeo and Juliet*."

"Oh? What's that?"

Eleanor leaned in close to murmur in his ear, "'O, wilt thou leave me so unsatisfied?'"

Jasper chuckled. "Never, my darling Eleanor."

He lowered his lips to hers. Eleanor was just twining her fingers in the hair at the nape of his neck when she heard it.

"Scoot over!" a soft voice hissed from the other side of the door. "I can't hear what's going on."

"You can't hear what's going on because they've gone silent." The speaker was recognizable as Clarissa.

"You don't think they're… *satisfying* each other. Do you?" Kate asked.

"What would that even entail?" Pippa asked, all curiosity.

Eleanor groaned, burying her face in Jasper's chest, which was shaking with laughter. Motioning for him to be quiet, she slipped from his arms and crept over to the door, behind which the conversation continued unabated.

"Eleanor wouldn't do that!" Pippa insisted, apparently having received an answer to her question. After a pregnant pause, she added, "Would she?"

"I wouldn't have thought so," Kate whispered. "But His Grace… I mean, Jasper… said something about a midnight rendezvous at the fol—"

Eleanor yanked the door open before Kate could finish her sentence. Surely enough, there were all three of her sisters. Kate and Clarissa jerked back guiltily. Pippa, on the other hand, lost her balance and would've fallen on her face had Eleanor not caught her.

"Greetings, sisters," Eleanor said dryly. "Fancy meeting you here."

Pippa waved her hands. "We were just, uh…"

"Eavesdropping?" Eleanor suggested.

"Precisely!" Clarissa said without an ounce of remorse.

Jasper had come up behind Eleanor and placed his hands

on her shoulders. She glanced up at him. "Are you sure you want these three living under your roof?"

"These two," Clarissa said swiftly. At Eleanor's quizzical look, she ducked her chin. "I still mean to take the position. As companion to Lady Francesca's great-aunt."

Eleanor studied her sister. "There's no need for you to do that now."

Clarissa's eyes took on a familiar mulish quality. "I know."

"And being a companion isn't necessarily an easy task. It may not be physically demanding, but if your employer is difficult, putting up with their antics can be exhausting in its own way."

"Frankly, I'm not sure that you're well-suited for it, Claire," Kate muttered.

"I know that," Clarissa said. "But I have reason to believe that this particular situation will suit me splendidly. And I want to do it. I really do."

Eleanor studied her sister. She could tell Clarissa wanted to take this position as a companion—or at least, that she thought she did. Eleanor couldn't fathom why.

But she knew herself well enough to understand that she had her own set of reasons for resisting the plan. For so many years, she had watched after her sisters, shepherding them along.

But they were grown now. Clarissa was five and twenty—firmly on the shelf, by most people's reckoning. Of course, she wanted a life of her own, and to make her own choices.

And really, once they arrived in London and received a proper wardrobe, what were the odds that her three beautiful sisters would not have a dozen suitors begging for their hands?

Things were about to change. For the better, to be sure, but change was difficult, nonetheless. The Weatherby

Wallflowers would be parted, and it would happen sooner than Eleanor wished.

She squeezed Clarissa's hand. "We'll talk some more, and you can explain why this is important to you."

Clarissa nodded, eyes bright. "Thank you, Eleanor."

Behind her, Jasper's stomach gave a great growl. He cleared his throat. "Shall we return to the breakfast room? I don't believe you ladies had the chance to finish your meals, either."

As they crossed the music room, Pippa said, "So. Jasper. Last night, Eleanor mentioned your regret at having fallen for the Robertsons' scheme, and not questioning it more closely."

"She told you right," Jasper said. "I am terribly sorry."

Pippa waved this off with a smile. "I've thought of how you can make it up to me."

Jasper arched an eyebrow. "Oh?"

Pippa nodded. "You see, for the first time in my life, I find myself without a single cat. I am catless, you might say!"

"Shall I arrange to have your three cats brought from Boroughbridge to the ducal estate?" Jasper offered.

"That is very kind of you. But a move can be very disruptive to cats, especially older cats who have lived all their lives in one home. I have just had a letter from Jane, the eldest daughter of the new family occupying our house. Ollie, Crumpet, and Pepper are doing very well. As much as I will miss them, I think it is best that I leave them there."

Pippa's eyes cut to Jasper, her expression sly. "But I cannot help but observe that Lady Milthorpe has four very fine kittens, kittens who are not firmly established in a home, and which I feel confident she will not want to deal with once the house party concludes."

The corner of Jasper's mouth twitched. "You are suggesting that we adopt them."

Pippa smiled brightly. "Precisely!"

Jasper tipped his head down toward hers. "I think it a splendid plan. After all, Beatrice and Benedick would never forgive me if I left those kittens behind."

Pippa squealed with delight, then hooked one arm through Kate's and the other through Clarissa's. The three sisters hurried ahead to the breakfast room.

As they passed a bay window overlooking the gardens, Eleanor spotted something that made her pause.

"What is it?" Jasper asked.

She found she could not speak as she watched the delicate yellow butterfly fluttering in the window frame.

"Eleanor?" Jasper asked, concern tinging his voice.

Eleanor watched the butterfly dance in the crisp fall breeze, then wheel off, fluttering toward the sunny gardens. A feeling of profound peace washed over her.

"Eleanor?" Jasper's voice came to her as if from far away. "What's wrong?"

"Nothing is wrong," she said, finally finding her tongue. She looked up at him and smiled. "Everything is going to be all right."

Jasper sighed, doubtlessly thinking of Felix. "I hope you're right."

She tugged him forward toward the breakfast room. "Don't worry. I always am."

As usual, she was.

~

Keep reading for a special preview of Book Two in The Weatherby Wallflowers quartet, *Snowbound with the Scoundrel*!

. . .

Would you like to catch up with Eleanor and Jasper a few years into their marriage to see how their happily-ever-after is going? I write a free bonus story for each of my books, exclusively for my newsletter subscribers. If you choose to subscribe, you'll receive updates from me about twice a month with Regency fun, all my latest news, and the occasional video of me starting a fire whilst dabbling in historical cooking. You can sign up at https://courtneymccaskill.com/newsletter/

In the Revenge of the Wallflowers series, the wallflowers are getting the last laugh! Read a new story from some of your favorite authors every week from now until March 2025. You can browse the full collection here.

PREVIEW: SNOWBOUND WITH THE SCOUNDREL

Coming November 12, 2024

First, he jilted her. Then, he humiliated her…

The Weatherby Wallflowers received their unfortunate nickname when Rupert Dupree, the second son of the Earl of Rottenbury, jilted Clarissa, then decamped for the Continent. When a gossip sheet published Rupert's letter forcefully rejecting their proposed union, all four Weatherby sisters became laughingstocks. Clarissa hadn't much been looking forward to marrying a stranger, but she has hated 'Rotten Rupert' ever since.

But you can't keep a Weatherby Wallflower down…

Now the consummate wallflower, Clarissa finds her true purpose: gathering information for the Home Office. It's the one advantage of blending into the wallpaper—nobody even notices that Clarissa is in the room, much less that she is surreptitiously listening to everyone's secrets.

Snowbound with the Scoundrel...

Clarissa's contact at the Home Office gives her the most important assignment of her career: to infiltrate the Countess of Helmsley's Christmas house party and protect a prominent Member of Parliament who has been subject to repeated assassination attempts. Nothing will stop Clarissa from reaching this house party, not even the snowstorm gathering over the Yorkshire moors. She manages to book passage on the last carriage leaving York.

But that's when Clarissa's luck runs out. Because it turns out there's one other passenger crazy enough to brave the moors in a blizzard.

And it happens to be Rupert Dupree...

~

December 1823
  York, England

The wind yanked at Clarissa Weatherby's cloak as she hurried across the River Foss. She grabbed it with her free hand to keep it from blowing away, but she did not slow her stride. The mail coach would leave the Black Swan Inn at a quarter past six, and she must be on it.

It was already six o'clock—full dark this time of year, but there was light enough coming from the shops and taverns that lined the street to prevent her from tripping over the cobblestones.

The houses became thinner, and the light scarcer, when she turned onto the Stonebow. It was still warm enough that the scattered snowflakes being blown about were melting as soon as they hit the ground, but now the sun was down, and the temperature was dropping precipitously.

She lifted her chin. It did not matter. She still had to get on that coach regardless of the worsening weather. She would just have to hope for the best.

The road widened into Peasholme Green, and Clarissa spotted the old building, its dark timber framing stark against its whitewashed plaster. She hurried through the door beneath one of its twin gables and approached the bar. "I need passage to Helmsley," she said, pushing her hood back.

The barman had a friendly look about him, with a balding head and a few white hairs in his thick mustache. "Helmsley?" he asked, pausing in the act of polishing a pint glass. "Oh, no, miss. You don't want to be going to Helmsley tonight. Not with the storm that's brewing."

Clarissa pulled a handful of coins from her pocket and began counting them out. "I don't much want to go. But I have no choice in the matter."

"Oh?" the barkeep asked. "And what is of such great urgency?"

Clarissa paused. The truth was, she did not know, and she would not know until she had the chance to read the letter her employer, Lady Winnifred FitzSimon, had pressed into her hand as she pushed her out the door.

But her ladyship had communicated that the errand, whatever it was, was of the utmost urgency. It was so crucial, in fact, that Lady Winnifred, who had been laid up in bed for the past three days, trembling with fever, had insisted upon sending Clarissa on to Helmsley by herself to complete it, even though her training was nowhere near complete.

The barkeep was waiting for an answer. "It's my mother," Clarissa lied. "She has been unwell these past few years. I had a letter from my sister, and she fears it is her time."

"Ah. I can see why you would chance it, then." The barkeep accepted the handful of coins Clarissa passed him. "It happens that there's one other soul crazy enough to try it in this weather."

"Oh?" Clarissa asked, hoisting her valise.

"A gentleman, by the looks of him," the barkeep confirmed. "Now, if you're wanting a hot brick for your feet, that will be an extra penny."

Clarissa did want the hot brick. It was colder than she'd thought it would be when she had departed the rented rooms she and Lady Winnifred had shared. Having finalized her arrangements, she headed back to the inn yard, where the red and black mail coach was waiting.

As there were so few passengers, the coachman allowed her to keep her valise with her. Clarissa climbed up, curious to see who her travelling companion for the next twenty hours would be.

The only greeting she received upon entering the coach was a soft snore. Her fellow passenger was slumped in a corner of the front-facing seat, head tipped back at an angle that seemed destined to leave him with a crick in his neck. Before surrendering to Hypnos's spell, he had spread his black, mink-lined cloak over himself like a blanket, meaning that Clarissa could only see his face. He looked to be around Clarissa's own age, which was to say, young for a man, and hopelessly on the shelf for a woman. She could not tell if he was handsome or not, with his head lolling back and his mouth hanging open, but she saw that he had blond hair and a bump on his nose.

Settling into the opposite corner of the rear-facing seat, Clarissa debated the merits of pulling out the letter Lady Winnifred had given her, the one detailing her mission. On the one hand, she was dreadfully curious about what it might say. It also seemed like a good idea to know what task she was to undertake before she went strolling into the lion's den. Besides, her companion gave every indication of being asleep.

On the other hand, Clarissa knew from personal experience that appearances could be deceiving. Pretending to snooze in a chair next to the fire was the preferred method Lady Winnifred employed when there was eavesdropping to be done.

Clarissa was ostensibly serving as Lady Winnifred's companion. When the world looked at Lady Winnifred, they saw the seventy-two-year-old aunt of the current Duke of Wroxley.

But Winnifred FitzSimon was more than that.

She was a *spy*.

Clarissa had been introduced to Lady Winnifred by her great-niece, Lady Francesca FitzSimon. Guests at the same house party, Clarissa and Francesca had struck up a friendship while rehearsing a scene from Shakespeare to enact for their fellow guests on a rainy day. It had been something of an unlikely pairing. Lady Francesca was the daughter of a duke, while Clarissa was the penniless daughter of a not-very-successful naturalist. Lady Francesca was beautiful and demure, and Clarissa was a tart-tongued spinster.

But the thing they had in common was that they both chafed at the roles society pressed them to assume. Lady Francesca had no desire to marry, but her parents were determined to see her wed to a lord within a year. Clarissa had no taste for marriage, either. Years ago, she had been betrothed to a man named Rupert Dupree, who was the younger son of the Earl of Rottenbury. It had been a match arranged by one of her dearly departed mother's distant cousins, Lady Milthorpe, meaning that Clarissa had never clapped eyes upon her intended.

This had not prevented Rotten Rupert, as Clarissa now thought of him, from penning a scathing letter forcefully rejecting the proposed union with Clarissa. Even worse, instead of having the letter delivered to Clarissa in private, he had sent it to every newspaper from Shetland to Cornwall. This had set off a brief but furious frenzy in which not only Clarissa, but also her three sisters, Eleanor, Kate, and Pippa, had been derided in the gossip pages. The gossip rags had even given them a nickname—the Weatherby Wallflowers.

It was fortunate that Rupert Dupree had decamped for the Continent by the time those newspapers reached Boroughbridge, the tiny village in Yorkshire where Clarissa had grown up. She might be slight in build and lacking in any sort of combat training.

But it would not go well for Rotten Rupert were he to encounter her in a dark alley.

Suffice to say, the blush was off the rose as far as marriage was concerned. Not that Clarissa had ever been one of those girls who began planning their wedding at the age of six. The thing that Clarissa wanted most in the world was the chance to make use of her wits. Were she a man, she fancied she would have been a Member of Parliament, ferociously debating the issues of the day and crafting legislation that would make the world a better place. She wanted to leave her mark, to do something important, not waste away in a tiny village, embroidering handkerchiefs and never making use of the six languages she had taught herself from books borrowed from the circulating library.

That also happened to be the reason Lady Francesca had thought to introduce Clarissa to her great-aunt. After her jilting, Clarissa had taken to wearing gowns in dull colors, which her sisters referred to as "Clarissa's dirt-colored dresses."

"Why would I want to draw the notice of a man?" Clarissa had asked Lady Francesca, who understood. "I *prefer* to blend into the wallpaper. Although perhaps my drab dresses are a little too effective in this regard. You would be astonished at the things I overhear sometimes. People don't even realize thatI'm standing beside them."

Clarissa would never forget the way her friend's spine had gone ramrod straight. Glancing about to make sure they were alone, Lady Francesca had asked, "Clarissa, have I ever told you about my Great-Aunt Winnifred?"

What Lady Francesca had proceeded to explain was that spies did not look the way they were portrayed in novels. A dashing young army officer in a red coat would draw every eye in the room, and arouse every suspicion as well.

The seventy-two-year-old woman snoozing by the fire, on the other hand? According to Lady Winnifred, old women were all but invisible to begin with. Close your eyes and throw in a fake snore and every villain from here to Thurso would discuss their wicked plans right in front of you, not even bothering to lower their voices.

And so, spies were always the last person you suspected. The old lady. The scullery maid.

And perhaps, the wallflower in the dirt-colored dress.

Lady Francesca had offered to make introductions, an offer Clarissa had accepted with alacrity. Surely enough, Great-Aunt Winnifred thought Clarissa had great potential, an assessment echoed by her contact at the Home Office, Sir Henry Kenchington. Sir Henry had spent a half hour peppering Clarissa with rapid-fire questions. He had seemed pleased with her command of French, Spanish, High German, Low German, Dutch, and even Russian.

Once the interview concluded, Sir Henry had removed his spectacles, rubbing his nose. "I have a theory, Miss Weatherby, that behind every weakness, there lies a strength, if you have the wit to see it. You have described yourself as a wallflower. Society derides wallflowers, of course, as spinsters in the making. They are unadmired, and most importantly, unnoticed." He had fixed her with his pale blue gaze. "Congratulations, Miss Weatherby. Your weakness is now your strength. I hope this is the start of a mutually beneficial arrangement."

It had been the best thing to ever happen to Clarissa. No longer would she be stuck frittering her days away embroidering handkerchiefs. She would be able to make use of her natural abilities. She was going to do something important!

She was assigned to train under Lady Winnifred. The two of them had just completed their first assignment, a simple mission to gather information regarding a gentleman who was smuggling French wine in Whitby. They had been heading back to London to await their next mission when Lady Winnifred fell ill in York. Her ladyship had sent a letter to Sir Henry to let him know that they would stay there so she could convalesce.

Sir Henry's reply was presently burning a hole in Clarissa's pocket.

With a cry from the driver, the mail coach departed from the inn. The man on the opposite bench seat lurched forward, then backward, his head thumping against the spare grey padding that lined the wall of the coach. But he did not awaken.

Clarissa peered at him. He really did seem to be asleep. And what were the chances he could make out the contents of her letter from across the dim carriage? She would be hard-pressed to make out the words by the carriage lamps as it was.

Were he to awaken, all he would see was a woman

reading a letter. There was nothing inherently suspicious about that!

Thus resolved, Clarissa removed the letter from her pocket and unfolded it eagerly.

Lady Winnifred,

I am more sorry to hear that you find yourself unwell than you can know, especially in light of the grim news I have received today. It concerns Mr. Oliver Baxter, a prominent member of the House of Commons with whom you are no doubt familiar.

There have been a number of unusual occurrences in Mr. Baxter's household this past month. A stray bullet that came through the window of his morning room, missing him by inches. A wheel that broke on his curricle in such a way that it was a miracle he was not thrown from the vehicle. And last week, a scullery maid who became sickened after tasting the crawfish soup to see if it had enough salt.

Mr. Baxter's wife became concerned and insisted that her husband contact Bow Street. Upon investigation, the soup was found to be tainted with arsenic, and the curricle showed signs of intentional tampering.

When the Runner went to notify Mr. Baxter of his findings, he learned that the entire household, consisting of Mr. Baxter, Mrs. Baxter, and one of her spinster cousins, had recently departed for Yorkshire in order to attend a house party being hosted by the Countess of Helmsley.

The Runner formed the impression that Mr. Baxter believed his wife had overreacted to this sequence of events, which he dismissed as mere coincidences. He therefore departed London with no idea that someone is trying to kill him. From your current position in York, you are by far the closest agent on hand. I therefore implore you, if you are remotely well enough to undertake the journey, to go to Helmsley Castle with all possible haste. I believe you are acquainted with Lord and Lady Helmsley, but I have provided a letter of introduction explaining your presence at the house party, as well as a letter for Mr. Baxter.

Hopefully, the would-be killer has remained behind in London, but we must take no chances. You are to therefore remain at the house party, watching for any signs of another attack. I have also enclosed an analysis of Mr. Baxter's political positions, and which of the house party's known guests would face significant losses were he to succeed in enacting legislation in accordance with those positions.

Given the urgency of the situation, I will send as many additional assets to the Helmsley estate as can be made available. In particular, one of my best men will return any day from a lengthy assignment on the Continent. I will have him on the first carriage north.

I remain yours &c.,

H.K.

Clarissa swallowed. Just her second assignment, and she was already facing a life-and-death situation. A part of her thrilled to have been given the chance to do something so important. But she was inexperienced, and she knew it. What if she was not up to the task?

She shivered, partly out of nervousness, but also because the brick at her feet had already lost most of its heat. The temperature was dropping precipitously, and she was shivering beneath her cloak. How she wished she had thought to don a couple of flannel petticoats and bring a thick woolen carriage blanket! Well, there was nothing for it now. There hadn't been time to pack properly, so she had hastily shoved a few things in her valise. The plan had been for Lady Winnifred to send her trunk after her the following day.

Clarissa wedged herself into the corner, trying to find a little warmth amongst the sparsely padded squabs. It would be an uncomfortable journey, but it wasn't far to Helmsley. She could endure it.

She read through the letter a second time. She was quite familiar with Oliver Baxter. Young and charismatic, his name was often mentioned as a potential candidate for Prime Minister should the Whigs regain power. He advocated for a number of reformist initiatives that Clarissa supported strongly, including eradicating slavery from the British Empire. He also advocated for parliamentary reform, including an expansion of voting rights to include the working and middle classes, and the elimination of so-called "pocket boroughs" whose populations had shrunk over the years, leaving a scant handful of voters whose support could easily be bought and sold.

Many a family fortune depended on these hotly debated issues, so it was easy to imagine that Mr. Baxter might have a few enemies.

Unfolding the second sheet of paper enclosed, she saw that Sir Henry's thoughts had gone in a similar direction:

Possible Suspects:

(1) Mr. Ulysses F. Humphrey- Mr. Humphrey's fortune is derived from a large sugar cane plantation on the island of Antigua employing slave labor. He stands to take significant losses should the emancipation proposals Mr. Baxter supports succeed.

(2) Mr. Richard Garroway- MP representing the pocket borough of Dunwich. Most of the town has fallen into the

sea, leaving only thirty-two voters in the entire constituency. If Mr. Baxter succeeds in passing parliamentary reform, Mr. Garroway will surely lose his seat.

A different hand, one Clarissa recognized as that of Lady Winnifred, had scrawled an additional name in the margin:

(3) Arabella Anstruther, Dowager Duchess of Kimbolton- a good friend of Lord and Lady Helmsley and likely to be in attendance. Mother of fourteen children including eleven boys. Mr. Baxter has argued quite forcefully that church livings and political appointments should be granted based on merit, rather than connections. He has been vocal in shaming those who grant positions in their gift to unqualified family members, or who sell them outright. This has made it impossible for a number of the duchess's shiftless sons to find livings, and I have heard her complain bitterly about the expense of maintaining them out of the family coffers. She will become increasingly desperate as more of her sons reach the age of majority.

Clarissa sat back. How like Lady Winnifred, to suspect not only at the male guests, but also the ladies. It was a good reminder that when she arrived, Clarissa must consider every possible suspect.

She noted her letters of introduction, both to Lord and Lady Helmsley and to Mr. Baxter, still folded and sealed. Tucking everything back together, she returned the letter to her valise and settled back against the thin grey squabs.

Just as the brick at her feet lost the last of its heat, the coach hit a bump, jolting her slumbering companion awake.

He blinked groggily, then did a double take as he saw that

he was not alone in the coach. "Blimey! I do beg your pardon, miss. Wouldn't have nodded off had I realized I wasn't alone." He gave a great, seemingly involuntary yawn. "I've come up straight from London, you see, so I'm just about fagged to death."

Clarissa did not see, not precisely, but she took it that this meant he was tired. "That's quite all right, sir."

He rubbed his eye with the heel of his hand. "Won't be much longer now, though. I'm only going through to Helmsley."

"Helmsley!" Clarissa exclaimed. At his curious look, she explained, "That is my destination as well. I don't suppose you are bound for Helmsley Castle?"

"Happens that I am. I'm en route to the earl and countess's house party."

"As am I," Clarissa said quickly.

He smiled at her, and something inside Clarissa shifted. He wasn't what you would call classically handsome. In addition to the bump on his nose, his smile was lopsided, and his hair a bit too shaggy. But in spite of these flaws, his features somehow came together in a way that was tremendously appealing.

She decided it was because he looked so affable, as if he were utterly delighted to find himself with her in that carriage, in spite of the fact that he was *fagged to death*, whatever that meant. And the impression that someone was genuinely pleased to be in your company held a special kind of appeal.

He shook his head, rueful. "But look at me—I've gone and put the cart before the horse! I pray you won't tell Lady H. how I prattled on without remembering to introduce myself." He smiled again, holding out a hand. "I'm Rupert. Rupert Dupree."

Snowbound with the Scoundrel will be available on November 12, 2024. Pre-order your copy today!

ALSO BY COURTNEY MCCASKILL

The Weatherby Wallflowers

Book 1: A Wallflower Never Surrenders

Book 2: Snowbound with the Scoundrel

Book 3: One Bed for the Bluestocking (Coming Soon)

Book 4: How He Won His Wallflower (Coming Soon)

The Astley Chronicles

Book 1: How to Train Your Viscount

Book 2: What's an Earl Gotta Do?

Book 3: The Sea Siren of Broadwater Bottom

Book 4: The Duke's Dark Secret

Book 5: Let Me Be Your Hero

Book 6: Romancing the Rifleman

Book 7: A Laird for Lady Lucy (Coming Soon)

My Favorite Mistake: An Astley Chronicles Novella

The Wicked Widows' League

Book 1: Scoundrel for Sale

Book 2: A Very Roguish Boxing Day

Other Books:

One Fine May (The Rake Review)

For more information, visit www.courtneymccaskill.com.

ACKNOWLEDGMENTS

I would like to thank my friends in the Brazen Belles Facebook Group for helping this Crazy Bear Lady come up with some cute cat names. In particular, Hayley B., Terri B., Lyn R., Liz O., Christa C., and Vicki N. suggested the names that I used in this book. Thank you all for your help!

I would be lost without my fabulous editor, Diana Bold, and my proofreaders Linda and Melinda. Many thanks to Dawn Brower and Amanda Mariel for kindly including me in this series. I am extremely grateful to the members of my ARC and Street Teams for all of your support and encouragement! Finally, all of my love goes to my wonderful family, especially V and J.

This one is for Jon, you absolute tosspot!

ABOUT THE AUTHOR

After reading *Black Beauty* for the 1,497th time, Courtney McCaskill was inspired to write her own stories. Reviews of her early work were mixed, with her fourth-grade teacher, Mrs. Compton, saying, "Please stop writing all of your essays from the point of view of a horse."

Today, Courtney lives in Austin, Texas with the hero of her own story, who holds the distinction of being the world's most sarcastic pediatrician. She is reliably informed by her son that she gives THE BEST hugs, "because you're so squishy, Mommy." In 2022, Regency Fiction Writers honored her with its Lady of the Realm award in appreciation of her volunteer work, both on its Board of Directors and as the Coordinator of the Regency Academe. When she's not busy almost burning her house down while attempting to make a traditional Christmas pudding, she enjoys playing the piano, learning everything there is to know about Kodiak bears, and of course, curling up with a great book. Visit her online at www.courtneymccaskill.com.